She reaches out to grab the end of it, and her hand makes contact with the tip of the spindle. For the first time in her life, she feels a sharp pang. It's a feeling, a sensation, coming from her skin. From *touch*. Which is impossible. And yet it's real—she *feels* it, and it . . . stings, hurts, flares, thrums, sending a shock through her entire body, making her dizzy.

And then, just at the break of dawn on the very day of her sixteenth birthday, she finds she is sinking through the dazzling sunlight, the aura of gold, falling, fainting, descending into memory, into a chaos of colors.

Dreams.

Flame.

ALSO BY LEXA HILLYER
Proof of Forever

SPINDLE FIRE

LEXA HILLYER

HARPER TEEN
An Imprint of HarperCollinsPublishers

HarperTeen is an imprint of HarperCollins Publishers.

Spindle Fire
Copyright © 2017 by Lexa Hillyer
All rights reserved. Printed in the United States of America.
No part of this book may be used or reproduced in any manner
whatsoever without written permission except in the case of brief quotations
embodied in critical articles and reviews. For information address
HarperCollins Children's Books, a division of HarperCollins Publishers,
195 Broadway, New York, NY 10007.
www.epicreads.com

Library of Congress Control Number: 2016949910
ISBN 978-0-06-244088-4

Typography by Carla Weise
Map by Diana Sousa
17 18 19 20 21   PC/LSCH   10 9 8 7 6 5 4 3 2 1
❖
First paperback edition, 2018

*For Minna Freya Grantham,
the beauty asleep within me
when this book began*

ÎLES DE GLACE

THE PALACE
OF AUBIN

STRAIT OF
SORROW

THE PALACE
OF DELUCE

AUBIN

LADY
ALMANDINE'S
ESTATE

RIVER ROAD

TRISTESSE
PASS

CORRAINE

CAPE
BAILLE

CONVENT OF ISOLÉ

SOUTH SEA

ILLUSTRATED BY
DIANA SOUSA

What was said to the rose that made it open
was said to me here in my chest.
—*Rumi*

THE ROSE LULLABY

One night reviled,
Before break of morn,
Amid the roses wild,
All tangled in thorns,
The shadow and the child
Together were born.

The bright sun did spin,
The moon swallowed day,
When one her dear twin
Forever did slay.

PART

I

AMID THE
ROSES WILD

1

Aurora

Winter seemed to come early in 1313, the year Aurora was born. For days that July, a mass of damp white flakes clung to treetops and roofs like snow.

Some thought perhaps it was the North Faerie's doing. They were wrong.

In her day—which was a very long time ago indeed—the North Faerie had been known for wreaking havoc on the skies whenever she lost one of her infamous chess games. But she had died many decades before our story begins, mysteriously murdered in her own home. That's why the White Throne, carved entirely from the tusks of narwhals, is now called the Red Throne; it's covered in her blood.

Aurora knows the stories well—she's read the entire

313-book collection of faerie histories in her grand library. Princesses have a great deal of time on their hands, after all. Especially princesses like Aurora, who have no sense of touch and no voice. These were tithed from her just months after her birth.

But it wasn't snow that came down that summer, for it didn't melt. And it wasn't any faerie's doing either. As everyone who was alive then and remains alive today remembers vividly, the ashes that rained over heads and homes and whole towns across the kingdom of Deluce had one very distinct quality: the acrid scent of spindle fire.

Wet wool.

Wood smoke.

Burning hair.

2

Isabelle

Mud. Murk. Dankness and blackness and bog land and fog so thick it entered the folds of the mind. This was Isabelle's world as a child.

Gradually, though, she discovered darkness was not an absence of light but a living thing, an infinitely tangible substance to roll around in and dig into. She began to fall in love with that darkness, exploring its wells of sounds and stirs.

The palace was full of dim corners where the king's unwanted daughter could play. The whole estate sits right on a cliff above the mouth of the Strait of Sorrow, whose tide pulls clouds to shore and traps them there, churning and unquenchable. This makes the air briny; it has the vague taste of sardines, and the softness of moss. The floors are always slick with moisture, the walls bright dusted with salt. Over time, Isbe learned the feel of every dent in these walls. Every variety of squeak and cry from the floor formed a language—*don't enter, turn right, someone was just in here,* or *you are alone.*

You see, she was blinded at the age of two; the very day of her half sister Aurora's christening.

Some people consider it a problem—or even a curse—to be forever trapped in darkness. But Isabelle no longer minds the dark.

Light too can be a curse.

It can illuminate things no one should ever have to witness.

3

Aurora

The double doors to the library fly open. Aurora quickly closes *The Song of Rowan* and tucks it beneath her chair cushion as Isbe tramples in, shaking snow off her boots. Her knotty chestnut hair is in its usual disarray, her plain blue-and-white dress torn in at least two places.

Aurora, on the other hand, believes that a princess is meant to look the part at all times, even if she is merely hiding out alone in her library reading romances. Today, for instance, she is wearing a burgundy underdress with an overdress featuring a complex pattern of golden birds and deep-green vines. She even wears a small hennin atop her head, with a long veil trailing behind it.

"Did Rowan take full advantage of his stony love yet?"

Isbe asks with a smirk, her eyes fixed on an invisible spot in the distance. She doesn't have to be able to see to guess: this isn't the first time Aurora has been caught in private, agonized rapture over the tale of Rowan and his true love, Ombeline, who was turned to stone until a thousand crows came down and pecked her free.

Aurora herself is still waiting to be released, in a way. Not from stone, of course, but from the long, silent hours of wondering, trapped in a world where she cannot speak and cannot feel. Will she find true love with Prince Philip of Aubin? Even now he and his brother are galloping toward the palace. . . .

"Ah, good. Some air. That's what this room needs." Isbe has popped open the secret pane in a stained-glass window, allowing delicate flurries to flutter in. Beyond the glass, the famous Delucian cliffs plummet down to the Strait of Sorrow, where Aurora can imagine the snow dissolving like sugar into tea.

Isbe throws herself onto the floor by Aurora's feet, as she is wont to do. Aurora's half sister is as extreme, with her very pale skin and very dark hair, as Aurora is soft, with her warm complexion and blond waves. They are like night and day, or winter and summer. And like both examples, one could simply not exist without the other.

The princess bends down and takes her sister's hand, tapping into her palm, using the secret language they've been evolving and deepening since early childhood. *Soon it will be Philip, and not Rowan, who occupies my time—and your filthy imagination.*

Occasionally Isbe misses a word here or there, but it's rare. Princesses—and their bastard half siblings—have plenty of time to perfect such things. The girls even have a symbol for the name Rowan—the tap for an *R* and then the pressure sequence that means handsome. This is how Aurora connotes all the heroes in her stories: the letter of his name, followed by an adjective: handsome, charming, loyal, strong.

Isbe flashes her big, jagged, unself-conscious smile at Aurora. "True." Then her face falls. "I'll *have* to rely on my imagination, since I'm sure you'll no longer have any time to fill me in on the details."

Aurora squeezes her hand. *No. I'll miss you every moment I'm with him,* she taps.

"Hopefully not *every* moment." Isbe grins again. Then she lets out a big sigh.

No reason for the dramatic sighs. Everything will be normal, Aurora taps.

"Well then," Isbe announces. "I was going to share some gossip. I've just overheard that Prince Philip and his younger brother, Edward, were spotted on the road two days ago at Tristesse Pass, along with their retinue. Which means they should be arriving sooner than we thought. Most likely by tonight. In time for your birthday!"

Aurora gasps, a sound that's almost inaudible. Her entire body buzzes with all the hectic energy of a chicken coop. Her planned marriage to Prince Philip is supposed to cement an important alliance between the kingdoms of Deluce and Aubin. Deluce has wealth, Aubin has military. The idea is that together they can stop the threat of the last living faerie queen, Malfleur.

If the rumors are true, that is. Word has it Malfleur has been building up her army using secret techniques unknown to the rest of the world, in addition to practicing levels of magic not seen among the fae in centuries. Just thinking about it gives Aurora a chill.

LaMorte is the only kingdom ruled by a faerie anymore. It used to be that *all* the positions of power were held by the fae, but that was long ago. Aurora's grandfather was part of the wave of human monarchs pushing the fae out, even as the faeries' magic waned. Now most of Deluce's aristocracy is human, though a faerie duchess or baron remains here and there. And while the fae allow females to govern alone (they pretty much have to, since female faeries generally outlive male faeries by many decades), humans do not. A human princess must marry to become a queen.

Aurora knows how important her upcoming wedding really is to the safety of her kingdom. But that doesn't mean she can't secretly hope that it will be more than tactical— that the prince will be her true love, and with that love, her whole life will change. That, like Ombeline from the story, she will finally be freed.

The veil on Aurora's hennin dances wildly in the open

air. Because of her lack of touch, she doesn't feel pain. So while the princess can tell that it's very cold out, the chill doesn't really bother her. It's just . . . *there*, a dim awareness like a heartbeat.

It's always windy up on the palace wall walks, where she and Isbe have come to look out for the banners of the approaching princes and their retinue. Through the crenellated parapet, Aurora can see the vast expanse of the royal village and the lands to the south and west sides, the mouth of the strait to the northeast, all covered in the soft drape of evening. It's especially blustery at this time of year and this time of day, when the sun has worn down to a crimson paper cut slicing sea from sky.

The wind is helpful, anyway, to her sister. It carries information—sounds and smells that tell her who is coming and how high the tides are, what will be served for dinner, and which of the soldiers guarding the front gates have bedded which of the housemaids.

Tonight, Isbe's face is alive with curiosity, and for what is probably the millionth time, Aurora wishes her sister could see herself, even for an instant. That she could witness the way joy and sadness write themselves so boldly in her expressions. How uncontained her emotions seem.

As different as they are—Isbe's features hard and wild and pale next to Aurora's rosiness, her sun-colored hair, and gentle curves—Aurora likes to believe that something invisible, something deep inside each of them, is connected, forged from the same fire.

Isbe races ahead along the wall walk, which is lit by torches ensconced in the iron brackets atop the seven cupola-covered drum towers. Her form flickers between light and shadow as she passes by each of the parapet's teeth. She is already climbing the stones of the southeast tower—the king's tower, which is also the best vantage point—by the time Aurora reaches the wide southern wall.

Aurora wants to call for Isbe to wait, but of course she can't. She just hopes they won't get caught sneaking around up here. Four years ago, the plague killed both of her parents, King Henri and Queen Amélie. Since then, the council's role has grown from keeping careful watch to issuing suffocating rules. And it's even worse lately.

Because Aurora's sixteenth birthday is tomorrow and the wedding to Philip will soon follow, the council has essentially kept her under lock and key within the lonely palace walls, even though Isbe is completely free to roam the ample grounds, romp through the royal forest, ride horses, snack on random pickings from the lower kitchen, and pretty much do anything she pleases. Everyone acts as if Aurora might collapse under a stray breeze—since she paid the tithe of touch as a child, she is constantly in danger of getting hurt and not realizing it. And it's true she has burned herself too many times to be allowed in the kitchens or too close to the fire. She has embarrassing scars on her knees from various tumbles as a child that led to scratches that bled for hours before she noticed them.

Following Isbe's disappearing form, Aurora hurries to the king's tower and tries to get a foothold in the still-wet stone. Before she gets very far, the familiar voices of the council members float over her head. The king's tower holds one of their meeting rooms, and with its jutting, thinly paned oriel windows, it is one of the easiest rooms to spy on, if you happen to be on the roof.

Aurora pauses, listening to what sounds like a heated exchange. It's very rare for the council to be meeting this late, particularly when such important guests are expected at any moment.

She tucks her dress and robes around her legs and crouches just beneath the oriel, peering in.

"They were supporters of Malfleur, I'm sure of it," one of the men is saying.

Another scoffs. "Nothing but peasants and petty thieves. A horrible accident, and that is all."

"It's not the time to analyze the attack! We are in a state of emergency!" cries another, slamming down hard on a table.

A horrible accident? Attack? A state of emergency? What could possibly have happened? She inches slightly closer to the base of the window, straining to hear.

"This is more than an attack; this is a political maneuver. It's a diplomatic crisis."

"He's right. It's an act . . . an act of *war*. This has to be Malfleur's doing. And without Aubin on our side, we are sunk."

"Aubin still needs us as much as we need them. Their

royal coffers are dry—we know that. Their precious war overseas has seen to that."

"Before we come to any conclusions, we must reconcile ourselves to the murder of the two princes and decide upon swift and immediate action."

At this, Aurora loses her grip and falls several feet to the damp stone floor of the wall walk. The fall doesn't hurt—of course—but the news rings loud and harsh in her ears. *The murder of the two princes.*

It cannot be true.

Philip is no longer coming to marry her.

He and his brother, Edward, are dead.

She must have misunderstood. She needs to go in there and confront them, find out the truth. But even as she thinks that, she realizes how silly it sounds. Aurora, confronting the council? It's unheard of. In the past she's made vain attempts to write her thoughts down with ink on vellum, copying the beautiful script found in the books she loves to read. But the council members have only responded with blank, befuddled stares. In fact, most of them are illiterate and find it simply unimaginable that a woman could have taught herself to both read and write.

The murder of the two princes. The words keep repeating themselves, tumbling over one another in her mind even as she scrambles up the tower toward her sister. She wishes once again that she could call out to Isbe. But with no voice, she is left to climb, higher this time, desperate to find her, to convey what she's heard.

The dome is slick and cold. She reaches the top of the tower and clings to the curved roof, inching her way toward the outer-facing side. She thinks she sees Isbe, just around the—

A gust of wind blows Aurora's veil into her face. As she tries to shake it free, she senses her shoe has become heavy. It must have soaked up some of the unmelted snow, which means . . .

Her foot slips.

She gasps, her balance giving way, then flails, losing her grip with one hand. Panic flies through her lungs, leaving her mouth in a silent scream.

The murder of the two princes, the wind sings back to her, and she knows. She is going to fall.

A shout pierces the darkness.

Isbe's face, torch lit, hovers above her. She has firmly caught Aurora's sleeve and yanked her back against the tower. "Aurora . . . I heard you. I'm here!"

Aurora's pulse races in her throat. She is shaking, marveling at her sister's ability to hear even the slightest skid of shoe against ice.

Slowly they move to safety, one chapped hand before the other, until they are just above the wall walk, where Isbe leaps down first and reaches up to assist Aurora, whose heart is still pounding so powerfully she fears she may faint.

But as her dizziness clears, all she can think is what she must communicate to Isbe. The princes.

Both of them. Murdered.

"Oi! What are you doing up here?" Two night guards are approaching.

Aurora frantically tries to grab Isbe's hand, but the guards rush them from either side and yank them apart.

"Told youse to stay off here!" one guard grumbles.

"Let us go!" Isbe cries as they are both dragged roughly down the steps.

"Escaped yer cage again, eh?" says the other to Aurora. She's thankful that Isbe can't see the sneer on his pocked face.

Isbe juts out her chin. "We were just trying to—"

"That's 'bout enough of that," one growls as they haul the girls through a passageway, up another set of stairs, and into the king's tower proper, where they are presented before the twelve gathered councilmen and -women.

"Sorry to barge in. But we caught 'em climbing the towers again. Princess almost took a bad drop," the older and fatter of the guards says. "*This* one was scampering up and down like a goat."

Before Aurora can so much as shake her head in protest, Isbe clears her throat, squeezing Aurora's hand tight. "He's right. It was all my fault, not Aurora's."

Meanwhile, Jules de Villeroy, the chancellor, tugs at his collar. "This is a most, *most* inopportune moment."

Aurora desperately taps into Isbe's hand. *The princes. Dead. Philip's dead.* She can't tell if her sister has registered the message.

Old hotheaded Humphrey bangs his fist on the arm of

his chair. "Dammit! Endangering the princess? At a time like this? I've had enough! All of our plans. The whole alliance . . . up in smoke in a moment if something were to—" He cuts himself off and takes a breath. "If we don't handle *that* one," he finishes, pointing fiercely at Isbe, "then I personally will."

Aurora looks nervously around the room at the council: ten men and two women. The men all have bare, protruding foreheads—the style of the time, though Aurora can't understand why—and wear high collars and deep frowns. The women, both financial attendants, look as shriveled as the pickled fish Aurora has watched servants eating in the kitchen. She can't remember a time when these women were young.

These are the men and women who have, over the past four years, become the unwanted surrogate caretakers for her and Isbe. She knows none of them has any true affection for her. She is a mere item to be bartered.

It's even worse for Isbe, of course. She is no princess, and she will be eighteen soon. So far, despite the council's best attempts, no one has been interested in marrying the dead king's blind bastard daughter.

Lord Ferdinand pushes his chair back from the table. Aurora can't help but notice that the corner of the rotund man's red robe is stained with either mud or gravy—more likely the latter, given how little he's known to venture past the castle walls. "With the permission of my fellow councilmen," Ferdinand says, "I see it fit we pursue our original plans regarding Isabelle immediately."

"Plans?" Isbe asks as Aurora's heart starts to beat faster.

"You are to be sent to a convent in the district of Isolé," says one of the stern old clerics at the back of the room.

"But . . . for how long?" Isbe croaks.

"For the remainder of your life," says the cleric.

"No!" Isbe tries to lunge forward; however, one of the guards keeps his fat hand around her arm, holding her back.

Aurora feels like she's been strangled. Isbe. Leaving. Forever. It's too much. Her knees are beginning to give out. Her sister shouldn't have said anything. She shouldn't have opened her big mouth, trying to be brave, trying to protect Aurora, like always.

Look where it's gotten her now.

Maximilien, one of the younger members and perhaps the kindest of the council despite being the chief of military, nods. "We were going to wait until after the wedding, but we might as well make haste. Aurora's safety and protection are of *utmost* importance."

Aurora doesn't know whether to be furious or devastated or simply afraid. Isolé lies at the southernmost point of Deluce, near the border of Corraine. That's miles and miles from the palace!

She fumbles for Isbe's hand again, but her sister pulls away.

"Why?" she blurts out. "Why are we to be parted if the wedding is no longer happening?" So her palm *did*

understand Aurora's hasty message.

Maximilien frowns. "I can see you have been listening in where you were not invited. Nevertheless . . ." He turns to Aurora. "You both may as well know that Princes Philip and Edward of Aubin are dead."

Aurora's heart plummets into her stomach like a bucket dropped down a well. Hearing it announced so bluntly is even harder the second time.

"I ask again," Isbe says, jutting out her chin. "How will Aurora marry if the two princes of Aubin are dead?"

"Luckily," another council member replies, "there is a third."

4

Isabelle

If human bodies had the firepower of cannons, Isbe is sure her head would have shot off and exploded, scattering burning black ash all over the council. (Aurora has read and described to her the exact mechanics of every type of weapon in Deluce's royal arsenal, and Isbe often entertains herself by imagining putting them to use.) Her fingertips graze the tapestries and portraits that line the walls as she stomps down the stone corridors, knocking over the Hercules vase in her rush—its nose worn down from years of her touching it. The piece is worth more than the dowry of seven duchesses. She hears it shatter. *Good.*

Over a century ago, this whole castle was actually the faerie queen Malfleur's own childhood home. She lived in it with her twin, Belcoeur, otherwise known as the Night Faerie. That was before Malfleur *killed* the Night Faerie and was assigned rule over the LaMorte territories. There's even a popular children's lullaby based on the story. But now ornate columns, thick rugs, and overpungent displays of flowers hide any trace of the palace's history, which becomes more like myth every day.

Isbe doesn't even let Aurora catch up to her as she traipses downstairs to her quarters in one of the western wings, not bothering to skip over the creaking seventh stair. She needs to be alone. She needs to think.

And for once, Aurora's advice, her calm wisdom, simply won't help.

Isbe knows that it's not Aurora's fault. It's not her fault that she's the only heir to the throne of Deluce. It's not her fault the kingdom could be on the verge of war. And it's not her fault she's so beautiful and well-behaved and perfect. Aurora is all light. She is fresh-fluffed cream and the smell of a spring bulb's first shoots pricking up through the earth, while Isbe has always been the expendable one, all anger and elbow, odd as a goose's honk.

For years the council has treated her no better than a glorified servant—any kindness she has received has been at Aurora's insistence. Isbe is the troublemaker, good for nothing except to serve as a companion for her younger sister. And now, apparently not even good for that. The truth that Isbe is simply no longer needed—by Aurora or by anyone—cuts into her, savage as claws.

She shoves open her door, and it slams into the wall with a terrible bang. It takes her a second to realize from the shift of heat and shadow, from the intake of breath, that someone is already waiting for her in the room.

"Think this here pillow has enough tassels?"

Gilbert, one of the stableboys and Isbe's oldest friend, shifts his legs on her bed, rustling her downy coverlet. She can smell the mud on his boots and the equine musk ever present in his hands and hair.

"Enough to strangle all twelve council members with?" she replies. "Unfortunately, no, Gil, I doubt there's enough frill in this entire castle to knot around their thick necks."

"Bad night?"

"To say the least."

"What is it?" Her bed exhales as he sits up—the few pieces of furniture in her bedroom have all learned to speak to her of movements, in creaks and whooshes and groans, in tics and aspirations. While Gil is, of course, technically not allowed in her room, not merely because he's the son of the palace horse farrier but also because he's a *boy*, he has nonetheless entered and exited these chambers for years without anyone knowing it, by way of a lilac trellis underneath her window.

"Isbe," Gil presses. "Just tell me."

"I'm leaving," she spits.

For weeks, months even, she's been agonizing about what will happen to her when Aurora marries. She loathes the fact that her fate is so dependent on her younger, more beautiful sister's, the way all her choices, when it comes down to it, are invisibly tethered to Aurora's. No matter how much she loves her sister, no matter how many years of their childhood they spent clambering up and down the winding passageway connecting their bedrooms . . . some part of her has always wished that for just one moment she could find out what her life would be like if Aurora weren't around.

Now she will know, and she hates herself for that terrible, shameful wish.

"What? You can't leave. I don't understand. Where are you going?" He touches her arm—his hand, familiar as Aurora's, is as rough as hers is delicate, a deep rein-worn crease cutting diagonally across his calloused palm.

She swallows hard. She can barely stand to explain what just happened. It's so mortifying; she feels hollowed out. Not only are they sending her away, but it has *always been their plan*. She's disposable, a *pomme sauvage*: a crab apple barely hanging onto the tree, not sweet enough to eat, sour and unwanted even before it falls to the earth to rot.

"The council wants to send me to a convent in Isolé. Apparently they were always intending it, but tonight we got in trouble, and the princes of Aubin—two of them, anyway—were murdered, and Aurora and I were caught spying, and now—" She takes a breath, steadying her voice. "Now I'm to depart at dawn."

Gil barks out a laugh.

Horrified, Isbe shoves him away. "This isn't *funny*, it's my *life*!" She marches miserably to her trunk and throws open the lid.

Gil comes up behind her. "Well, this is perhaps perfect, then!"

"Yes, it's—wait, what?" She turns.

"I'm leaving the palace too," Gil says.

Automatically, she reaches up and places her hands on his cheeks, feeling the dimples and familiar smile, the honesty, the *Gilbertness* of him. It's a habit that started many years ago with her half sister—Isbe would touch her face to try and read the emotions there, since Aurora has no voice to betray the feeling behind her words. It was Isbe's way of staying as connected as possible to Aurora . . . and then it became so second nature that she began to try it out on Gilbert too. He never refused.

"You're not joking," she says now, both feeling and hearing his seriousness.

"No. And it isn't funny, actually." His jaw clicks softly. "My brother's wife died last month in childbirth. I only just found out. Lost the baby too. Roul is . . . well, you can imagine."

"I'm . . ." She fumbles, taken aback. "I'm very sorry." Isbe hasn't seen Gil's older brother in many years, and never knew Roul's wife. To her knowledge, Gil never met her either.

Gil clears his throat. "Anyway. He didn't send for me. You know Roul; he wouldn't do that. Too proud. But a messenger let it slip. He could use my help at the farm, what with the two young ones. Isn't too many miles south of here."

Isbe nods. She remembers when Roul left to take over a

farm in one of the vast, faerie-owned fiefs farther inland. He had to pay several tithes of luck to a faerie baron for it.

"He'll take us *both* in, I'm sure," Gil goes on. "Needs all the help he can get, I'd think. I wasn't certain if I should go. That is, I didn't *want* to leave. But now . . . see? You wouldn't *have* to go to Isolé. You could just come with me."

Isbe doesn't know what to say, only that her face feels as though it has been splashed by a pot of scalding water. Embarrassment and gratitude fight each other for space inside her chest. She has no idea what farm life is really like, but it must be better than life in a convent. At any rate, life there with *Gil* would be immeasurably better than being alone.

"Besides," Gil goes on, "just picturing you at a convent is hilarious. Girl like you? Wouldn't last 'til the first sundown."

"A girl like me?"

"Wild. Big mouth. Says whatever she pleases."

"Hmph." She's not sure if it's a compliment or an insult, but she lets the point drop, instead crouching down to cram dresses and sheets into her trunk. She must keep her hands and mouth busy, otherwise who knows what she might be tempted to do—muss up Gil's hair, or kiss him, or . . .

"Poor Roul," she says instead, attempting to distract herself from the fact that she is preparing to leave her home, and Aurora, forever. "I'm sure there's many a country girl waiting in line to be his next wife, though." Everyone used to say he was tall, dark-haired, and handsome, even when they were all kids. "Perhaps," she adds, nudging Gil with her shoulder, "he'll have extras lined up for you as well. Some delightful farmer's daughter for a wife. A nice girl who always says exactly the right thing."

The idea brings her a mix of happiness for Gil and something else too: jealousy, maybe, though it shouldn't. She knows that.

Still, she wonders whether in moments like this he ever thinks back to that day, about three years ago . . . the day she was wading in the tiny stream just past the cattle pastures.

Isbe had "borrowed" Freckles again, the frisky young mare few others had the patience to ride, for one of her expeditions to spy on the royal military. These rides very often ended with Freckles bucking Isbe into the thick mud at pasture's end. The council did not condone this behavior, of course—said she'd likely die someday for taking such risks—but for Isbe it became a game, trying to figure out where she'd landed and how to get back.

Since she has grown up without sight, Isbe has rarely known the pleasure of running freely through field or forest. It's too dangerous—the world rushes up at her, random and disordered. But on the back of a horse, she can experience the thrill of speed, of the air racing through her hair, of her lungs heaving as the animal becomes her legs and her eyes. And she has never cared about the odd bruises and scrapes from falling or fumbling her way home—these are simply the world's way of proving its own existence, the souvenirs of a life actually *lived*.

On this particular occasion, Gil had found her doing her best to wrench the mud from her garments in the stream's eddies. In late spring, when the sun is hot, the stream flows over a low ledge, creating a nice current below. She and Aurora fondly call this spot the Waterfall, even though the drop is only a few feet. Sometimes they also call it Nose Rock, due to the boulder at the base of the ledge that resembles a man's face with, well, a very large nose.

Gil had scolded her for riding alone, and to defend herself, Isbe began an enactment of the military exercises she'd learned from spying—or at least, what she presumed them to be, based on the shouted commands she'd overheard, the hollers of the soldiers, the clang of swords, and the shuffle of hooves.

The more Gil laughed at her attempts, the more determined Isbe became to prove she'd truly learned how to fight. Her demonstration easefully transformed into a water war, and she remembers the exact moment she fell against Gil in the stream, and his hand became entangled in her long, loose hair, and the mossy, mineral scent of the water mingled with the damp touch of his body against hers, his laughter slipping away on the wind as their lips met.

The kiss had been both surprising and seamless, both endless and somehow fleeting. His lips were warm and soft, so unlike the other, more calloused parts of him she was used to. His tongue was there, communicating with her own in a foreign language—and there was so much, so much to say with just their bodies, with just their lips.

But then he'd pulled back—their first-ever awkward moment. "We shouldn't," he'd said. Something like that. She couldn't understand what he meant, why he said it, why he didn't want to keep on doing what they had been doing: for hours, for days, maybe forever.

And then, with a sudden and terrible weight, she knew. Of course she knew: Isbe was not beautiful. Not like other girls. Certainly not like Aurora. Even without being able to see her the way others did, Isbe knew how gorgeous Aurora was, from the way she moved, the way she smelled, the way people inhaled abruptly when they saw her, the way men spoke about her in whispers and murmurs they thought no one else could hear.

No. Isbe was different. Awkward and tall for a girl, with messy dark hair that never lay flat, a pointy nose and hard cheekbones and too-big eyes.

Gil didn't see her *that* way. He didn't want those things from her, the things boys want from beautiful girls.

After that day, Isbe had become as firm and hard as Nose Rock, wild and spiked and merciless as a morning star club, brave and bold and quick—too quick to let feelings of doubt or embarrassment about her appearance ever catch up to her again. She doesn't need to be beautiful. And she doesn't need love. She can live without it.

But now her comment lingers uncomfortably in the air between them.

Gil clears his throat. "I should prepare us two horses. We'll ride just before dawn."

"Gil?" she asks as he stands to leave.

"Iz?"

She turns her face away from his, feeling exposed. "Thank you."

And then he is shoving her window open, and with a gust of cold air, he is gone.

———

Isbe is still packing when a rustling in the secret passageway announces Aurora's approach. A second later the tapestry swishes open and Aurora's slippers pat across the room. She kneels next to Isbe, and their elbows bump. Even though Isbe's swimming in a sea of confused and contradictory feelings, she is just as aware as ever of her sister's fragility. It's Isbe's job—as it has always been—to be strong for Aurora. Even if, in this moment, Aurora can't be strong for *her*.

Aurora takes her hand and begins to tap. *I didn't need you to stand up for me. You shouldn't have.*

Isbe can feel the pent-up frustration through the tips of Aurora's fingers.

Maybe if you had kept quiet, you wouldn't have to go.

"Aurora, that's silly. Even if I hadn't said a thing, they would still be sending me away. I'm not needed here anymore. You're getting married. I no longer have a use. It's a wonder they didn't send me sooner."

It's not fair. I'm not a child, and I should have a choice. It's not up to you.

"It's not up to *either* of us. It's up to the council." She feels a little calmer when she thinks of Gilbert's promise to help. Maybe once Aurora is settled with her new prince, she can be reunited with her sister. "Besides, I'm not *going* to the nunnery, so you needn't worry."

What?

"I'm not going. I'm running away."

But I'll still be here, lonely and miserable.

Isbe tries to ignore the mild sting in her words. "You won't be lonely—you're marrying a prince. *I'm* the one being kicked out of our home. I'm sorry if I can't say I pity you."

Please don't be jealous of me, Isbe. You know how much I need you. We need each other.

"Jealous?" She snorts. Jealous of the princess who can't speak or feel, who's forced into a marriage with a prince she's never met? "As if I'd *want* my life to be anything like yours!" she blurts out.

She can feel from the tension in Aurora's body that she has hurt her sister.

Slowly Aurora taps. *In that case, maybe it is for the best that you're leaving.*

She doesn't mean it, Isbe knows—she's just offended. She's just worried and upset about everything that's happened in the past few hours. But still Isbe yanks her hand away—a sharp cruelty. Without their hand-to-hand connection, her sister can't communicate at all. She's trapped in her own silence.

Well, she'd better get used to it.

"Please, just leave. I need to be alone." The words burn her throat, and as soon as her sister swishes through the tapestry and her distressed footsteps fade from the secret corridor, Isbe slumps down onto her plush bed, a flood of dread and sadness pushing up against her on all sides, threatening to drown her.

She rolls over, pushing her face into a pillow. Its fresh linen-y smell only makes the pain welling up inside her worse. How many times has Aurora insisted on Isbe's comfort, even at the expense of her own? How often has Isbe tended to Aurora's scrapes and cuts and beestings—not because they hurt her but precisely because they *didn't*? Sometimes Isbe could swear *she* felt the pain that her sister could not, held it for her, in case that was how pain worked and someone had to bear it.

How many mornings did they wake side by side, having stayed up too late telling each other stories? How many games and jokes and codes did they create—not to mention an entire secret language of hand taps—building a world that was all their own, an impenetrable fortress belonging just to them?

Isbe longs even now to crawl up the secret passageway to Aurora's room and apologize, to get into her bed and refuse to let go of her, refuse to be parted.

But it's an impossible wish. Her life until now has been a lie, an indulgence. And the horrible suspicion that Aurora *pities* her—that, on some level, maybe she *wants* Isbe out of her way—is what gives her the resolve she needs at last.

Isbe would always rather face the truth. Even if it crushes her.

When she hears the pebble against her window several hours later, she doesn't hesitate. If she turned back now and ran to apologize to Aurora, she might lose her nerve. So she walks toward the wind blowing her open shutters back and forth.

Night has a very different smell from day. It is purer, sweeter somehow. In the night, there are no boundaries between herself and the world around her. She is equal to it.

Isbe heaves her trunk onto the windowsill and, when Gil calls softly up to her, drops it into his waiting arms, fleeing her room—and her sister and her home and her life up until now.

As the cold air embraces her and she grips the lilac trellis for the last time, she could swear her own palm tingles, as though from a simple long-and-short pinkie tap. *Good-bye.*

5

Aurora

Aurora is startled from fitful sleep by a loud rustling of feathers . . . and a voice. "Evening, caged bird," it says.

She opens her eyes and scans the room. The door is closed. A fire mellows in the hearth. Perhaps one of her maids came in to stoke it? That must have been the noise. Or maybe she was dreaming. She leans back against the pillow. Her eyes drift closed again.

"Any pastry? Better yet, mouse's head?"

This time Aurora sits up with a start. On her window ledge stands a small, smoke-black starling silhouetted by moonlight. Its tiny dark eyes shine, and it cocks its head as though curious, or hungry. She must have left her window open a crack. Since the cold doesn't bother her, she sometimes forgets to worry about it. The bird in the window is watching her. It's almost as if the *bird* was the one to speak. . . .

But that's old magic, impossible magic.

Then, as she watches, the bird opens its mouth. "Me. What." Each of the words a separate caw. "What. Is. Me."

Aurora's chest tenses. A talking bird. Like something from one of her tales. She throws back the covers and steps cautiously toward the window. Around the bird's ankle is a fine metal brace, and if she's not mistaken, it bears a familiar image: a thorny ring surrounding a small crow. The crest of Malfleur.

Aurora stares in awe. People say that unlike most faeries, Queen Malfleur still knows how to wield magic of great power and influence—has made a special study of it all her life, which has been long. She reigns over the scattered territories of disgruntled and largely disorganized citizens in the remote LaMorte Mountains, and Deluce has little to no traffic with LaMorte, so there's not much evidence to prove whether the rumors of the queen's gifts of magic are true.

In fact, Deluce has issued many trade sanctions against them, and has repeatedly taxed all passage between the two kingdoms in an effort to discourage the unhappy, unhealthy, and often uncivilized people of LaMorte from crossing over to the lands of their far wealthier neighbors. Aurora has always assumed Malfleur's skill in magic had been vastly exaggerated throughout the years—more myth than truth to it.

But studying the bird now, Aurora realizes that in fact the rumors about Malfleur's powers may have been accurate all along. If the faerie queen can make birds speak, what else can she do? And why has the bird come here?

Aurora shivers again, trying to picture the faerie queen, with the dramatic white scar that supposedly crosses her left eyelid.

The bird flutters its wings. "Me freak? Me . . . fiction?"

Aurora shakes her head no.

"What is me?" the bird asks, and she cannot tell if the words are a taunt or a test—or a sincere question. "Vermin. Wonder. Failed experiment. Or success?"

She shakes her head again.

"Magic in guts. Magic inside. Words inside. Like dust. Eating dust. Like fire. Me? Alone. Alone," the bird says.

Its voice is cold as iron, and she can't tell whether it knows what it's saying. Whether it's asking for help.

"Cat got your tongue?" the bird caws. "Cat got your tongue?"

Aurora shakes her head a third time.

"No words, human?" The starling caws again, and it sounds like a harsh laugh. "Like scarecrow."

At this, Aurora loses patience and shoos the bird out of the window with a hard wave of the back of her hand. The bird cries once more, fluttering back and taunting her with a final, mocking word. "Useless." Then it's winging away into the night.

As soon as it's gone, Aurora closes her shutters quickly,

tears pricking at her eyes, mortification stinging her cheeks. Is she losing her mind, or did a starling really just speak to her—and not just speak, but tease, call her useless, and compare her to a scarecrow?

She gets back into bed, either to sleep and dream, or else to wake up from this eerie nightmare, but neither happens. Instead she lies awake, the starling's words lingering in her ears. *Useless.*

She sits up and pushes back the covers. She goes to the hearth and lights a lantern, then wraps herself in her robe and hurries into the secret passageway to Isbe's room. She has to tell her about the bird—maybe her sister can help her understand what it means. But when she flips open the tapestry, she sees wind rattling the open shutters. The fire is out. The room is empty. Isbe has gone.

Aurora adjusts the heavy cloak around her shoulders and lifts her lantern higher as she steps into the thick, moon-bright snow, reminding herself why she's doing this. She forces herself to think of the talking bird. She will not be useless. She will not let Isbe go. She has always needed her sister. Now her sister needs her. She's not going to let her just run away like that. She'll find her, bring her back, fight for her to stay.

Suspecting Gilbert's aid, the first thing she does is look for hoofprints, which are easy enough to find in the new-fallen snow. She traces them past the stables and along the dark woods at the edge of the castle village. She passes the unruly thicket where she and Isbe used to imagine that evil monsters dwelled at night, the branches twisted into an ornate latticework glistening with frost. The path of snow prints leads her to the main southerly road, which first winds closer to the shores of the strait and then curves west, veering toward the vast expanse of land beyond the royal grounds. Peasants sleep later in winter, and the area appears deserted. She rapidly loses the meager set of hoofprints amid the mud and slush and chaos of horse tracks in the road, all silvered in a predawn haze.

She turns, half tempted to go back. Though she has only gone a few miles, she is as far as she's ever been from the castle.

Sneaking away had in fact been easy, which gave Aurora an *un*easy feeling. She's never considered simply leaving the palace before—why would she?

Now she's hoping that there will be so much to do in the morning in preparation for her birthday feast that it will take everyone a little while to realize that the princess herself has vanished, and the bastard sister too. She knows the council members will be quite busy doing their best to hide their fears about the princes' murders, while dispatching soldiers and guards to fortify the LaMorte border.

And if all goes well, she'll catch up to Isbe by the afternoon, and they'll return safe and sound in time for the celebration.

A horse-drawn cart clops toward her, and she moves to the side of the road as its giant wheels shoot mud up her ankles. She's partly hoping that its driver will stop and ask if she needs help, but she can't bring herself to wave him down, fearing she could be recognized and sent home as soon as the driver realizes she doesn't speak.

She keeps her head down and continues walking.

The road is disturbingly quiet. It occurs to Aurora that she really has very little sense of Deluce as a nation, of what it's *really* like to live here. She's been introduced to a variety of lords and ladies, dukes and duchesses, noblemen and noblefaeries alike, but she's never once been invited to *their* homes, nor seen the great population of peasants at work.

There's a rustle in the trees, and a bird darts out of the underbrush, flapping into the sky. Could it be the same starling? Worry blossoms inside her. There are so many things lurking in this world about which she knows so little: magic that has the power to give birds speech, tensions that drive men to murder. Her heart races as though trying to speak for her, to tell her to stop, to turn back. This is no way to spend a sixteenth birthday—wandering alone.

Another bird shrieks.

A distant scream rings out—maybe an owl.

Or could it be the howl of a killer, covered in the stale blood of two princes, hungry for more?

To be safe, Aurora steps off the road and into the soft thickness of the surrounding woods. Even with her lantern, it's dark—so dark. It's too late, or too early, for a girl—a princess—to be out alone.

This was a mistake. She'll turn home and demand that the council send out a proper search party to discover Isbe's whereabouts and bring her back. She'll find a way. Perhaps she can refuse to marry Prince William—the third and youngest son of the late king of Aubin—until this one wish has been granted.

Yes. That's what she'll do. She'll double back, sticking to the woods, which are speckled slightly with the last dregs of moonlight.

But even upon turning around, pushing past underbrush and dodging the low-hanging branches of the trees, many still covered in snow, she begins to find herself disoriented. She'd been only a few feet from the road, hadn't she? But the road, of course, isn't lit, and so she can't quite tell. Better to chance bandits on the road than wolves in the forest. She moves a few feet in what she is sure must be the right direction, but only finds herself surrounded by more woods. Is this the royal forest? She begins to run, urgency pumping through her veins. Her dress tangles in roots and branches, and she hears a tear, but she doesn't care. She trips and falls onto her knees, dropping the lantern. The flame sputters out. With no way to relight it, she leaves it on the ground and gets up quickly, her fear spiking. She runs toward the road.

The road isn't there.

She turns around again and sees a glimmer of light. That *must* be it: the moon against a frozen puddle. Pulse hammering in her temples, she runs harder. She finds herself not beside the road at all, but near a cottage. Its windows are shuttered and completely covered in ivy. It must be one of the many old homes the royal families of the past used to summer in—ideal for hunting excursions. There are several of these throughout the royal forest, Aurora knows, many now long abandoned. Her father enjoyed hunting when he was young and decreed that all the deer in the forest be reserved for his use alone—but he apparently gave up the sport when he married her mother. Since then, the royal forest has become thick with foliage and busy with game that no one is allowed to hunt.

This cottage is large but extremely humble in comparison to the palace, with only two levels and not a single tower. The light she thought she had seen is not the moon but a strange cluster of fireflies huddled at the base of the front roof. As her eyes adjust, she can make out the shape of a small wooden swing tied with two ropes, lightly swaying in the wind.

She has no idea where she is, or which of the several old summer homes this might be, but at this hour an abandoned cottage seems far safer than the woods. When the sun has fully risen she'll resume her search for the road.

Ivy winds along the doorframe, and Aurora wonders when the door was last opened. After tugging and shoving, dust flying into her face, the heavy door eventually budges inward with a groan.

Aurora glances over her shoulder into the whispering woods around her before entering the dark home. She leaves the door open a crack, hoping the faintest of outdoor light will penetrate the heavy blackness of the air within—and wishing she had just a small portion of Isbe's bravery, her facility for moving about in the dark.

Think, she urges herself. Servants usually leave a lantern on a shelf just inside the door of every room. Her hands fumble along the inner walls until she trips and hears a clatter. A metal lantern. It must have been on the floor.

She bends down and feels for the handle. Thankfully, there is an old candle inside and a tinderbox attached. Hurriedly, with trembling hands, she shakes a bit of dried kindling into the lid and removes the flint, then rubs the flint against the firestone, watching the faintest of sparks fly off.

It takes several minutes before the kindling catches—a tiny, winking orange ember, which she gathers toward her mouth and blows on until it becomes a small flame. Quickly she uses the flame to light the candle before stomping it back out. It's the first time she has lit a candle like this in all her life—normally, the servants keep fires burning in every room of the palace, for all but a very few hours of the night, and it's far easier to light the lanterns using the already leaping hearth flames.

The dust in the air is thick—so thick she fears the air itself will somehow catch on fire. The house has clearly not been inhabited for many years, but feeling she has no better choice, she finds her way to the staircase and heads up, looking for something resembling a bedroom, where she can close the door and sleep the remaining hour or so until sunrise.

At the top of the stairs, she enters the nearest room, and can see dimly that it's a children's nursery. An old doll sits in the window, a clock—still ticking!—is perched on the mantel, and two small beds line opposite walls. There's an open wardrobe, and inside it hang the forms of little girls' dresses, glimmering as though woven not of fabric but of precious metal.

A whistle chimes, and Aurora nearly loses her breath before realizing the sound has come, oddly, *from* the clock. A tiny mechanical bird's face is popping in and out. It whistles once more, and then the bird's head retreats behind a little door below the six. She's never seen anything like it before.

She turns and notices something luminous in the corner of the room. A large golden wheel with spokes, bigger than one you might find on a horse-drawn cart. It looks like a glowing sun, and it's resting atop a low stand, also made of gold. Spilling from a small spool at its side is a long, shimmering thread.

Aurora moves closer to inspect it. To her surprise, even in the candlelight, it appears the thread *itself* is made from gold. She examines the strange instrument from which the thread flows. It must be some sort of elaborate spindle, she realizes. She's never seen one, though she's read about them in books. Her parents always told her that spindles were instruments of evil, bad luck to be warded off at all costs. Since it was only one of many of their superstitions, she hadn't given it much thought before, but this particular contraption seems magical, mysterious, wonderful.

Enraptured by the spindle's foreign beauty, she sets down the lantern and spins the great wheel with her hand, watching as it pulls the remainder of the golden thread onto the spool. The sun begins to break over the horizon just then, sending a splash of brilliance into the room, making the thread glow. She reaches out to grab the end of it, and her hand makes contact with the tip of the spindle. For the first time in her life, she feels a sharp pang. It's a feeling, a sensation, coming from her skin. From *touch*. Which is impossible. And yet it's real—she *feels* it, and it . . . stings, hurts, flares, thrums, sending a shock through her entire body, making her dizzy.

And then, just at the break of dawn on the very day of her sixteenth birthday, she finds she is sinking through the dazzling sunlight, the aura of gold, falling, fainting, descending into memory, into a chaos of colors.

Dreams.

Flame.

6

Belcoeur,
the Night Faerie

Threads of pink, silver, and pure light weave through her fingers as if of their own will. The soft *click-clack* of her loom is a love sound, warp mating with weft, over and under, over and under, until an image begins to emerge: low silver clouds mirrored in a pond, trees bending protectively as two little girls race through streaked sunlight. In the distance, a summer cottage, its windows dim. A scene she has created so often her body knows it as well as breathing.

"My Sweet Bee," the queen of Sommeil says to her loom, "how tirelessly you work for me." Her eyes graze over the instrument's contours to its name, carved carefully by hand into the breast beam. *Sweet Bee.*

A thread catches, pulling her attention back to the

tapestry. A memory pierces her heart. *Someone is coming.*

Her breath quickens. Belcoeur licks her finger and feeds another strand of silk through the eye of a needle. With careful precision, she hand stitches a new detail, seen only partially through one of the cottage windows: a table with a minuscule teacup on it, steam rising from its lip. Beside it, a bowl heaped with sugar. In case the visitor is thirsty.

Hours, days, and even the trees beyond the castle walls swirl by, rippling in mist. Belcoeur hangs her tapestry on the wall beside the others and steps back to take it in.

But something is not right. A coarse, coal-colored cord has braided its way into a corner, creating shadow. Before her eyes, the image on the tapestry morphs, the shadow creeps . . . and the door to the tiny knit cottage is thrown open.

PART

II

ALL TANGLED
IN THORNS

7

Aurora

Aurora is on fire. The world is on fire. Her whole body is alive and tingly and in shock, yet she feels so strange, like she's dying—no. Like she's being *born*.

She's lying on a hard wooden floor. She sits up, blinking, unsure how long she's been asleep. It is now full morning, and sun pours through the window of the nursery room, warm and full. Outside, birds chirp haphazardly. Everything looks the same except for the spinning wheel, which has vanished. Could it have been stolen? But if the room was raided, wouldn't she have awoken?

She feels an ache in her hand and holds it up, where she sees a tiny pinprick of blood. How can it hurt so much? How can it hurt *at all*?

How . . . ? she wonders.

Just as she's wondering it, someone says the word aloud.

She scrambles around, but no one's there.

What . . . ? she thinks, only once again the word is not in her head but audible, as though an invisible person is mimicking her, has crawled into her mind and read her thoughts.

Make it stop! she wishes—and it happens again.

A scream erupts from somewhere, so powerful it shakes her entire body, sending her crumpling to the floor covering her ears. Every time she heaves for breath, the sound gets louder, wailing in rhythm to her breathing.

And that's when it occurs to her.

No one else *is* here.

She is the one screaming.

Which isn't possible. It can't be.

She hears footsteps pounding up the creaky wooden stairs. Someone's coming. She pushes to her knees, tries to get her mind to focus. Maybe she should hide in the wardrobe, or—

The bedroom door flies open and a young man enters.

Instantly he is at her side, one arm around her. She experiences this stranger's unexpected embrace in a way she has never experienced anything before. The heat of him, the closeness—it's too intense. Too overwhelming. She yanks herself away.

Touch.

"Are you all right? Can I help you?" he's saying.

She finds she is shaking. She can't tell if this is a dream or a nightmare.

"Shh," he says. "Take a deep breath. One, two. Good."

She settles somewhat and looks at him. Her attacker? No, her rescuer. He can't be much older than her. His eyes are a blend of browns and greens like summer ponds, their depths unclear—not how she imagined any of the heroes in her stories. In her mind, Rowan always had shiny gray eyes, like the still-hot ridges of a burnt log. This man is no prince, either. He's barefoot, with the deep tan and streamlined muscles of a field worker—and thin too, as though there is nothing to spare in his life. He's carrying netting, a bow and arrow, and a large coil of rope on his back.

"What are you doing in here?" he asks, reaching out to help her to her feet.

The gesture is unassuming, easy, and yet as their hands meet, she once again feels a heat so strong it burns. Every line in his palms, every rough crease in his fingertips makes noise against her skin. She pulls away again, as though stung.

"How did you find this place?" he asks.

Aurora doesn't know what to do. She opens her lips to respond, but it's so rare that anyone addresses her in this manner, actually expecting a response. Only an awkward croak comes out.

"Tell me your name. Where did you come from?"

"I'm—" she tries, trembling again at the sound of what must be her own voice. "I'm . . . Aurora," she manages.

"Crown—crown princess of Deluce." The words feel scrambled on her tongue.

"How did you find the cottage? You must know it's not safe out here."

She shakes her head, already exhausted from the few words she's spoken.

He steps back, suspicion written on his brow. No, he is definitely not Rowan handsome, she can see, nor Ansell strong. And yet there's something about him—a muddy mingling of adjectives her hands certainly wouldn't be quick or clever enough to tap into Isbe's palms.

"Prove you're not an Impression," he says quietly. She notices his hand moving toward the hilt of a dagger at his belt.

"I don't—"

But before she can reply, he takes her wrists roughly in one hand and points his knife to her throat with the other.

She gasps, blinking rapidly, shocked that he has dared to threaten her when only a moment ago he'd wanted to help. . . .

"Tell me," he says slowly and carefully, "how you got here."

Aurora swallows. Her throat is still raw from the scream. Her wrists in his hand make a silent scream of their own. Her whole body is *buzzing*, yet her back against the wall is so final, somehow, it muffles her fear. "A gold—golden wheel," she begins, shifting nervously and trying not to think about the blade, so close to her neck. She focuses instead on the feeling of her own lips and tongue, the subtle vibrations of air passing through her throat. "A . . . a spinning wheel. I touched it. It . . . it . . . *harmed* me. I . . ." But she can't go on. Her voice is harsh and high in her own ears; it echoes in her skull, making it impossible to think.

"A gold spinning wheel," he repeats.

He slowly draws his knife away from her throat, and she takes a big, shuddering gulp of air. If the pinprick of the spindle hurt, she can't fathom what a knifepoint might do to her. Just the thought causes her to sway, light-headed.

Very light-headed. How long has it been since she's eaten, or rested? She blinks rapidly.

He sheaths the dagger and catches her before she faints. Again she is overcome by the heat of his chest, even through his tunic. She breathes in the crisp scent of grass on him and tries to steady herself as he rights her.

This man practically assaulted her a minute ago! It must have been a misunderstanding. She looks up at his jaw. Not as square as the eldest prince of Aubin. She would know. She's studied many sketches of him.

Then again—she remembers with a cold shock—Philip and Edward of Aubin are both dead.

She has to get home. "Where are we?" Urgency causes her skin to prickle. The two princes were killed, possibly by Queen Malfleur's forces. Her marriage was supposed to seal the alliance between Aubin and Deluce. The council must be looking for her. And Isbe too.

"That's an odd question in the Borderlands."

"Borderlands?" It's getting easier to speak, as long as she allows each word its own pace, giving her mind and ears time to catch up. And as long as he's not touching her. "Is that . . . part of the royal forest?"

His face is a mix of surprise and puzzlement. "Moments ago we might have found ourselves in the forest. But who knows what we'll find when we step outside the cottage this time? Hasn't anyone ever warned you of the Borderlands? Almost no one makes it out alive. There are only Impressions out here."

"Impressions?"

"*Impressions*, yes, have you never heard of them?" he asks, frowning as he leans against the doorframe, blocking any potential escape. "Deceptive creatures. They find the lost and lead them in circles. Right over the edge of cliffs, if you're unlucky enough. You really don't know about Impressions?"

She shakes her head.

He glances to the side for a moment. Then, in a lower voice, he goes on. "Impressions will drive you mad, like the queen. They have no past, no memory, and no future. They don't *feel*—or at least, they can't feel anything new. Their emotions—like their words, and their bodies, and their desires—never alter. That's why I kept asking you how you ended up here. An Impression can only respond in one way, over and over."

She doesn't tell him that her life up until now was worse than what he has described. She couldn't respond at *all* to people's questions before today. She shudders, thinking of the talking bird that taunted her . . . the one bearing Malfleur's crest.

"The Borderlands are full of them. However you got here, you've wandered into the deadliest part of Sommeil. Deadlier than Belcoeur."

Aurora shakes her head. *Belcoeur is dead,* she thinks. *Slain by her sister.*

She shivers, even though the room is warm. For years, she and Isbe would play at being Malfleur and Belcoeur, taking turns at the ultimate battle between faerie sisters. If only Isbe was here now.

"Are you sure you're not an Impression?" he says, pulling her back toward him, so close that their foreheads are almost touching. His not-square jaw is lined in stubble. *Surely the princes of Aubin's faces are freshly groomed,* she thinks. *Were.*

He pushes her long hair over one shoulder and moves the collar of her cloak away, then leans in, almost as if to kiss her neck. She's so surprised she freezes in place, his fingertips tickling her just below the ear. She shivers uncontrollably. She has never known what it was like to be tickled—she has no words, and no context, for the shock of it. His lips almost touch her skin, and then . . . he sniffs.

"What are you doing?" she blurts out.

"You smell real," he answers.

Heat rises up her neck from where his breath lingers, until her cheeks feel hot.

"Aha." He runs his hand through his messy hair and

looks at her, holding her gaze. Then he grins slightly. "That's good too. That's a relief. Now I *know* you're not an Impression."

"What? Why?"

"Because," he says smugly. "Impressions don't blush."

Her face burns hotter. "Who—who *are* you?"

"I'm Heath. And I'm here to save your life. Now let's get out of here."

She glances around at what is clearly a children's room. How can this place be dangerous? But she doesn't have time to wonder, as he has already begun to head down the stairs.

"But . . . my sister," she protests as they descend. Then she stops talking and grabs on to his arm with both her hands, overcome by the alarming sensation that the stairs are disappearing beneath her feet, as though made of clouds she might sink through at any moment. Like in a dream.

She's relieved when they make it into the front room. It must have just been another moment of light-headedness. Then she realizes her hands are still clutching his sturdy arm. She lets go quickly, the burn of contact simmering through her.

In the daylight she can see that the cottage's furnishings are sparse, but there's a small chair in the corner, curiously turned so it's facing the wall. It gives her an odd, unsettled feeling. Something is not right about this place.

Turning around, she spots another doorway. She cocks her head, confused. The door is at the side of the room, which, if she's correct, should lead directly into the staircase on the other side of the wall. But the open doorway leads to another room. The cottage seems to have no internal logic.

"We must hurry," Heath says, turning back toward her.

But she's drawn to the unexpected doorway. She peers inside the next room—a smaller sitting room, this one with a table. On it, by another window—which, by her calculations, has no right to be there, as this ought to have been an interior wall—sit a teacup and a sugar bowl. As she gets closer, she can see that the sugar bowl is heaped high. Beside it, there is an inch or two of tea in the teacup. She dips her pinkie finger in, and yanks it out with a yelp. The tea is scalding. Automatically, she sucks on her finger to try and soothe it—something she has seen others do. The pain of her finger throbs inside the warmth of her mouth.

She stares at the tea set. *Someone else has been here recently.*

"Aurora, please do not mistake me," Heath says behind her. "If we don't leave now, we may never get out of here. The cottage has a way of, well, disappearing."

"How can it . . . disappear?" The last word ghosts off her tongue almost without effort, despite the fact that her mind is reeling over all of this:

Belcoeur—the Night Faerie—is not dead but alive and mad, ruling over a place called Sommeil.

A royal forest that shifts and sways.

And her voice, her sense of touch. She's never known a faerie tithe to come undone before.

"I've come upon this cottage many times," Heath explains, "but it's never in the same place twice. I might not have found it today had it not been for your screams."

Heath leads her away. They pass through the parlor room not once but twice, and then a third time before reaching the front door.

"It's happening already," Heath says, pulling her over the threshold.

Once outside, wind grasps at Aurora's cloak and her hair, whirling them in a frenzy around her. For a few seconds she feels she *is* the wind.

She's so distracted by the myriad sensations racing across her skin that she doesn't realize what she is seeing: the trees in the royal forest. *Moving.* A dark green mass of pine needles swaying, limbs branching before her eyes, trunks rearranging themselves—the entire woods shuffled like a deck of cards.

Heath begins to run, and she struggles to keep up, dazzled, dizzied, nearly tripping several times and almost losing her cloak to the creaking reach of a tree branch. If she weren't so disoriented, she might be tempted to slow down in wonder as shafts of sunlight interplay with the shifting forest. It's more beautiful than anything she's ever seen.

And then, with a gasp, Heath stops, thrusting his arms out to catch her. Aurora crashes into him. He holds her steady as a swirl of mist surrounds them, the green of the forest blending into the gray of fog. She sees with terror that they are standing at the very lip of a precipice that drops as far as the cliffs of Deluce, though she cannot tell whether land or water waits at the bottom.

One step farther and she would have fallen.

Thunder rumbles from the chasm, and then a massive flock of blackbirds shoots upward in a frenzied cloud, circles overhead, flapping hard before flying off.

Heath's breath is in her ear; his chest rises against hers. "Wait," he whispers. "Wait."

Slowly, as though in a foreign dance, he steps back, guiding her body against his. Then to the side. Then a turn. Then they are no longer by the side of a cliff but instead staring at a high stone wall that seems to go on endlessly in either direction.

Heath sighs, and she does too, finding relief as soon as he has let her go.

"Come, help me find the rift," he says, tracing his hands along the ragged face of the wall.

She's never been more confused in all her life. "Rift?" The word floats out of her and away. A forest, and then a cliff, and now a wall, each trading spots with the last as though rearranged by an invisible hand.

"Somewhere," he says, reaching back to her and placing her hand against the cold stone. "We may not be able to see it, because of the illusion."

Aurora has so many questions she doesn't even know where to begin, but she wants to get out of here as badly as he seems to. Her sister—and a prince, and an entire kingdom—are waiting for her. So she reaches up and out, beginning to inch along the wall as Heath does.

Aurora takes in the wall's story through the pads of her

fingers—she's unused to all the information that can storm her body this way. Her fingertips tingle and ache. It's like the cold texture of the stone carries an emotion. Touching it makes her feel raw and exposed.

"Ow!" she cries, pulling her fingers back. "Something . . ." *Like the prick of the spinning wheel.* "Sharp."

She squints through the fog and then sucks in a breath.

"What is it?" Heath asks urgently, coming to her side. "Did you find the rift?"

She shakes her head. "There's . . . there's something *in* the stones. Can you see it? There's . . ." Terror and disgust rise to her head like a toxic fume. Through the mist, she makes out a suit of warped armor.

But it's not just armor. It's the anguished form of a dead soldier, his body crushed by the stones.

And yet . . . somehow, he's become part *of* the stones. She can see the mangled profile of the man's face, his arm wrenched backward, his helmet jutting out jaggedly—that's what she'd scratched her hand on.

She shudders, her ears ringing, her chest frozen with shock.

"The queen's guards," Heath says, his voice barely more than a whisper.

She continues to gape at the scene of desperation and violence, preserved in stone like a gruesome sculpture. "But why would her own guards be trying to get through to her? Wouldn't she keep them close?"

"They weren't trying to get *in*," Heath says. "They were trying to get out."

She backs away. Her arms are trembling wildly. Around them, the forest has risen up again, and she's afraid that if she turns her back on the wall, it won't be there anymore. That even *Heath* won't be there anymore. She grabs at his sleeve. "I don't like this."

Heath's voice is hard as he moves on, continuing to investigate the wall. "Neither did they. Four of her best men. Story goes they hacked through with an ax, and that's what left the rift. Long before I was even born."

Aurora's beginning to feel completely overwhelmed from running her hands over the stones, every variation a forlorn mystery, when finally something *changes*.

She hears Heath's quick intake of breath. "This is it," he whispers.

The wall *appears* intact, but Aurora discovers she can pass her hand straight through the stones. She pulls it back hastily. What if the wall clamps down on her, as it must have done with the four guards?

Heath lunges forward.

In seconds, he is enveloped by the illusion, and dread replaces all other sensations. For all she knows, he has disappeared, leaving her alone. She cringes, tense, waiting to hear the horrible sound of stones moving, of crunching bones.

But then Heath's hand and face reemerge, and he grins. "You coming?"

She holds her breath, reminding herself that she has no other choice. Not unless she wants to remain alone in the Borderlands.

She closes her eyes . . . then steps into the mist and stone.

Penetrating the illusion is like walking through ice. She feels the wall's resistance, a deep sorrow tinged with bitterness. The word "stop" clenches all around her. She starts to hyperventilate.

This is wrong. This is all wrong. She needs to get out. She needs to turn back. She needs to—

Heath's hand wraps around hers, and tugs.

8

Isabelle

Normally, noisy crowds frustrate Isbe; she ends up disconnected in all the commotion. But the cacophony at Roul's dinner table tonight is strangely comforting—it may not replace the loneliness she feels when she thinks of her sister, but at least it serves to lessen the raging questions in her mind: What is Aurora doing at this very moment? What would she think of this table, of this meal they must eat almost entirely with their hands? The many interweaving voices talking over one another, the laughter and the sounds of dishes rattling on the warped wooden table make the entire room seem warmer, cozier, and more alive than she has felt in a while.

A neighboring family has joined them for their evening

meal—a kind couple and their five children, making it seven kids in total, in addition to the five adults. The neighbors contributed their own pheasant eggs and helped to prepare a rabbit stew. Isbe senses for them this is quite a feast, and after a week of hard work, she too is savoring the strong scent of the stew and the satisfying toughness of the meat in her teeth.

Isbe has been learning everything she can about the farm: how to follow the fence to the goat pen, where to draw water, what grain sack to feed the pigs from. Before they came, Roul clearly hadn't lifted a finger to straighten up his small home since the death of Celeste, and it reeked of mourning and of dirty children, of sweat and sour goats' milk. Isbe spent the first day scrubbing the floors, rubbing dry lavender and sage into the cracks to freshen the place up.

She can't imagine what it must be like to have lost an unborn baby *and* a wife in one strike. Roul's son, Piers, is too young to help out, so he runs loose all day, reminding Isbe of herself at that age. When there's nothing else to be done, Isbe plays with Aalis, whom Roul had otherwise been strapping to his back every day while he worked.

There has been almost no break. In just a few days, Isbe's back, arms, and legs have gathered a deep, unfamiliar ache. The nights are short and cold; the days begin before dawn.

Sometimes Aalis wakes screaming from bad dreams, and Isbe holds her warm little body against her own, singing her the rose lullaby until the girl relaxes and drifts back to sleep. Though she might not admit it aloud, the familiar lullaby comforts Isbe too. "One night reviled, before break of morn, amid the roses wild, all tangled in thorns, the shadow and the child together were born . . ." Somehow the words make her feel connected to the life she led up until now—the life she left behind.

When Isbe and Gilbert first got here, Isbe brought her fingers to touch Roul's leathery cheeks, to explore the sharp ridges of his face. Gil—despite the roughness of his hands and garments—is so familiar, so *constant*, she thinks of him as smooth, like an oft-handled river stone. Roul, on the other hand, is all broken bits and hard edges. It's strange how haggard he has become in just a few years; he isn't much older than Gil, after all. But life beyond the royal village has not been kind to him, and Gil now exceeds him in both height and the broadness of his shoulders.

Gilbert is sitting to Isbe's right at the table, and she can feel his shoulder grazing hers. "You look somber," he mutters into her ear.

She hates how aware she is of his breath whispering against her skin. That if she turned too soon, her mouth would collide with his.

"I'm afraid this life is harder on you than either of us knew it would be," he goes on quietly, beneath the din of the rest of the group.

"No," she replies immediately. The last thing she wants to admit is how shocked she's been by how different things are for the peasants. Even though she was treated more like a servant at the palace than royalty, she had freedom to choose her activities. No one's livelihood has ever *truly* depended on her before.

But there's a deep satisfaction in being of real use for once. "I'm not afraid of hard work," she tells him.

"All right. No need to get defensive," he says, poking her in the ribs.

She gives him a half grin. "Better than when I'm on the *offensive*, though."

He laughs quietly. "I like it when you get aggressive."

"Oh, do you?" she challenges.

Even though the room is noisy, she can hear him breathing again. They are sitting very close, his voice directed only at her. "Yes," he says, sounding serious. "I do."

And then he flicks a bit of his stew at her face.

"Hey!" she says, turning to him.

"It wasn't me!" he protests.

"Oh, don't try and blame the children." She grins wider this time, picking up a soggy carrot from her bowl, not caring as broth soaks into her sleeve.

"Isbe!" he says. "You're making a mess of your—"

She tosses the chunk of carrot at him and he squeals with laughter. She's always loved his ridiculous laugh.

"Truce," he says now, leaning closer to her again, then tenderly wiping a bit of broth from the corner of her mouth.

She freezes, holding her breath at his touch.

"It's so nice to be able to relax for once," one of the neighbors cuts in. "It seems everyone's been so tense, what with the murders."

The word "murders" quiets the rest of the room.

"Good riddance, if you ask me," says the wife.

"What do you mean?" Gilbert asks carefully.

"Aubin? Trust that filthy dog's nation?" the husband says in response. "Never bought that alliance bein' a good idea. Not for one minute. Them princes better off dead."

"Better off without 'em in these parts," the wife seconds.

"Well," Isbe begins. "Many at the palace fear the approach of Malfleur and the forces of LaMorte."

The husband laughs. "All mule dung! LaMorte? Them mountains been silent since before time I was a kid. An attack from LaMorte? Likely as God bringing down a flood."

Roul grunts. "You ask me, it's all stories. Scare us into more taxes, like they always do. Never enough. Levy on the grain. Next it'll be a tax to use my right foot and 'nother to use my left."

"I don't know much," says the wife. "But I ain't ever trusted the council."

Isbe bites her tongue. She's not sure, in fact, what to think. She's not exactly full of warm feelings toward the council at the moment. But would they *invent* a threat just to manipulate the poor people of the kingdom? It's something that simply never occurred to her before.

"Palace deserves what it's had," the husband adds. "All them just gone and *asleep*. Well. They been sleeping on the job for years, you ask me."

"What are you talking about?" Isbe asks. Her body has gone cold.

"You ain't heard?" the wife puts in. "What a tale. And they're saying it's all the fault of the princess herself. Wandered off and fell right down where she lay. Well, of course they tried to bring her back. But anyone what's so much as looked at her fell down sick in their spots."

All at once, Gil's hand is on Isbe's arm.

"What's that?" Roul is saying. "We haven't heard of a disease here."

"Ain't heard of the sleeping sickness?" says the wife. "Say it's worse than anything. Hits you before you know it. May as well be dead, all of 'em."

"All of them?" Isbe blurts out, her pulse leaping into her throat.

The husband replies: "Princess. Most of the palace too. All them like children, just sleepin' right there on the ground. No one can wake 'em. Soon the flies'll come, you ask me."

Isbe stands up and shoves her chair away from the table, the smell of the stew now nauseating to her. "I don't understand. I don't know what you mean."

"Course, some are saying it's no sickness at all," the wife says, clearly enjoying herself. "Old faerie magic, you ask me."

"Isbe," Gil says, wrapping his arms around her. "Let's go outside for a moment. You look like you need a breath of clean air."

Numbly she lets him direct her out of the house, where the chill of the evening attacks her immediately on all sides. She begins to shiver uncontrollably. "Gil, what can they mean? Is it true? What do we do? I have to help my sister, I have to go to her, I have to—"

"We *can't* go to her, Isbe. It isn't safe. Didn't you hear what they said? The roads are closed off. It's catching."

"So, what, I'm just supposed to go about making rabbit stew and gossiping with neighbors while my sister suffers? She could *die*, Gil!"

"We don't know that. We don't know enough yet," he insists. "Just try and stay calm, and—"

"Calm?" She shoves his arms away from her. And yet she feels disoriented. The night, usually so soothing, now seems swollen with unfamiliar sounds. *"Calm?"* She'd like to take a battering ram to those peasants and their story.

"Bad choice in words," Gil says, letting out a sigh. "Look, you heard what Martine said. Maybe . . . maybe there's more to it than a sickness."

"What are you saying?" Isbe asks, feeling a tiny glimpse of hope, the way she can sometimes feel, just from the subtle coolness of shadows giving way, when the sun is about to peek out from behind the clouds. "You think there's faerie magic involved?"

She imagines Gil shrugging. "Maybe."

Isbe doesn't know what to believe. Magic like that . . . none of the faeries she has ever met can do more than parlor tricks. But it's possible. It's an idea. And curses, unlike diseases, can potentially be reversed. "Are there any local noblefaeries who might understand it? Anyone at all?"

"Lord Barnabé," Gil says slowly. "He goes by Binks.

Roul says he's not very trustworthy, but what fae are? It might be worth a try."

And then she remembers: Binks tithes human luck. She wonders now whether Roul's lack of luck could be blamed for the death of Celeste and their baby. She shudders. But then she straightens her shoulders. "Yes. It's definitely worth a try."

There's a long moment of silence. Isbe feels her heart clawing at her throat. Without Gil's help, she's lost. She'll never be able to seek out Binks on her own.

Finally he speaks. "We'll head out first thing tomorrow."

———————

There is an old saying in these parts: "Never trust a faerie with something to gain." But sometimes, there is no other choice.

Late the following afternoon, Isbe finds herself covered to her knees in muddy snow, her toes completely numb, as she makes her way down the long private road that leads to Binks's estate. Knowing that Aurora is in trouble makes Isbe too feel trapped, as though the earth itself has risen up to bury her alive.

As she and Gil approach, a long caravan made up of three mule-driven wagons winds closer, rattling noisily. Isbe turns to Gil as they move out of the way to let the procession pass. "What's with the wagons? He's not leaving, is he?"

"Not that I can see. But the wagons are piled up with furniture," Gil says wonderingly. "Never known a faerie to move . . ."

Isbe huffs, frustration rising inside her. "Excuse me, sir," she says, calling out to the driver and turning her face upward, to where the mule driver must be seated. The wagon comes to a clunky halt. She can't tell what the driver looks like, of course, but she can guess by the smell of him that it isn't nice. "Can you tell me what you're doing with all this furniture?"

"Payment," the man grunts.

"For?"

"Won it fair and square, got the documents to prove it."

Isbe gapes. "You mean to say that you won these things by *gambling* for them?"

"That's what I said, didn't I?" the man replies, his breath reeking of dried herring. "Now move out of the way. We've a long journey."

The caravan rumbles away. Isbe's curiosity and unease grow as they approach the manor itself. Gil describes its impressive size and the flashy, bright-colored drapes that line the front windows—a rarity even among royals. It takes a long time for someone to answer the front gate, but finally metal slides against metal. "Were you scheduled?" a man—a servant, presumably—asks dryly.

Isbe nudges Gil, who clears his throat.

"Lord Barnabé is not expecting us, no, but we come on important business from . . . from the palace," Gil announces.

The servant sucks in a breath. He disappears, and for a moment, Isbe is sure they've been refused. Then the gate begins to lift, and the heavy door grinds open.

"In. *In*," the servant barks.

Isbe and Gil shuffle forward. The inside of the home is somehow colder than it is outside.

"Follow," says the servant, his voice echoing within the cavernous entry hall. So they do. Their soggy footsteps slosh and echo on marble, and Isbe loses count of how many turns they make.

And then she hears the screaming.

No, not screams—more like squeals . . . amid men's overlapping voices, angry and excited.

The servant grunts. "Fights," he says, as if that explains everything. "This way."

The squealing gets louder now, and then Gil says, "Oh! *Oh*."

There's another sound beneath that of the squeals . . . a shuffling, a grunting, a groaning, a . . . *snorting*?

"What?" Isbe demands impatiently. Gil doesn't answer, clearly too stunned to speak. "What *is it*?"

"Gah!" shouts a male voice, not Gil's. "Absalom, NO! Go for the neck!"

More grunting, like something part metal, part beast, being dragged roughly across a bumpy surface.

There are multiple men in the room, many of them in heated argument. Large ale goblets clatter against wood as the men slurp and slosh, laugh and shout. Isbe can tell there are flung-open windows that must be facing the outdoors: a courtyard, where the screams are coming from. By the way sound travels, she guesses this is some sort of spectators' room. One voice stands out from the rest: "Who are *they*?" Lord Barnabé.

"Business from the palace, sir. About the sleeping sickness," the servant explains.

Before the lord can reply, there's a wild sound—a cross between a howl and roar, then a loud thump. Gurgling, gleeful laughter squeaks from Lord Barnabé's throat, strangely high-pitched, as though he's wearing a too-tight collar.

Then Isbe can smell it: blood and bodies and mud and something *animal*. It reminds her of when she sometimes used to follow the military squads on their boar-hunting missions. They'd perform these hunts to train for battle, forced to wrestle the wounded animals in hand-to-hoof combat. She would hunch over Freckles's muscular back from a distance, weaving her fingers through the mare's coarse mane, listening with disgust and fascination.

"Boar fighting," Gil confirms.

A wave of nausea rises in her chest. Humans fighting wild animals as a form of training is one type of gruesome, but setting the beasts against *each other*, simply for sport, is sick and cruel. "Lord Barnabé. Binks," she says loudly. "We are here on a matter of some urgency."

"Gentlemen, one moment," Binks says irritably. Then, to his servant: "Show them to my private quarters."

Isbe is immensely relieved to exit the spectators' room and its offensive smells and sounds. She can tell the next room is heavily upholstered because of the way it seems to swallow up their footsteps. She doesn't trust heavy upholstery. It hides things.

As they're offered seats in Binks's office, Gil reaches over and squeezes her hand. "Short," he whispers hurriedly. "A bit of a belly, large nose, ridiculously dressed including a chaperon with a *feathered* tail trailing down the back of his head . . ."

He stops talking and lets go of her hand as Binks enters the room moments later, closing the door.

"So," he announces, sitting down almost silently. Isbe imagines he has trained even his chair to wear a poker face, to reveal nothing. "What business do you seek here?"

"We're here for answers," Isbe blurts out. "About the sleeping sickness."

"What help do you think I can give you?" Binks asks stiffly.

Gil is the one who answers. "Faerie magic, sir," he says. "We thought someone like you might know something about this affliction we've been hearing of."

Binks taps something against his desk. Possibly a large ring. Isbe longs for Aurora, as she has moment after moment, day after day, since leaving the palace—especially at times like these, when her sister would have been by Isbe's side, slyly tapping everything she was seeing into Isbe's palm.

"Hmmm," Binks says at last. "I'm afraid I simply can't help you."

Isbe sits forward. "But—"

"*However*, since you've come all this way, may I at least offer some entertainment in the form of a game? I'd invite you to my gaming room, but it's woefully low on furnishings at the moment."

"We're not here to play." Isbe can barely contain her fury. "My sister, the princess, may *die*. We need your help."

Binks taps again. He must be wearing *several* heavy rings. Isbe begins to realize he is lightly hammering a sort of pattern. "Who did you say you were again?"

She sits taller. "I'm Isabelle of Deluce. Daughter of the late King Henri of Deluce."

Binks makes some sort of weird gasping, snorting sound. "The bastard girl. Ah, of course. I remember you." And then, more quietly, as though studying her intently: "*Of course.* Struck blind as a child. Yes. Yes."

She feels a tiny whoosh of breeze and a flicker of light and shadow, as if he's waving his hand in front of her face. She knows that gesture—he's testing whether she really can't see him.

"Stop that," Gilbert says, and Binks sits back again in his seat. "Can you or can you not help us?"

"Help you *how*?"

"By *telling* us what faerie might have the strength and motivation to have—"

"So they kept it a secret from you, did they?" Binks says. "Interesting. Perhaps they thought it best. Perhaps they didn't take it seriously. To be honest, none of us did."

"Take what seriously? What do you know?" Isbe demands.

"That Violette," Binks says, seemingly to himself. "I

wouldn't believe she could do it. There's something else at work here too, I'd wager. I'd wager quite a *bit* that there's more to it. What a scandal. *What* a scandal."

"Please," Gil insists. "Tell us what you know. Is there a faerie called Violette we should speak to? Would she know more about the source of the sickness and how to end it?"

"Oh, I *doubt* that," Binks spits out. "If you could even secure her attention, which I also doubt. *Hmmm.* Are you *sure* I can't interest you two in a little game? I could make it worth your while, of course. . . ."

"Worth our while how?" Gil's voice has turned deeply suspicious.

But Isbe senses an opportunity. "We will play one of your games, on the condition that if we win, you will tell us the entire story of Violette and the sleeping sickness—every single word of it. Everything you know."

"And if you lose, I get a tithe of luck from you. Or better yet," Binks says, "from *you*." He clearly means Gil. "The girl doesn't quite strike one as lucky, now does she?" he asks with a laugh.

"No," Isbe says firmly. She can't let Gil risk his luck for her. "I'll be the one to play."

"Absolutely not," Gil interjects. "The game is between you and me, not Isabelle."

"Gil," Isbe hisses. She feels a wave of nausea. Gil's never been that good with cards. Isbe may not be able to see them, but when she and Aurora partnered against visiting nobles in the past, her incredible memory meant they almost always won.

"Very well, then." Binks is tapping his desk again. *One-two-three-four-then-the-thumb. One-two-three-four-then-the-thumb. One-two-three-four-then-the-thumb. Switch hands.* "Fox and geese? Or . . . knucklebox? Hmm. No. Heart of harts. One of my favorite games," he says, pulling a stack of cards from his desk and shuffling them.

Not heart of harts, Isbe thinks. She's somewhat familiar with the game: a hellishly complex one that depends on reading the opponent's facial cues, counting, knowledge of actual hunting strategy, risk management, and sheer random luck of the draw.

Binks deals the cards, and Isbe tries not to hold her breath as he and Gil play round after round, the lord's servant continuously entering to refill Binks's goblet of ale. The cards make a satisfying smack as they hit the table—must be a thick, valuable set. Gil is a conservative player, much to Isbe's relief—in no round does he bid on a stock card, while Binks throws in plenty of coins each round in the hope of increasing the value of his hand.

Throughout the game, Binks continues his rhythmic tapping. The sound becomes mesmerizing as Isbe begins to lose track of the game, so she's startled when the tapping seems to skip a beat at one point . . . the second right thumb tap, if she's not mistaken. Isbe wonders if it's just that Binks has become distracted, or if perhaps it's a sign that he has a weak hand. Could it be his tell? She would nudge Gil or try to send him some signal to pay close attention, but there's no way to communicate with him without Binks noticing.

Finally, in the seventh round, Binks reveals a set of four queens atop the ten of hearts. He has slain the hart.

"I've won!" he declares, not even bothering to clean up the table as he stands to collect the debt. "Let's shake on it, good man," he says to Gilbert.

Isbe's heart sinks. She can tell from the weight of Gil's silence that there's no doubting the play. Binks has indeed succeeded in collecting all four queens, despite the fact that they constituted a full third of the cards in play: an *extremely* unlikely occurrence. Then again, Binks's tribute is luck; he has an unfair advantage when it comes to elements of chance.

Gil stands and takes Binks's hand, then gasps and steps backward, knocking into his chair.

"What is it? Are you all right?" Isbe asks, standing too.

"It's fine, I just . . . it stung."

"May not be faerie magic powerful enough to put a palace to sleep, but it does the trick when it comes to collecting," Binks says, his voice snide, all the joy from winning now morphed into a thin, twisted pride. "Better luck next time!" he adds. "My servant will see you out."

Binks creaks back down to reshuffle his deck with a smug *ruffle-snap, ruffle-snap, ruffle-snap.*

They can't be sent away. Not this easily.

"It's all right," Gil whispers as they follow the servant out into the hall. "We'll find out who this faerie Violette is.

Somehow we'll get our answers."

"It isn't fair." Despair, frustration, and rage are shuffling through Isbe's mind just like that stupid deck of cards, making her feel shaky, like she might just grab the next *bec de faucon* she can find and smash all the fancy chandeliers she hears clinking overhead. She'd like to take a saber to Binks's face, which she imagines must be puffy as an overcooked pastry and crumbly to the touch. "He's disgusting. A single ring from one of his stupid fat fingers would pay for all the food Roul eats in a year."

"It's the system we live in, Isbe. Binks wears ten matching rings and gambles away his lot, while people like us must dress like *this*," he says, tugging at her sleeve, obviously hoping to cheer her up.

But something he said has snagged in her mind. "Ten matching rings?"

"Rubies, all of them."

Isbe freezes. *One-two-three-four-FIVE-one-two-three-four-FIVE.* Except sometime in the fifth round when he momentarily lost his rhythm. . . .

Or had he?

"Miss, miss!" the servant barks as Isbe turns around, desperately trying to feel her winding way back to Binks's office. For a moment she bursts into the wrong room and stands there in silence before realizing her mistake. She backs out and heads farther down the hall, Gil joining her. He grabs her elbow.

"What are you doing?"

"Please," she pants. "I need to see Binks."

Gil wordlessly steers her to the right door.

"Master is busy," the servant says, running up behind them.

But Isbe doesn't listen. She shoves open the door to the office where, as she suspected, Binks is still sitting there, smugly shuffling his deck with a *ruffle-snap*. "It's customary," she says, before he can speak, "to allow the spectator to handle the cards at least once. To verify the legitimacy of the deck."

Binks huffs. "You're welcome to count them. They're all here."

"I'm sure they are," Isbe says, holding out her hand.

"I'm sorry, sir," the servant says from the doorway. "I tried to stop her."

"Not to worry. I've seen many a sore loser in my life." Binks hands her the deck of cards. "Count away, my dear. And might I recommend a visit to my groom on your way out? Someone should do something with that unruly mane of yours."

Isbe ignores the dig and feels the cards he has laid into her palms. They are definitely sturdy. Possibly gold or silver leafed. She doesn't count them, though. She just quickly goes through each card, placing it at the bottom of the pile, feeling the surface of each, until . . .

"Which card is this?" she asks, holding one up to Gil.

"It's—it's the queen of clovers. Why?"

"Lord Binks has cheated you," Isbe announces. "The card has been marked."

"I don't see a mark," Gil says, taking the card from her.

"No, I imagine it's not easy to see. But I felt it—a soft scratch, from something sharp, like the beveled edge of a ruby."

"Preposterous!" Binks blusters.

Just as Gil says, "I'll be damned." His voice is amazed. "You're *right*."

"It's too late," Binks snarls. "Your luck is mine. There's no way to get it back."

Isbe has never hated anyone so much in her life. If she could see his eyes, she might tear them out.

"We didn't come back for Gil's luck," she says, forcing her voice to stay steady. "But you still owe us. You promised us a story. It's time to pay up."

9

Binks,

a Male Faerie of Modest Nobility,
Who May or May Not Be Important to This Tale,
Except That He Happened to Be in the Right Place
at the Right Time

Y ou can often tell a bad day by its smell, and this one *stank.* Yet Binks crinkled his nose in delight; he'd won a feisty game of clovers that had gotten him through the castle gates, and today he was attending the royal christening of the baby Aurora, an event to which only an elite few were invited, and where only the most delectable of crumbling cakes, juicy bird meats, lemony fishes, and pungent wines would be served.

Binks was mostly here for the wines. Barrels from previous centuries would be excavated from Deluce's famous cliffside cellars and served in achingly tall goblets. Perhaps a round or two of card games, as well—klaberjass, say, or latterlu—would leave his pockets full of gold and his luck at

82

an all-time high. He could never be sure which fed which—the luck needed to win at gambling, or the gambling needed to acquire more luck.

Binks noticed he was not the only faerie in attendance. Right away he recognized Claudine, the gourmand, with her bright white-blond hair and plump cheeks. She had little power but seemed to have maintained political influence simply by knowing everyone in the kingdom, for she never missed a party, as far as Binks could tell. Claudine's tithe was, generally, taste; she went around collecting more and more of it—and of course, *enjoying* it—and the evidence showed in the red of her cheeks and bulge of her ever more prominent behind.

When it was Claudine's turn to bless the child, he watched as she approached the cradle, offering the quietly mewling baby a sweetness of temper and beauty of face, in exchange for the child's voice.

King Henri and his wife, Queen Amélie, looked at each other in surprise, and Binks knew he wasn't the only one who had forgotten this predilection of Claudine's. Though she mostly collected taste, she was also proud of her singing voice and desired to maintain it. Her voice had been the very thing that used to garner her invitations at the highest level of court. It was rare for a faerie to have more than one tithe, and Binks suspected she was showing off.

He watched as Queen Amélie nodded at King Henri, who stepped forward and announced: "Very well. A princess of sweetness and beauty should have little need of a voice.

In fact, more daughters ought to make such an exchange, I'm sure."

Claudine granted her gift and reclaimed her spot, humming softly to herself, even as the baby girl inside the cradle went eerily silent.

Next was the faerie Almandine, whom Binks couldn't quite place until she separated herself from the crowd. She was willowy and seemed to flow rather than walk. She was a known sensualist. It was said her entire estate had been transformed into a replica of ancient Roman baths and that she spent most hours of most days bathing in the nude and accepting new lovers, both human and faerie, both male and female, into her private quarters.

"My gift," said Almandine, her eyes trained smugly on the child, "is a dancer's elegance and grace. And the price I seek is the girl's sense of touch."

Once again the king and queen put their heads together to discuss the offer before finally agreeing to this exchange as well. "Surely it will save her from ever feeling pain," the queen said, gazing fondly down at the quiet, tightly wrapped bundle that was her daughter.

And so Almandine granted her gift and accepted her payment. Binks wondered whether the rumors of her lust were true, and if so, whether she'd be interested in *his* company later in the evening. But before his thoughts had a chance to unfold from there—and indeed, before Violette, the third faerie, had a chance to grant a final gift—the heavy double doors blew open with a slam.

Binks got a direct view of Malfleur, queen of the LaMorte Territories, as she stormed into the hall, Vultures flapping in her wake. The scar over her left eyelid glared white against her pale skin, accenting her exquisite, angled beauty rather than marring it.

He was not, it must be said, altogether surprised by her appearance. Everyone knew Malfleur was obsessed with youth, and what could be more appealing than the youth of a princess possessed both of wealth and beauty? Everyone knew that in exchange for the military protection her army offered, she'd tithed away the youth from many a female in her own kingdom, leaving them shriveled and old.

Malfleur kneeled down beside the cradle. "My dear Princess Aurora," she began in a voice deceptive in its softness.

"No!" the king interrupted her. "We will give up much, but we will not stand for the loss of her youth. You were not invited, Malfleur. Please see yourself out."

Malfleur looked up at him placidly, then cocked her head. Even from several yards away, Binks could practically feel the clever cogs in her mind spinning and throwing off hot sparks.

"Of course," she said, standing and bowing. "I cannot ask a tithe without granting something in return."

The queen too stood. "We do not want your gift, Malfleur."

For just a moment, Malfleur's eyes snapped thin like a cat's. "Well, that makes things easier. Gifts come at a cost, but *curses* come for free."

Gasps rippled through the gathered crowd. No one had heard of a faerie casting a curse in their lifetime. Long ago, a faerie curse would have been considered very frightening indeed, but now people eyed one another and mumbled skeptically. Surely no one, not even the last living faerie queen, had the power to enact a curse of any real consequence. But the gall to even suggest it was enough to shock everyone, and Binks noticed that Queen Amélie had begun to weep in panic. For whether the curse would come true or not mattered less than the fact that their daughter's reputation was about to be sullied.

No one would marry a princess with a curse, rumored or real.

But it was too late. Malfleur reached into the cradle and lifted the child. "Aurora will grow up to be just as beautiful, graceful, and good-natured as her parents—and the world—could possibly wish. So beautiful that all who lay eyes on her will adore her, and her sweetness and obedience will bring great joy into her parents' lives. She will be the treasure of Deluce. That is, until she reaches the prime of her youth. On her sixteenth birthday, she will do harm to herself. No . . . no."

Malfleur looked up from the child and turned to face the crowd of nobles and faeries watching in horror. She seemed to be thinking quickly as her eyes flashed light and dark. "Though it was many, many years ago, some of you may recall the evil of the Night Faerie, Belcoeur, from whom I *saved* you all. And yet here you stand now, ungrateful. Oblivious to all that I've done for you. Well, this curse is in the name of Belcoeur, who was ever so fond of spinning. When Aurora turns sixteen, she won't just hurt herself—she'll prick a finger on a beautiful, rare spindle, and she will die."

The pronouncement lingered in the air for a few seconds, harsh as the snapped string of a vielle, and then the queen of Deluce let out a sob and clung to her husband's robes.

Malfleur went on, directing her speech now at everyone in the room. "Aurora's death will be a reminder to all who choose to ignore my wishes, to all those who have forgotten my greatness, forgotten what I have done for you, and the little I have asked in return."

With that, she placed the pretty, silent baby back into her cradle and left.

Binks swallowed. He did not like the taint of bad luck in this room. There would be no foreign wines uncasked *now*, he was sure of it.

It took several moments of silence before Violette, who stood in a corner, stroking her vibrant red hair in a long wave over her shoulder, finally put away the small hand mirror she kept close to her heart and approached the queen, who was now weeping softly into her husband's shoulder.

"As we all know, it is neither easy nor advisable to reverse a faerie curse," Violette drawled. "Many dangers can befall those who attempt this challenge. But I am willing to give it a try, for the right price."

"Please, please help us," the queen said, dabbing at her eyes.

The king took a step closer to Violette. "Tell us what you need," he said. "We'll give you anything—anything you ask."

Violette licked her lips and looked around the room. "In exchange for amending Malfleur's curse, I ask for the light in your daughter's eyes. I ask for her sight."

Queen Amélie once again grasped the king's robes, shaking her head. "We've already allowed too much to be taken," she whispered.

"We don't have any choice," the king muttered.

The queen picked up the baby and held her to her chest. "I can't," she said. "It's too much. We've gone too far." Then she looked up, wild-eyed, at the crowd, and her jaw opened slightly. Binks felt himself standing straighter.

"Violette," the queen went on slowly. "We *will* give you the sight of . . . of the king's daughter." Her voice was calculating. "But first, tell us how you will help us."

Violette smiled narrowly. "On her sixteenth birthday, the princess Aurora will indeed prick her finger on a spindle—*but*." She held up a hand before the room could break into more murmuring. "She will not die. Instead, she will enter a sleep so deep, that only . . ." She paused, frowning, evidently at a loss, and trying to invent something convincing. "Only *true love* may awaken her."

The queen looked at King Henri with hope written on her face, even as Binks heard Almandine snort and caught Claudine rolling her eyes at the phrase "true love."

"And now, for my price," Violette said with a satisfied little purr.

The queen handed the baby to the king. Standing tall, she shouted into the crowd, "Where is Isabelle? Bring forth Isabelle."

The crowd parted, and a small child Binks had never seen before stumbled out, as though shoved, blinking nervously at all of the adults surrounding her. The girl had a mess of tangled dark curls and was wearing some sort of raglike garment that only poorly resembled a dress. Binks couldn't help but wrinkle his nose.

"What is this?" Violette asked.

"This," the king said, looking first at his wife and then at the faerie, "is my other daughter. The queen promised you the sight of the king's daughter, but . . ." He returned Violette's narrow smile. "She did not specify which."

10

Gilbert,

Former Groom at the Royal Stables of Deluce and Isabelle's Best Friend of Eighteen Years

Gil and Isbe dismount from the spice merchant's cart in a fit of coughing. Even after he has driven off, they cannot shake the heavy scent of pepper and cloves from their clothes. The merchant himself wore a thick cloth over his nose and mouth, though Gil wasn't sure whether it was to protect himself from sneezing all day or to hide his misshapen face, which reminded Gil of molten rock.

Gil carries their luggage toward a cluster of trade ships bearing the yellow seal of Aubin; Isbe follows, her hand resting on his arm. Ever since they heard Binks's story, she has been worrying it over like a bit of wool in her hand until it has hardened into a plan. If you threw that plan over the pier, it would sink straight through the salt spray, past the icy layers of waves to the very bottom of the sea. It has weight to it, her plan.

"We've got to undo the sleeping sickness—the curse—according to its rules," Isbe had explained after they left Binks's manor. "We need to bring back Aurora's true love. The youngest prince of Aubin."

"Prince . . . William?"

"It's got to be him," she insisted. "They are engaged to be married." Her eyes went dark and solid, impenetrable as iron keyholes in the dead of winter, and he knew there would be no persuading her otherwise.

Still he tried. "Who's to say the prince is in love with a girl he has never laid eyes upon? Everyone knows their engagement is political and nothing else. Besides, it was his older brother who was supposed to marry her in the first place."

Isbe's jaw got as hard as her eyes then. "Oh, he may not love her yet, but he *will*. Gil, every single man who sees my sister loves her immediately. Most women too."

"If that were true, then anyone at all might awaken her. But it isn't. *I* never fell in love with Aurora."

Isbe huffed, causing stray curls to lift away from her face. "Are you saying she isn't beautiful and graceful, that she doesn't smell of wild raspberries late on the vine, and that her hair isn't the color of the sun first thing in the morning, or that the curves of her body aren't soft and perfect as the hills and valleys of Deluce, or that kindness doesn't radiate from her smile?" she demanded, reciting a list of qualities she had heard repeated countless times by others.

Gil half had the urge to laugh and half to pick up Isbe by the waist and toss her into the nearest stack of hay. She was so stubborn . . . and so oblivious to his true meaning. "Sure, I suppose Aurora's all of those things," he said with a sigh. "That wasn't my point."

Isbe folded her arms. "Well, in our case, it must be the prince who breaks the curse so that he can be credited with saving Deluce, further solidifying their union. It's the only way we can show Malfleur that we are a stronghold against her magic. We'll show the faeries their curse means nothing to us."

He stared at her, studying the determination written on her face, which made it all the more stark and beautiful. Her lips were pursed, just slightly, and he had to fight away the images that arose in him. Images of touching those lips with his own. "You've really thought this through, haven't you?" he said quietly. "But since when are you so eager to save us all from the evil of Malfleur? I thought this was about your sister's health. And I didn't think you put any stock in those rumors. . . ."

"Ever since the murder of the two elder princes, and now this mysterious faerie curse, I have thought of little else but the vulnerability of Deluce. This isn't just about saving Aurora. This is about saving *all* of us. And let's face it—no one else is going to do it."

"You don't know a single thing about Prince William," Gil said, feeling the familiar twins of frustration and awe creep into his voice. In the easy way he knew he'd always win an arm wrestle with Isbe despite her wiry strength, he also knew he'd never win a single argument. Still, he made one last attempt. "And what about Aalis and Piers? And Roul?"

Isbe sighed, and he could swear he saw softness shift across her face like a drifting cloud. "Roul will find a new wife to help him with the children. He never lacked admirers when he was young. *Neither* of you did," she added. It should have been a compliment, but it felt like a dig.

And he hated to admit why.

Because it meant Isbe saw him as more than a friend— she thought of him as a *man*, even a potential husband . . . for *someone else*. He wanted to tell her, to let loose all the jumbled desires racing like fine chargers inside his chest, pounding their hooves in his veins. Sometimes he feared by holding it all in he was creating some sort of inevitable stampede that would one day kill him.

And yet.

Even as a bastard, even as a runaway, she was still a royal. The daughter of a king. And he would never be more in her esteem than a beloved groom. A childhood companion.

"I don't like the idea of you traveling so far, Isbe," was all he finally admitted. "Especially not when times are so unpredictable. It's always been my job to keep you safe. You would have been trampled by a wayward mare 'fore you could hardly walk if it wasn't for me."

Could she sense the purpose in his words? Isbe placed both her hands on his shoulders, then let them wander up to his face as she had so many times over the years, reading his expression—altering it subtly with her touch as she did, so that he was left with the unsettling suspicion that she understood not what he was truly feeling, only what she wanted him to feel.

"I am certain this is the best course, Gil," she said at last. "There's only one thing of which I'm not *fully* certain yet." Already she'd begun to pack a small store of food and a change of clothes.

"And what's that?" he asked.

She stopped what she was doing and stood to face him again, her eyes landing just at his chin. He sucked in a breath. How he wished so often he could grab her in his arms and make her really understand him. . . .

"Whether or not you'll be joining me," she said.

———

And so here they are, on the pier, about to board an oil vessel that will sail right through the strait, just under the noses of the sleeping castle village, and out across the North Sea . . . to Aubin. Even now, the sails slap one another in the crisp winter air, as though applauding Isbe's recklessness.

Gil doesn't need to have his luck with him to know this is a bad gamble.

But there is one thing of which he can be certain: he'll always gamble on Isbe. He'll do anything—barter any sense he owns—to be near her, to remain a part of her. Even though she may never know.

11

Aurora

T ime may have stopped; seconds or centuries may have
ticked by while she remained held within the wall, but
finally Aurora parts the stone—parts *from* it—though the
cold still clings to her like a shadow.

She begins to take in her surroundings . . . and an eerie
sense of *recognition* floods her. But it must be a coincidence.
It has to be. She's still shaken from moving through the
wall illusion—and from seeing all the soldiers deformed,
crushed, morphed into stone.

Across a barren field, an old castle rises up from a tangle
of dying vines and rotting tree trunks. Some sort of ivy,
dotted with dried purple flowers, climbs from window to
window, many of them boarded up. One entire tower has

collapsed in on itself, and stone rubble litters the grounds. The day—if this even *is* the same day—has waned; purple-pink light veins the dried grass, almost obscuring the long, narrow road that snakes to the mouth of the gate. In the distance beyond the estate, she can see that the road leads to the low, lopsided peaks of huts and even a church—though it's all blackened and in obvious disrepair, as if the whole village was razed by a bad fire.

"What is this place?" she whispers.

Heath smiles at her, all the wariness and urgency he exuded in the Borderlands now gone from his face. "Welcome to Blackthorn," he says. "Home of Queen Belcoeur."

Blackthorn. So she was right, in a way. She *did* recognize it. The Blackthorns used to hold a great spread of land in the rocky LaMorte Territories. It's where Queen Malfleur now rules. From there, it is said, the faerie queen can look out across the mountains to her entire kingdom, and can even see, if she squints, the gleaming cupolas of Deluce's palace, her childhood home, in the distance.

But Aurora and Heath aren't in the mountains. And *this* Blackthorn is inhabited not by Malfleur, but by her dead sister—who is not, Aurora reminds herself, dead at all, apparently. She can't help but wonder if she's tumbling through a dream.

Then again, she has never dreamed with her lost senses.

"You live here?" Aurora stares at the castle, distress creeping into her lungs.

"Most of us do. Our grandparents, and their parents,

were Blackthorn's staff. But now we're more like tenants. We live here, and we work here, but we don't really work for *her*. We don't even see her. She doesn't leave the north turret. For all we know, she subsists by eating the stray moths that find their way through her windows."

Aurora looks at Heath. She is having a difficult time separating her confusion about *him* with her overwhelming curiosity—and wariness—about this *place*. She clears her throat, picturing whittling her words into a knife, one that can cut through the fog. "I need to get home. My sister . . . and the prince . . . and . . ."

"Home," he repeats, as though the idea were an uncanny one.

"Deluce. The palace. Yes."

"I'm afraid that may be a bit complicated," Heath replies. "Come on, evening is approaching. You and I have much to discuss. Very much to discuss."

"We do?" No one has ever had much to discuss with her, other than Isbe.

But he is already hurrying ahead at a half jog. Aurora follows, then abruptly stumbles, landing hard on her knees with a sharp cry. She has fallen countless times before, but this is different—it takes the breath out of her. Her legs feel wobbly, and one of her ankles throbs.

"Aurora!" Heath runs to her side.

She sees the object in the grass that tripped her: a glass jar, lying in the dusty earth, which looks almost blue in the ebbing light.

The jar is cool and firm in her hands . . . and full of dead fireflies.

She lets it drop back to the ground as Heath helps her up. "Here, lean on me."

All of the lifting, the touching, the shuffling—hand to shoulder, arm to back—it's too much. But she has no choice. Her ankle is weak. It is singing a silent song of despair. She can't listen to it anymore, but the pain won't go away. It's constant. She never knew what it really was to be hurt, even a little.

She swallows, and swallows again, trying not to cry, trying not to faint. Other people, she reminds herself, *live* with a sense of touch. They are not consumed by it. She breathes deeply and tries to distract herself.

"What . . . what was that?" she asks.

"Part of the queen's enchantment," he says. "They're everywhere, these jars. If you tried to collect them all, you'd find still more would crop up, as though naturally occurring."

Enchantment? Another riddle. He seems full of them, like so many imprisoned insects. Isbe used to collect fireflies too, with Gil when they were kids. She'd bring them back for Aurora, to light the secret passageway between their bedrooms. Aurora used to be disturbed by the way the bugs' bodies would glow as though aflame, and then go dormant, one by one, until she realized they were suffocating. She always wondered what it would be like to light up from the inside, like some beautiful cry of warning.

They reach a broken wooden fence, then pass through a gate and down a dirt path. The last of the sun streaks the ruined castle in shadow as Heath raps a special knock on the door.

Aurora holds her breath. They are entering the home of the Night Faerie. . . . But it's a young boy, no more than eight or nine years old, who answers. He's dressed in a frayed tunic twice his size. He blinks out at them, his little face smudged with dirt. "Heath!" he exclaims with a wide smile.

Heath ruffles the boy's head. "Flea. Be good and don't let anyone know we're here just yet, all right?"

"Too late!" The boy grins as what looks like the rest of his family appears in the doorway—a father, mother, and two older sisters, one carrying a baby boy in her arms, the other with a rounded belly suggesting her own child will come soon. All of them have a gaunt, skeletal appearance, with deep circles beneath their eyes.

"We were expecting you to bring home a *deer*," the girl holding the baby says.

"Your family?" Aurora asks him, feeling self-conscious in her now-tattered cloak, which is still likely finer than anything these peasants have ever worn.

"Not exactly," Heath says, then turns back to them. "This is Aurora. She's—well, I'll explain later."

Aurora notices the wife and husband catch eyes.

"Well, come in, of course," the wife says quickly. "Dinner's almost ready."

"Actually, Greta." Heath swipes loose hair out of his

face. "I'll have Wren bring Aurora's dish up to the tower later. I don't want everyone asking questions."

The sisters stare at him. "The tower?" the older one asks.

The younger of the two has her mouth crunched quizzically to the left. "And what if *we* have questions?"

"Trust me," he answers easily, "I've got more questions than you." He pulls Aurora past them, through a large open hall in which a number of other peasants stop their chores to stare at her, then down a corridor and into a kitchen full of rich scents, where he grabs a bottle of something from one of the side tables. Then he leads her into a back room lit by torches. He hangs up the rope he had been carrying on his back. He helps her down a series of walkways, toward a flight of stairs.

But it's all happening too fast, and his arm around her is both guiding her and making her dizzy at the same time. "Heath, I can't stay here," she manages. It feels good at least to say something firm, something definite. "I have to get back to Deluce. They need me," she adds. *The third prince will be waiting.*

He turns to face her, placing a finger on her lips. "*I* need you."

She's too startled to reply, or even to understand what he means. Her lips tingle, and she tries to rub them with her sleeve to make the sensation go away.

At the top of the stairs is a tower bedroom that looks, to Aurora's surprise and relief, much like a parlor she might have seen in the home of a Delucian baron or chevalier,

100

except that a layer of dust covers the once-vivid red and purple brocades on the chairs and settees. A thick canopy hangs over the bed. One window has been thrown open to let in the springlike air. The fireplace is unkempt, ashes piled high. This could be any number of rooms she's been in before, and yet it feels odd, like something is missing from the room, and the room itself knows it.

"This should do," Heath says. "You'll have privacy from the rest."

"The rest?"

"We don't have many private quarters. Some people live five or six to a room here." He helps her into one of the chairs. "Are you comfortable?" He almost seems nervous, even though just moments ago he'd been all grin and swagger. "Here, let me see your ankle," he says, pulling a stool up to her chair for her to place her foot on. Then he kneels before her and gingerly removes her boot, lifting the edge of her dress to reveal her ankle. He takes the bottle from the kitchen—some sort of fragrant oil—and dabs a little on his hands to rub into her bare skin.

She winces.

"It doesn't look too bad, a minor twist," he says. He begins to apply a poultice.

Her teeth grit together, sending pressure along her jaw to the back of her skull. She's so tense she can hardly move. Finally she lets out a small cry.

He looks up at her in surprise. "I'm sorry, was I too rough? Are you all right? You look pale." His hand goes to her cheek, and she reflexively jerks her head away. "Why are you afraid to let me touch you?"

"I . . ." How can she explain?

"Did I offend you in the cottage? I apologize for my rough behavior. I'm so used to defending myself, and it simply didn't occur to me at first that you could be *real*."

"It's not that," she says, and then sighs, trying to release the tension in her body. Trying to breathe in the pain in her ankle and breathe it out. It is just a fact; no more, no less. "It's just that I've never felt like this before. I've never felt at all."

"I don't understand."

And so she tells him, haltingly: about her christening and the tithes the fae took in exchange for their gifts. With each word, she feels a little bit braver, freer, more confident.

"What kind of parents would allow that to happen to their child?" Heath asks quietly when she finishes.

"Oh, it wasn't anything malicious on their part," Aurora says. "They believed the exchanges were worthwhile, or else they wouldn't have accepted them. They wanted to improve me."

"By allowing your senses to be robbed from you? I suppose they thought beautiful and silent makes an ideal princess."

His words abrade her more harshly than his touch did. She opens her mouth to respond but finds she can't. She doesn't know what to say.

Because he's absolutely right. And the truth of it—hearing it spoken aloud like that—is stunning.

"They wanted to protect me," she whispers at last. That much he cannot deny.

He clears his throat. "But not all touch is painful, Aurora." Once again he reaches toward her cheek, and this time, she tries not to cringe or move away as he traces his fingers, ever so lightly, along her jaw.

It makes her want to cry. Because he's wrong. All touch *is* painful—this kind of touch even more so. It makes her feel as though she is starving, lost, alone.

"Aurora."

She'd been looking at the ground, avoiding his eyes. But now she focuses on him, takes in the warm tone of his skin; the light, messy shading of stubble along his jaw; the unkempt sweep of hair not much darker than her own. They catch eyes. He too has been staring at her.

"Forgive me." He clears his throat. "I shouldn't have done that, or said any of that. I just haven't ever met someone like you, someone from . . . out *there*. I didn't—we weren't ever sure if it was possible."

"Possible?"

"You see," he says, gently finishing tying the bandage, "we've been imprisoned in Sommeil for generations. In the past there were countless suicides, horrible infighting between those who believed in the real world and those who had already begun to forget it. Eventually, knowledge of the other world they had come from began to fade. Now my generation knows no other way of being but this." He gestures at the room around them. "We've simply inherited this . . . this *feeling*. Of smallness. Of being trapped."

Aurora swallows. She understands the feeling of walls closing in, of the world around her shrinking rather than expanding. Even when the council is focused on other things—which they usually are—she has always imagined their control over her like an invisible yoke. But it's not just the council members watching her, holding her back, keeping her in. It's the people of Deluce and their expectations of a crown princess. Maybe even too the ghosts of her dead parents, wanting her to uphold their honor.

"Many no longer believe the stories," Heath goes on. "About the other world. Your world. But I always have. When the queen made Sommeil, she had to have created a way out."

"The queen . . . *made* Sommeil?"

Heath nods.

Aurora shifts, tempted to flee despite the continued ache in her ankle. His words have unsettled her. Part of her wonders if *all* conversations are this confusing, if she simply isn't used to talking normally with people, and that's why everything out of Heath's mouth sounds so strange. But then she thinks about what he's saying: *Belcoeur, the Night Faerie, made a world of her own. And now she rules here.*

Aurora runs through her 313-book collection of faerie histories in her head. She seems to remember something about the Night Faerie tithing. . . .

"Dreams," Heath says, just as she's thinking it. "The queen wove Sommeil out of dreams, or so the story goes.

She has complete power here. She hides out in the north turret, protected by enchantment after enchantment, while the world around us grows more desperate and more treacherous by the day. And for as long as any of us has been alive, no one has found a way to escape. And no one new has appeared. Until you. Don't you see? You're the proof. You're the answer."

"But I don't have any answers."

"You must, though. Maybe it will come to you. Maybe you'll remember."

"Surely the queen must know the way," Aurora protests.

He shakes his head. "We've tried everything. She won't die, and she won't answer our demands. She won't even come out of hiding. She's protected by too much magic."

Aurora believes him. It would probably take another faerie—a powerful one, like Malfleur—to kill Belcoeur or to break the spell keeping them all in this world. "I don't know how I can help," she says again, hating to disappoint him.

"Just tell me what you know," he says quietly.

And so she does. She tells him all about Deluce: the political upheaval, the planned alliance, the murder of the two princes. The threat of Malfleur, who has, apparently, been lying for more than a century about the fate of her sister. "She has always claimed to have killed her. But could it be she took pity on her twin and simply banished her here instead, wove a spell trapping Belcoeur in a world of her own making, perhaps?" she wonders aloud. "If that's the case, we'll never find a way out."

"Go on," Heath prods. "What happened after the murders?"

She tells him about Isbe, and how she fled into the night to find her but discovered instead the abandoned summer cottage. Her chest expands with breath as she tells of the spinning wheel, golden and glimmering, as big as a forest beast, and how she woke up here in this place so unfamiliar to her. With every detail, she feels a warm honey glow rising up inside her until it seems her voice must be the brightest light in the room. "All I can guess," Aurora finishes, "is that the spindle must have been enchanted too. Belcoeur was a weaver, correct?"

Heath nods. "It's all she does, even now."

"Perhaps the spinning wheel belonged to her then, before she left my world for Sommeil."

"But if what you say is true," Heath ponders, "then why would Malfleur banish Belcoeur here, only to leave a way into Sommeil?"

"Maybe Malfleur *didn't* banish her after all. Perhaps Belcoeur . . ." Aurora pauses. "Perhaps she came here of her own free will. Perhaps *she* is the one who left the way in."

"Left a way in but not a way out?"

Aurora shrugs helplessly. There's nothing about this in any of her faerie histories. "I already told you, I don't have any answers. I'm more lost than you are."

He gets up and paces. "I want to get you home, Aurora. And if we do—*when* we do, I'm coming with you. I've waited all my life for this. I will never be happy here in

Sommeil—I've always known that. I'll never stop thinking about what it's like out there. I am going to figure this out. And until then, I'll make sure you're safe here."

There's a rap on the door, and a petite girl around Aurora's age pokes her head into the room.

"Oh, good. Wren, come in," Heath says.

Wren enters with a tray of soup, a small hunk of meat, and a rough piece of bread. The girl has delicate features, a turned-up nose, and small mouth. She's ghostly thin, her skin the color of tree bark when starlight hits it. Though her black hair is tied messily and her ears are overly pointy, she is very pretty.

"I know I can trust you to be sure Aurora is comfortable," Heath says.

"Of course," Wren replies, her voice soft and lulling. Her thin lips pull down to one side. "Any friend of Heath's is a friend of mine," she says to Aurora.

Heath leaves the room, and Aurora can almost feel the chill in his wake.

"You're cold," Wren says, setting down the tray. She goes to the hearth and looks for the flint box.

"Thank you." Aurora notices her fingers fumble. "Are you all right?" she asks the girl.

"Yes. But . . . I wish . . . ," Wren whispers. "Forgive me for saying . . . I wish you wouldn't . . . encourage him too much."

"Heath?"

Wren turns to face Aurora, her eyes big and dark. "No

one can be happy if they are always searching. That's what I think, anyway. If you believe you're living in a shadow, you will never feel the light. Do you see what I mean?"

Aurora tests her ankle and stands up, wincing only a little.

"Miss! Sit back down!" Wren comes toward her.

"No, no, I'm fine." Aurora waves her off lightly. "Let me help you. I want to help."

She approaches her, and even though Aurora has only ever lit a fire a few times, she takes the flint box from Wren's trembling hands. After a couple of tries, she manages to catch a spark and kneels down to place the lit tinder into the fire. However, something in the fireplace catches her eye. A glimmer.

She gasps. "Wren. Are these . . . *jewels in the ashes*?" she whispers, nearly dropping the tinder. She scoops up the gleaming stones—a necklace made of pearls separated by tiny rubies. "Why would someone leave these in the fireplace?"

"I'm sorry, miss. The room hasn't been cleaned. We don't usually put guests here. We don't usually have guests at all."

Inspiration flies into her. "You could trade these, sell them—you could buy food for everyone in Blackthorn!"

Wren sighs, kneeling beside her. She takes the lit tinder and lights a log. "There *is* no food to be bought," she replies softly. "We rely on the hunters, like Heath, to bring back meat. We ration the grain, which struggles more to thrive every year that goes by. . . ."

She helps Aurora back to her feet, and both of them step back from the growing flames.

Wren's light hand on her elbow sends a message through Aurora that overwhelms her with its tenderness. She looks down at the beautiful stones coated in a light layer of ash, which have left black dust in her palm. "But still," she starts, then trails off.

Aurora would gladly hammer out all of the emeralds and sapphires in her crown to help the people of Sommeil, if she had it here. But perhaps Wren is right that the jewels would do no good. It has never occurred to Aurora to feel embarrassed by who she is. Or worse . . . ashamed. She's lived a life of tasseled pillows and billowing gowns, while these people suffer.

She traces her fingers over the string of pearls, then slips it into the pocket of her gown as a reminder.

"I'm sorry," Aurora says now. "I want to help you. And Heath. All of you. I wish I knew what to do." Her voice has begun to come to her with ease, but the answers have not.

Wren looks at her curiously. "Sommeil must seem a sad place to you. But it isn't. Not entirely. The evils here are no worse than the evils anywhere, I imagine. Why should I want to learn of another world, a vaster world, if it means regretting my whole life until now? Who wants to be made to loathe what they have? Small as it is, my life is mine."

"But . . . there's so much you're missing. There's a great wide expanse of a world to explore where I'm from," she protests, her heart swelling with love for Deluce. Though even as she says this, a dull voice thuds through her veins . . . *has* she ever thought to explore her own world?

"Just promise me you won't give Heath false hope," Wren says, taking Aurora's hands in her own. And Aurora has the wild desire to tap into her small palms. "You'll only break his heart."

A moment later, Wren lets go and moves back to the silver tray, where she lifts a lid off the soup dish. "I'll let you eat and rest now."

Aurora tries to taste her food, but all she can think of is the look on Wren's face. If she ever gets home again, she is going to appreciate her world. She's going to tell Isbe every day how much she cares. She's never going to be ensnared by her own fears again.

But for now she's not home, she's here. *Sommeil.* She rolls the word around in her mind as she takes off her travel clothes to change into the nightgown Wren left out for her. It's the first time she's ever had to dress or undress herself, but she can't stand the idea of someone else doing it for her, not now. Not when a mere breath against her skin sends her into shivers so intense she's not sure if they're pleasurable or sickening. Even now, as she steps into the lightweight gown, every thread whispers around and against her.

She climbs into the bed, settling into its deep embrace.

She's exhausted, but her heart burns with curiosity. Deluce needs her. Isbe needs her. The last faerie queen in *her* world could be marching at any moment, could even now be committing more unthinkable murders. And yet . . . what will happen if—no, *when*—Aurora returns? Will her voice and sense of touch immediately snuff out like a candle? She doesn't know *why* these senses have returned to her—can only imagine that the faerie tithes at her christening somehow don't hold weight here in Sommeil, that Belcoeur's magic, evil as it may be, nullifies any other. This *is* a world of Belcoeur's making, after all.

And what did Wren mean when she said Sommeil was full of beauty?

The worn softness of a pillow caresses her cheek; she is penetratingly aware of every single stitch in its fabric, a grammar of its own, a way of being she never knew before coming here. She thinks of all the everyday objects that she's never fully *known*. She would like to meet them all with her hands, to feel the secret code of their physical forms, the silk, the paper, the wood, the string. Marble and grass and fallen leaves and a baby's hair and the ears of a goat. They are all as utterly foreign to her as the unusual birdlike clock she saw in the nursery room in the cottage. And the enormous golden spinning wheel that pricked her finger and gave her the curse, or gift, of pain.

The ghost of Heath's fingers sighs along her jaw. Will it haunt her forever when she leaves this place? She has only just learned this form of closeness, and already she fears how much she craves it, craves *more*—how devastated she would be never to have it again.

She extends her hand to the bedframe, touching its old, polished oak. She presses her fingers against it as though it were Isbe's palm. *I'm afraid,* she taps, wishing her sister could hear her. She thinks of the words Heath said to her earlier that startled her so.

I need you, she taps.

12

Isabelle

Evening wind whips at her neck. Isbe inhales, clenching her eyes against the freezing ocean spray. There are rumors among the sailors that the waves have been angrier than usual this winter, ever since the purported death of someone they refer to reverentially as the Balladeer, a figure much spoken of but rarely seen.

The Balladeer is said to have roamed the North Sea for many years, singing to the water in the water's own language, using music to draw fish straight into his wide nets. Some believe he was one of the fae, but others say that cannot be, for the fae are driven only by greed. Very poor seaside villages in the north had, over the past ten years or more, reported enormous bundles of fresh-caught herring and eel, cod and pike, and sometimes even oysters appearing on their shores, as though left there by some benevolent god, and they swore they could still hear the final notes of the Balladeer's song in the air as they collected these unexpected gifts. But—whether god or faerie or human—the Balladeer is gone now, and the waters, turbulent and brutally cold, seem to know it.

Clinging to the rail of the rocking ship with one hand, Isbe dips the other into her pocket, feeling for the lock of hair there, coarse and curly. Gil was horrified when she demanded he hack away the long tangles that had been blowing in her face for nearly eighteen years. At first he'd refused to help, but when she determined to do it for herself, he conceded, not wanting to stand by and watch her wield a rusted old fish knife so close to her own skin.

She brushes her fingers against the reminder of what they've done. It was necessary, along with binding her chest and donning the garb of a young sailor. Before boarding the ship, she and Gil were both questioned. No one wants to carry the sleeping sickness abroad with them. But using the last of the coins Isbe had taken from the palace before she left, they managed to convince the captain to change his mind about allowing Gil and his blind "brother" aboard the ship.

The echo of lifeboats rattling along the ship's sides greeted them as they boarded. She was surprised by how many deckhands there were, and unsettled by the fishy, oil-lantern stench mixed with manly sweat.

Now, as she turns to make her way below decks, the odor increases. She has spent most of the day trying to stay out of the way of the experienced hands, listening to the *thunk* of oil barrels in the cargo hold and the thickly accented calls of the sailors in a language she barely recognizes as her own—*avast* and *abaft*, *dead rise* and *draft*—wishing she could participate, but knowing how dangerous it would be to get in the way of a swinging beam or changing sail. And the last thing she needs is to draw unwanted attention. She must not jeopardize her goal of reaching William of Aubin safely.

At her request, Gil described the various spears and daggers strapped to the wall. The voulges she'd heard of—they resemble a meat cleaver but with a longer handle—and the ranseur too, tridentlike with short sides. At the helm sits one foreign weapon that neither Gil nor Isbe recognize: a giant spear that springs forward like an arrow, but with a long rope attached to the end.

She can tell from the quiet now that the decks are mostly cleared, save a few sailors who will man the ship through the darkest hours. Though she dreads another night in the crowded, low-ceilinged cabin below, the air thick with grunts and snores and the scurrying of rats, she knows that, come sunrise, they'll be within rowing distance of Aubin's shores.

Unused to the violence of the waves, she fumbles for ropes and beams to guide her—ten paces to the hatch, seven rungs down the ladder. Belowdecks, no one can stand to his full height, and certainly not Isbe, who is as tall as many of the men and feels a bruise forming on her forehead to prove it. She ducks, using her hands to trace the rough-hewn sides of the narrow bunks until another hand wraps around hers, silently indicating for her to stop.

It's Gilbert, already lying in his bunk. Even out at sea, he still smells faintly of leather and fresh hay. She climbs onto the hard bunk below his. Though she'd hate to admit it, there's no way she could make this journey alone . . . she can't even find her own bed without help.

Her bones hurt. Her head feels heavy, her body tight and cramped. She longs for an open field to ride through, for the earth's quantity of steadiness. And for peace of mind. Every night Isbe has been turning over her plan and the many ways it might go wrong. Getting into the palace shouldn't be hard. Traders and messengers are constantly coming and going, and Isbe knows her way around a palace. But what if she's stopped before gaining conference with the prince himself? Or what if he rejects her plea? What if he agrees to help but it's already too late? Gil was right—this *is* a foolish, wild mission.

The vessel creaks and groans. Waves beat against it. Sleep undulates around her, a dark water.

——◆——

. . . Arms are rocking her. A voice sings. *One night so mild, before break of morn.* The words are in her blood, thrumming in her ears—except part of her remains awake, aware that the words to the famous lullaby about Belcoeur and Malfleur usually say "reviled," not "so mild."

116

Still the song goes on, swirling around her: *Amid the roses wild, all tangled in thorns, the shadow and the child together were born.* She is cradled. She is small. She is warm, helpless, held. But then the voice, soft and not quite recognizable, changes key.

> *The girl and her twin*
> *As sisters did play*
> *'Til darkness did win*
> *The light from the day.*

Isbe tosses in her sleep. That isn't the version of the lullaby she knows—the version *everyone* knows. The meaning of the new words swims inside her, confusing her. It's not entirely different, but the phrases have been rearranged and altered in her dream. *Play* . . . the two girls are playing. That's not part of the original song. How does it usually end? *One her dear twin forever did slay.*

Tears fall on her skin. She is rocked, cradled, dreaming but not dreaming. Something in the voice. Who is singing? *Mama,* Isbe wants to cry out, but she cannot speak, and the desire rips through her chest, a stabbing pain.

Isabelle, the voice sighs. *My sweet Isabelle. My sweet . . .*

"Leopold. LEOPOLD. ISBE!"

Gil is hovering over her as she wakes; she can feel his breath on her cheek. He is shaking her, addressing her with the fake boy's name they decided on.

The world around her convulses. Even in the roiling

cabin, she can smell that it is still night. She can only have
been asleep an hour or two. But the sailors are rustling and
shouting and moving about, clambering up the ladder. Is it
a storm?

She sits up, banging her head against the upper bunk.
"What's happening?"

"I don't know. Come on," Gil says, pulling her up.

They stumble toward the ladder. Isbe's whole body is
shaking with excitement. And something else too—the
memory of that dream, that voice. She hasn't had a mother
dream in years, but she used to have them a lot. They always
leave her feeling light-headed and hot. She never before realized how strange it was that there are two separate versions
of the rose lullaby: the one everybody knows, and the one
she just heard in her dream. Her mother, whoever she was,
must have sung her own version to Isbe as a baby. Maybe she
simply didn't like the gruesome nature of the original.

A sound of clattering rings out above, as though the
twenty men have tripled. Her hands grip the rungs. She
hears the captain hollering to the rest: "A pod! 'Sa whole
host of 'em, an *nars* too!"

Gil turns and shouts down at her, his voice crackling like
a lit match: "Narwhals."

———

Above deck, all is chaos, and Isbe gets instantly turned
around. She is shuffled this way and that. She falls to her
knees. The vessel rears up like a giant startled horse. Men are
screaming directions at one another. The rack of weapons

clangs loudly as they grab for spears. She thinks of the foreign weapon rigged to the helm, and its name and purpose emerge out of all those days spent learning from Aurora, not just about fascinating devices used for warfare but also those used for hunting. This one could slay enormous sea creatures, from five feet long to thirty.

A harpoon.

She scrambles to her feet, feeling like such a fool for not realizing sooner: all these men and all these weapons . . . this isn't just a merchant vessel bearing oil from one shore to another. It's an active whaling ship.

And now they've discovered a pod of narwhals, which are among the most treasured creatures of the sea because of their long, unicornlike tusks. Isbe remembers Aurora telling her the famous White Throne—on which the North Faerie was murdered years ago—was carved and constructed solely from their ivory.

"Isbe!" she hears, and Gilbert grabs her arm again.

"What is that sound?" she shouts, trying to understand why it's as though sixty men, and not twenty, are pounding across the deck.

"Drums."

Isbe pauses, understanding. "To lure the animal."

Through the noise, she can hear the captain shouting "All hands!" A thrill flies through her, and she hardly feels the cold wind lashing her. She used to think adventure was sneaking out her window to play in the fields with Gil. Or stealing strips of meat from the kitchens to try and lure the sharp-toothed foxes in the royal forest. But for the first time since leaving the palace, it strikes her how far she has come. With the roar of the sea in her ears and the violent sway of the boat beneath her, she realizes that the very notion of adventure is a lie, for it predicts an arc that ends in its hero triumphing over challenge. This? This is no adventure; this is life, pure and raw, and she can feel the difference, can taste it—its elation and its terror, but most of all, its wild uncertainty.

"Iz," Gil whispers close to her ear.

Her hands find his. She feels the strength of his arms and shoulders as he tries to steady them both, to steer her back toward the shelter of the hatch. The boat sways and they stumble together; her back hits a low wall. He pulls her down to the floor again, leaning over her, protecting her from the spray and the wind and the sailors pushing past them.

He puts a rope in her hands. "Stay here. Hold this. Wait for me."

"But—"

His hands are on her shoulders, on her chin, cupping her face. *"Wait here."* The whisper is so quiet and yet so clear, it is like a cloak finding its hook.

She pulls him closer. They cling to each other and she finds his ear. "Gil . . . what are you . . ."

But his head turns before she can finish, and his mouth brushes her jaw. Instinct, as unplanned as a breath, guides her lips to his. His cheeks and jaw are slick with ocean spray.

Salt stings her tongue. The kiss is hungry and hard and over before she can understand it.

She grasps for him, but he slips out of her hands. Another sailor is there, trying to move past them, shoving them forward and apart. "Quick like!" he barks, and Isbe finds herself banging her elbows and legs as she's thrown to the side and then down into a wooden basin, which is being rapidly lowered.

It's one of the dinghies at the side of the ship, she realizes quickly, and there are several other men on board who are passing around weapons and oars.

"Gil! Gilbert!" she cries out, flailing her arms.

But she has lost him, and it feels like she has lost herself. The tiny lifeboat tosses in the rough waves, and she falls again. And again. Metal slashes the air just beside her face. Saltwater stings and burns like ice. She kneels and clutches at the air but can't get steady. She can't think, between the howling of the sea and the shouts of the sailors and the thrumming of blood in her ears and the conviction that she is going to die out here in the water's vast, roiling, unknowable passion.

A spear is thrust into her open, shaking palms. Most of the crew knows she is blind. Why would one of them give her a weapon? How could they not realize . . .

But ah—it is night, and dark, and sighted men do not do well where they cannot clearly see.

More barked orders—formations and directions in words she doesn't comprehend. Something about smallest men to the bow. She is shoved to the front of the tiny craft. Fear clenches down inside her, becomes an iron nail hammered tight to her heart. As she grips the rusted handle of the spear in one hand and hangs on to the side of the dinghy with the other, she at last grasps what's happening. She is part of the hunt.

———

The drums are beating. The sailors shout their commands. "Lean into it, lad!" a man commands from just behind her. He's talking to her, but she doesn't have an oar, doesn't understand the command. Does he mean lean into the motion of the boat? Perhaps it's like riding a horse, where one must allow one's body to move with and not counter to it.

Though she cannot see, there are things Isbe knows. She knows, for instance, that the man who just gave her orders has a thick beard. Even amid all this madness, she can smell how it traps the rancid odor of his last several meals. She knows his muscles are likely bulging from the effort of rowing the dinghy—she can tell this from the arrhythmic thrashing of wood against wave, the pauses, the creaks, the panting of effort, the warble of worry in all the men's voices.

And she knows something else too, knows it deep in her bones like an echo in a long corridor: the beast is nigh.

Nearly as soon as she experiences the buzz of that thought, the dinghy lurches, the bow flying upward into the crashing waves. She's thrown onto her back and swallows a huge gulp of seawater. Sputtering, she tries to sit up again, conscious that the spear is still in her hand, and that she could have stabbed herself—or someone else—with it.

"Gil!" she cries again fruitlessly. Her ankle throbs—it's twisted at an unnatural angle.

"Encirclé!" she hears. The command has come from a different boat. They are surrounding one of the whales. She tries to picture the giant narwhal, with its long, majestic, glimmering horn. Tiny boats on all sides, getting closer. Men poised with their weapons. The great fish diving and surfacing, trying to get away. *Faster,* she thinks. *Hurry. Escape.*

Of course she knows where and how Deluce gets its oil—from the fat of these animals. And Isbe has witnessed many a hunt during her lifetime. Yet somehow this is different. She is flooded with awe, wonder, and repulsion.

Then she hears it: the *zing* of the harpoon's spear flying through the air, followed by a noise Isbe can only describe as murderous. The creature has been hit.

It's as though the whale's cry contains the varied cries of whole families, of past and future beings: a strange and tragic symphony of mangled horns and snapped strings.

And then the world goes mute. Even the sea waits, eerily still.

Now a high, songlike wail breaks the silence. There's a loud, angry splash. All the men begin shouting over one another again, and she hears weapons rapidly drawn.

"Round 'bout, Adeline! She's diving! Sophia, Sophia! Losin' line! All hands! 'At's the pull! We're losin' 'er!" It's the captain's voice. He's calling directions to the smaller boats, each of them given female names: *Maria, Sophia, Adeline, Clementine, Clarabelle* . . .

Then a frenzy of spattering and screaming as they try to stab the beast, many losing their spears if not their footing. A few have gone overboard, from the sound of it. She doubts they'll be saved. Her breath clatters in her chest. Is Gilbert among them?

She tastes rust—and blood—in the salty air.

"The rope! Clarabelle!" the captain shouts.

"Close now! 'At's you, lad!" Isbe is shoved, hard, in the shoulder.

She tries to breathe, but her lungs burn. The spear is slippery in her hand. The hunt has somehow, unthinkably, come down to her. The whale leaps, and her boat is jerked forward. It feels as though her heart has leapt up too, to clog her throat. Their oars are tangled in the harpoon's line.

She chokes on saltwater. At any moment, they'll all be tossed into the sea and likely battered to death by the giant, writhing fish.

The rope whines as it's pulled tauter and tauter. The whale is yanking hard. It will drag them down with it, into the depths of the sea.

She realizes, with terror, what she must do, if she wants to live. The boat tilts and heaves again, and she's nearly thrown over, but someone grabs and steadies her.

"Now! Now! We canna hold 'er much longer!"

She doesn't know who made the command. The words

surround her, coming from the wind itself. *Now. Now.*

The waves roar. The whale bellows. The rope hisses.

She only has one spear, one thrust, one chance to get this right. It's impossible.

She clenches her eyes, listening hard, leaning into the movement of the dinghy even as she tries to feel for the movement of the agonized creature beside and below and before them. *Now, now, now.*

The waves lash. The whale moans. The rope sings.

Her heart stops.

The spear flies.

13

Claudine,

a Faerie of Considerable Stature
(in More Ways Than One)

Claudine would not have believed the rumors had it not been for a lack of jam. She finds herself this morning quite short of the sweet preserves that normally provide her only pleasure in waking up. Her maid trembles at her bedside, holding out a wobbling silver tray with a large hunk of rye bread on it, bare as a baby's head. Claudine backhands the tray, which flies from her maid's grip and clatters to the floor.

"So it really is true, then," she mutters, adjusting herself against her giant stack of pillows; her body—a mountain underneath the thick burgundy quilt—heaves with the effort.

She's heard the story by now. News travels fast in winter, when there's nothing else to do but gossip: Princess Aurora of Deluce was found motionless on the upper floor of an abandoned summer cottage, lying next to an enormous golden spindle. A maiden's scream drew others to the site. The princess, presumed dead at first, was in fact sleeping far too deeply to awaken. The maiden who'd discovered her promptly fell into a similar state. Others were able to send a messenger to gallop back to the palace for help.

The council sent out six of their best men and a wagon through the rutted, frost-covered roads to rescue the young princess. As the men loaded her onto the cart, however, one of them grew weary and hardly made it out of the woods before falling to the ground in an unshakeable sleep. The others hurried on their course, wrapping the princess in thick cloaks. But on the short ride back to the palace, the remaining councilmen too succumbed.

So the tale goes. The horse driver hardly made it past the chains of the drawbridge glimmering in the morning sun before he fell asleep on his perch. The horse, confused, whinnied and tried to bolt, yanking the cart the rest of the way into the palace, where the strange contagion continued to spread.

There has been no movement since, no message, no wave of a flag from within those walls to signify life; all roads to the palace have been cordoned off.

Strange stories, Claudine thinks. Faerie curses. She'd be amazed if any of the fae still have the power they once did. These days, a faerie curse carries hardly more magic than it takes to boil a kettle. And yet, the unlikeliness of the princess finding that particular abandoned cottage . . . it reeks of faerie magic.

"A sleeping sickness . . . ," she says now to her maid. "It reminds me of something my cousin Violette once said. At the child's christening."

"The child?" the maid asks timidly.

"The *princess*, of course," Claudine says. "Now leave me."

She lumbers out of her bed, humming to herself in a voice far purer than should belong to someone of her age. She waddles to the window, throwing open the sash and shutters and breathing in the harsh air. It is winter outside, and it is winter too, *always*, within her. Nothing can fill the void. Nothing satisfies the hunger. Nothing can take root, no matter how much sweetness she consumes.

Except something *has* taken root. For even now, a thick, dark-vined briar pushes its way out of the hard, frozen dirt surrounding the cottage where Aurora was found. Thorns splinter along its stems as it grows eagerly, with a hunger as powerful as Claudine's own, stretching along the path through the royal forest, reaching the road and eventually winding toward the palace itself, thickening as it grows long, doubling, tripling, quadrupling, pressing onward, blossoming with purple-white buds, and rising, rising, rising.

14

Isabelle

Timing is everything. One might even say it was bad timing that Isbe was born in the same year the king decided to banish all of his mistresses from the land, ensuring the new queen would never be made jealous—and that Isbe would never know her own mother.

And because she understands how crucial timing can be, Isbe is not surprised to hear her spear whiz a few feet into the air before splashing uselessly into the sea, missing the rope entirely. Her palm stings; her skin's raw, her pulse loud in her ears. Throughout the din of the hunt, she had been listening carefully to the high, faint whine of the harpoon's rope as it pulled taut. It was the sound of fraying, of fibers untwining and splitting. She had tried to point her spear not at the whale but directly at that sound. Even though she missed, she was right about one thing: there's a terrible wrenching sound as the narwhal gives a final angry heave— and the rope snaps.

A tiny spark of hope lights in Isbe's heart even as her body is thrown backward from the aftershock and the icy waves envelop her.

The whale has gotten free.

She thrashes, as the beast had done. She tries to scream underwater. She burns from the inside. Her body struggles for many minutes, and then begins to let go, to soften. Her mind follows, turning numb. From that numbness, a faint pressure emerges, a pattern against her open hands. It's a message. The sea is speaking to her in the same way Aurora does: by tapping in their secret language. Or maybe it isn't the sea but Aurora herself, or a memory of Aurora. *I'm afraid,* the water pulses into her hand. *I need you.*

The tapping becomes angry, nonsensical, frantic. It is no longer a message. It is . . . wood. The end of a stray oar. Isbe grasps for it, but it eludes her. She tries again, her mind beginning to awaken. The desire to live shoots through her with the power of cannonfire and she grabs again, holding on as the slippery oar yanks her upward, toward the surface—and her face breaks free.

She gags on saltwater as air whooshes into her lungs.

Someone is pulling the other end of the oar.

Someone has saved her.

PART
III

THE SHADOW
AND THE CHILD

15

Aurora

Night is a gasp, and then over.

Opening her eyes, Aurora needs no gauzy sway of a curtain to signal the wind's presence. The unseen forces of the world all have bodies, she understands now. Phantoms fill the air.

A soft moan comes from her throat. The pain in her ankle has subsided into a distant throb. Yet the bed, the sheets, the weight of the blanket over her, the tickle of fresh breeze across her brow—these gather into a complex melody that makes her *want*.

More and more every day.

She's not even sure *what* she wants, but she knows that obedience, grace, kindness . . . these no longer form the only standards by which she can live. Not with this new, lush thing borne inside her: desire . . . for touch, for the breath that inflates her chest, for her voice, for life—the *feeling* of it.

She sits up, letting memory slowly sift back into her like flour through a sieve. She had tried to keep track of the days at first, but Sommeil has a way of blurring things together; time seems to glide by almost invisibly, like a skitter bug across a lake. How long has she been gone?

Sleepily, she lists the facts to herself: Deluce needs her. She must return, marry a prince, and protect her kingdom, though these things have begun to seem like mere strands of a book she once read. The one that stands out the most is this: she has to get back to Isbe. Which means somehow finding a way out of this place.

Aurora's stomach stirs. She flips back the covers and dresses quickly, with ever-increasing confidence. Even hunger has a different—and greater—impact here. In Deluce, she'd often go hours forgetting to eat, especially when caught up in a good book. But here she feels the pang and immediately begins to imagine the juice of a fresh peach, the smooth spread of butter on warm pastries, even though she knows they don't have such luxuries. In Deluce, servants brought breakfast to her room, and Isbe always joined her before they started their day. But everything is different in Sommeil. She eats with the others—her rank doesn't matter. And her sister isn't here.

Isbe ran away, a voice reminds Aurora as she slips on her boots. *She was content to live without you. She loved you, but she pitied you*. She has once again kicked the wasps' nest of thoughts that always lies just to the side of her path. Her heart races as she tries to ignore her doubts.

She glances out the window. From the tower, Aurora can see all the way across the desiccated fields surrounding Blackthorn, butting up against a thick, dry forest. There's no sign of the stone wall from here, the one that protects the estate from the Borderlands; the one she and Heath, unbelievably, passed through together.

Below her, there are already peasants up early, moving about near a run-down barn. And in the distance, a figure approaches the woods alone.

Heath. Going off to hunt once again. In the Border-lands. Over the past few days, she has watched him return home dragging the bodies of whole harts and wild boar with arrows aslant in their chests, sacks filled with bloody pheasant and duck parts, and once, a net of fish, some still writhing. And she has watched too, as Wren greets him each time with something more than gratitude in her posture, in her smile.

You'll only break his heart, Wren had said to her on that first day.

Many nights he goes straight to his chambers without eating dinner, hunched over a lantern, making notes to himself. At first she was impressed that he could read and write, though only rudimentarily. And then she became curious. He explained that he was keeping a hunting log because game has grown increasingly scarce.

135

With everything she learns about Sommeil, Aurora has only become more concerned for its fate, has come to realize that escape may be necessary not just for her, or for Heath, but for all of them.

But in the meantime, she has been trying to help however she can. Here there's no complex hierarchy of household staff to run the palace and maintain its grounds and outbuildings. Instead, chores are assigned based on family, with many peasants who don't appear to have any role at all. Greta and her family man the kitchens along with several others, and though Aurora has no experience, she's made herself useful there—hanging herbs to dry, grinding grain into powder to make flour, scrubbing vegetables from the gardens until her hands, usually prized for their daintiness, have grown ragged and chapped. This may be a world wrought from dreaming, but for Aurora it has provided her first taste of real work and real life—life the way the masses live it, both here and, she can only assume, at home.

She doesn't bother to pin up her hair. She grabs a piece of vellum that she'd asked Wren to procure yesterday and flings open her bedroom door, runs down the stairs and out onto the grounds, making her way after Heath. She inhales the morning dew as she calls out to him repeatedly, but he doesn't turn around.

Aurora's beginning to fear her voice has somehow been imagined this whole time, both by her and by others, when finally he hears her and turns.

"What are you doing out here?" he asks, sweeping hair

out of his eyes. She's noticed how often he does that around her, and she wonders, fleetingly, if she makes him nervous.

She tries to catch her breath. "I thought I could come with you today. Help take notes for you. I'm a very skilled writer and I have excellent penmanship. I—"

"Aurora, it isn't safe. You need to go back."

"But I want to be of *use*. Every day I've been biding my time, wandering alone, and I haven't gotten any closer to an answer." Her limited contributions leave plenty of time to roam the castle, looking for evidence, for a sign, for a way out—as though she might simply stumble upon a lost key to a hidden door. Maybe, she has thought irrationally, she'd find another spinning wheel.

But she has not. And her own sense of urgency has already begun to wane. Isbe comes to her as a sharp pang of need but then fades from her mind again. Sommeil itself has this effect on her. There's a poignancy to every breath here, and it distracts her, reminds her of early mornings when she was eleven or twelve, just discovering the tomes of epic romance in the library. How she'd take her latest treasure down to the kitchens, where she'd sit in a window to read while the warm scent of baking biscuits drifted and curled around her, steaming the pane.

Sommeil gives her that exact feeling: those brief hours when you are holding an unread story in your hands and don't yet know how it will end. You would be content if the biscuits never rose and were never consumed, the irises in the garden never bloomed and faded, the rain hovered but never fell. The not-yet-ness tastes sweeter than the thing you're waiting for.

"I thought I could help you. At least I could get out of the estate and—"

"And get yourself killed in the Borderlands?" Heath sighs, his arm muscles flexing as if by instinct. "I can see you are beginning to feel what this place does to people. That restlessness. Half sweet, half deadly. You don't need to get lost, or be lured by an Impression, to go mad here. Sometimes it happens all on its own."

"But you've been ignoring me—*avoiding* me, even," she adds, realizing that it's true. "We agreed to help each other find a way out of Sommeil. I thought—"

"I made you no promises."

"But you *did*," she insists, feeling baffled and dismayed by the way he won't even look in her eyes.

"I said I would protect you, and that's what I'm trying to do right now. As for a way out . . . I had hoped you might have answers, but you don't. In the meantime, Blackthorn needs me." His hands clench and unclench.

"But the game dwindles," she counters. "You can't just turn back to your life, knowing one day the food may run out completely!" The heat of their argument is warming her cheeks.

"What do you know about hunger? You grew up a sheltered, spoiled princess!"

The accusation stings, even though it shouldn't. Her

royal upbringing shouldn't be an insult. "I didn't *choose* my own parents."

"No, but they chose everything for you," he snaps.

"What does that mean?"

"It means now that I've thought more about the corruption of your world—the way human senses are bartered out of vanity—I'm less convinced I want anything to do with it."

Aurora's jaw drops. He can't mean that. He is just lashing out because of his disappointment. His disappointment *in her*.

Shame roils in her gut. She draws in a breath, trying not to stare at Heath's mouth, trying not to imagine, as she has done every night in her bed, him touching her face tenderly again, the way he did on the first night.

"Fine," she says. "You can stay here and hunt until there's not a single deer left in the forest. I'm going to find my own way home." She marches off, an unfamiliar emotion sparking and raging in her throat: *anger*.

———

Back inside the castle, she finds her way to the study where she has seen Heath retire to make his notes. He doesn't think she knows what it's really like to be one of them. Well, why should she? No one's told her; no one's given her a chance to understand.

Pushing her way into the small space, she sees piles of empty, dirty cups, indicating he has stayed up late many nights, working and thinking. At the desk beneath the window lies a stack of pages. She sits down to rifle through them. Except they aren't notes, really. They are more like charts and graphs with all sorts of scrawled labels. Depictions, she realizes slowly, of the Borderlands. He's been keeping track of its patterns, how it changes. He must think that by decoding how their world operates, he will find a secret loophole, and with it, an exit. But how many years has he spent on this project, with no success?

Aurora touches the pages. It strikes her that perhaps Heath is missing the point: what if there simply *is* no exit? The prick of the spinning wheel's flying bobbin sent her here, or so she has gathered. It's possible the spinning wheel has some significance, but does it really represent a pattern, or is it just a disconnected clue? Why, in a world built from the power of dreaming, would anything follow logic?

She drops the vellum and leaves his study. Everyone has warned her repeatedly to stay away from the north turret. It's dangerous to get too close to the queen's quarters, they say. But what good has cowering done them—or anyone, for that matter?

She moves through parlor room after parlor room, trying to avoid those peasants who don't work—the ones who huddle in corners with dark looks. They unsettle her. Hunger seems to have hardened in them like tree sap; she can almost see a bitterness crystalizing in the whites of their eyes, the way frost solidifies over a leaf in winter. She has the sense that if she stares too long, she too will succumb, and freeze.

140

She clenches her stomach and forges past them.

The must and mildew of the back halls fill her lungs as she makes her way toward the forbidden wing. Finally, after several twists and turns, she reaches the locked door at the end of the long and narrow north hall.

Aurora balls up her fists and bangs on the door.

She bangs and bangs, but nothing happens. The harder she pounds on the echoing wood, the more her frustration mounts. How dare Heath accuse her of being sheltered and spoiled, when she's done nothing but try to help?

If she's honest with herself, the insult has wounded her for a deeper reason. She is not only an outsider to him, but someone with qualities he doesn't admire: wealth, privilege, innocence. Qualities she'd thought made her special. He believes that her father and mother were self-serving, cynical, greedy. That they allowed her to be deprived of touch and voice for their *own* benefit instead of for hers.

But that's not true. It can't be. Can it? Even as she wonders about these things, her past begins to unfold before her in a new light, and it makes her feel sick. Maybe Heath is right. She thinks of the way her mother treated Isbe, as though she was not a family member at all.

Maybe her parents *were* cruel.

She sinks to the floor beside the locked door and pulls out the necklace she's been carrying around—the one she found in the hearth on her first night. A bead is missing.

Why is the bead missing, and why does this detail bother her so?

141

She has the sudden, desperate conviction that if she can fix this necklace, she can still save some final piece of her childhood.

But it's all so disgustingly obvious, isn't it? Aurora has been a pawn. She has been used. She has meant nothing to anyone, except as a figurehead.

She thought, like Ombeline, that she wanted to be freed from stone, that she wanted to speak, and to feel. But now she's afraid of all the bad things she might feel—is *already* feeling. Of all the things she might say. She can hurt people now, and be hurt by them, in all new ways.

But what really hurts is seeing that her life until now was a lie. The only one who even cared about Aurora—not as a princess, but as a person—was Isbe.

She fumbles with the jewels in her hand. A tear streaks her face. She wipes it away, and another pearl comes loose from the strand. The pearl rolls away from her and under the locked door.

Slowly, the door opens.

Aurora scrambles back to her feet and then, with caution, she glances around her, before approaching the doorway. Almost despite herself, she walks through it.

She enters an enormous, windowless hall lined with cobwebs . . . and, she squints to see, beautiful, plentiful tapestries. There are so many they overlap on the walls. Some are coated in a thick layer of dust; others seem freshly hung. *The Night Faerie's work.* She shivers.

But no one is in here, so how did the door open on its own?

Aurora can hear the tiny rattle of the rolling pearl, though she can't see it in the dim-lit room. Her footsteps click faintly, as though the sound has come from a distance. The air is dense and stifling, and the weak light from the open door behind her only serves to highlight the dust motes in the air, making it even harder to see.

Though she's been exposed to plenty of artwork before, Aurora is awed as she moves closer to the tapestries. They are especially elaborate, each depicting a landscape with immaculate detail, and she pauses, taking them in individually in the near darkness of the room. There's something about each that she recognizes. They must be based on the queen's memories from the real world.

It occurs to her that *all* of Sommeil has been constructed out of the queen's memories of the real world—warped, dreamlike versions of real things. Blackthorn. The royal forest. She wonders what other pieces of her world have a double here.

She has the sensation of moving through water—a murky, reedy lake—as she walks farther into the room. She comes to a portrayal, this one newer, less dusty, of the cottage in the Borderlands. And within the window, a table set with tea, still steaming. The image, eerily familiar, sends a chill through her. It's as though the silk itself wavers, like steam. As though Belcoeur purposely wove the steam over the tea so it would still be hot when Aurora arrived . . . like she knew someone was coming.

Aurora had forgotten about the rattling sound, until now. Abruptly, it stops.

She turns.

At the far end of the hall, someone has bent down to pick up the pearl. Someone with long, disheveled white hair . . . and a large crown. The old woman—the queen, Aurora realizes with a quick intake of breath—continues turning the bead over in her fingers with apparent consternation, like she's trying to recall something. Then the queen looks up.

Aurora freezes, terrified. Her instinct is to run, but she can only stare. The woman was obviously once beautiful, but now old. Thick makeup streaks her face with a jester-like horror, as though applied by a child's hand. Her crown looks overlarge and jagged on her petite head. This is not the fearsome Night Faerie Aurora has always imagined, the one with enough strength—and evil—to rival Malfleur's.

She doesn't know why everyone here says it's so difficult to get to the queen, and she doesn't know why the locked door came unlocked, but here she is. She draws in a breath. This is it. This is her chance.

"Belcoeur," she says, trying frantically to gather her courage, to channel Isbe's bravery. "Why—why did you create Sommeil?" She stands taller. "Your people are suffering. You—you must release us."

"Are the cherry tarts ready?"

"I'm sorry?"

"The tarts!" the queen hisses. "Bloodred. They must be red as blood. For the visitor. Someone is coming. Someone is coming." Her hands shake. Then her clear green eyes lock on to Aurora's. "Who are you?" she demands with renewed clarity. "Why are you here?"

"There was a spinning wheel," Aurora stutters.

"But I don't know you. You're not the one I'm waiting for." She shakes her head. "Everything is wrong."

Aurora clears her throat. "Just tell me how to get back to the other world, the one you came from. The one *we* came from."

The queen shakes her head again. "I don't know how to make it right. I wish I could, but I can't."

"Surely you can help. You have greater power than any other living faerie."

The queen stares back at her again, trembling now. "I'm trapped too." Her voice, raspy and low, is unnerving.

"But that doesn't make sense. You *made* this place. Why?"

There's a pause.

The queen continues to stare at her in grief, a look that drives through Aurora's chest like one of the deadly sharp icicles that hang from the Delucian gates in winter.

"I don't remember." The queen's hoarse voice crawls into Aurora's ears, making her shiver.

A series of shouts cause Aurora to turn. Through the open door there's a light bobbing.

"Aurora?" It's Wren's voice. Relief floods her. "What are

you doing here?" Wren asks urgently as she bursts through the door to the north hall carrying a lantern.

"I was just—" Aurora turns around, but Belcoeur has vanished.

She blinks rapidly. Not only is the queen gone, but there is no other exit to the room. She looks around. Despite the dust hanging in the air and the dimness, diminished only a little by the lantern, Aurora sees that the walls are completely bare. All of the tapestries have disappeared. She swallows hard, her head swimming through the murk of the room and the conversation she just had. Could she have imagined it all?

No. *No.* Belcoeur *was* here.

"There you are. You shouldn't be near the north turret; it's not safe," Wren says, taking Aurora by the elbow. "The queen's enchantments are particularly strong here. Many have gone in search of her and never returned. I've told you already, the rooms become a maze with no end and no center."

"I . . . I saw her. I saw the queen," Aurora says. "A pearl rolled under the door and unlocked it somehow, and . . ." She trails off, no longer trusting her own impression of what happened.

Wren wrinkles her pretty brow as she leads her out of the empty hall. "Heath was so worried when you were missing at dinner, and we realized no one had seen you all day," she says quietly as they wind their way back through the castle. Through the large windows in the east parlor, Aurora sees that night has fallen. But it felt like she'd been in the tapestry room for minutes, not hours.

"Heath said . . . he said you two had an argument earlier," Wren goes on. "His moods can sometimes be stormy," Wren says apologetically. "We've never had an outsider before. None of us knows quite what to believe. Many of the others fear—"

"What do they fear?"

"That you are not real. If not an Impression, then some other creation of the queen's. A trick, an illusion, an enchantment."

"That *I'm* not real," Aurora marvels.

Wren squeezes Aurora's hand. The quick pulse reminds Aurora of Isbe and sends a lump straight to her throat. "But don't worry. Heath believes you, and I believe you too."

She delivers Aurora to her room.

"Thank you, Wren," Aurora says, still clutching her hand. But despite the young woman's kindness, Aurora has never felt more alone.

16

Isabelle

"Far's I can take ya, lad." The stranger who saved Isbe from drowning now pats her shoulder with a rough hand as their boat bobs, quietly knocking against a pier.

She nods, her mouth dry from salt and vomit. "Honor be w' you," she says, trying to keep her voice masculine and devoid of the polish of nobility. It seems an inadequate phrase, but she's at a loss for words. The man rescued her for no good reason. He asked for nothing in return, only stated with a half laugh, "A' thought you'd were the ghost a the Balladeer hisself out there, I did," as he pulled her aboard.

Isbe's entire body now screams in stiffness and pain as she wobbles out of the small boat, pulling herself onto the abandoned pier. The immense cold had ceased to bother her for the last hour, but moving has reawakened the bone chill, and she shivers uncontrollably as she sits on the dock listening to the man row away.

She inhales, taking a moment to consider this new depth of aloneness, cool and echoey as a wine cave. She has *never* been this alone—never without Gilbert's or Aurora's hand to guide her through unknown territory. Or when they weren't there, she always knew they'd be close by, looking for her. Now the world yawns open around her, a giant blank. A terrifying mystery full of mixed sounds and smells and unpredictable dangers.

The air here is fresh and bright, though. A marbled fog constantly stifles the Delucian palace—the maids always complained of the challenge of drying laundry, and Isbe grew accustomed to the smell of damp sheets and mildewed braies—but here she finds herself squinting in the sun. There must be a glare off the water. She listens to the wood licked by the gentle Aubinian waves: *glog glog ricket-glog.* Nothing like the ravenous *kush-kash* of the Delucian surf against the cliffs. Deluce is a peace-loving nation surrounded by violent breakers, while Aubin, it seems, is a militaristic state hugged by friendly seas.

But the friendliness ends at the shore. Isbe and her anonymous, gruff-voiced sailor savior had been turned away from three ports already, told that Aubin's borders were closed off to prevent the spread of disease. The country has not only heard of the sleeping sickness but believes it to be the next in a rash of plagues that have decimated the population over

149

the last few decades, and they aren't taking any chances, especially not on bedraggled riffraff like them.

After the third refusal, the sailor decided it was wise to split up and find their own ways past the harbor guards. Isbe knows Gil would never even consider leaving her in such a situation. But he *has* left her, however unwillingly. They never found each other after getting separated during the hunt. She doesn't know if he managed to scramble back aboard the merchant vessel or if he made it safely to Aubin in one of the smaller dinghies like she has, or . . .

She can't bring herself to think of the third possibility. The screams of the many men who were dislodged from their positions—lost their footing and found their way into the sea—echo in her memory. And Gil was never a particularly good swimmer.

If he *did* make it back onto the larger vessel, they would likely have been turned away at the harbor too. Which means they probably would've returned to Deluce to recover. She can only hope that in another day's time, Gilbert will have found his way back to Roul's house. But knowing Gil, he'd make every effort to set out again to find her.

And then she remembers something else: Gilbert gambled his luck away to Binks. The thought falls inside her, heavy as a rock. But surely, *surely* she would know somehow—she would *feel* it—if Gil had died. Wouldn't she?

Her jaw clamps hard, and she runs her hands through her shorn hair, trying to think . . . or to stop thinking. Stop remembering their fierce, fleeting kiss before he vanished. Stop desperately wondering what it meant. She touches her face, feels the harsh but familiar angles of her cheeks and nose. Feels the wetness coming from her eyes. Wipes it away.

She sucks in a shaky breath. She may never know if Gil is alive or dead—just like the injured narwhal, he has entered an unknowable darkness. However, she reminds herself that *if* Gil is alive, she can do nothing for him right now but wish and hope. And wishing and hoping don't get results. Action does. She left on a mission, and she's still far from accomplishing it.

She pushes herself to standing, feeling her way carefully along the rickety pier with one foot in front of the other. She needs to get to the prince.

———

The stench hits her before she stumbles onto dry land, and it immediately becomes clear why this point of entrance has been left unguarded: sewage. Isbe gags, then tears off part of her sleeve and ties it around her mouth and nose. This must be the narrow waterway that lets Aubin's royal sewage out to sea. No wonder no ships dock here. She walks a little bit taller. The discovery is disgusting, yet convenient. It means she can follow the little inlet straight into the heart of the castle village.

There have been many times during Isbe's childhood when she questioned her rightful place at the palace—her rightful place *anywhere*. But Gil often assured her that these distinctions of class are less important than we'd like to believe. "Rich or poor, noble or peasant, everybody shits," he'd say with a laugh.

And so, as the day blooms above—doing little to melt the glacier within her—Isbe labors along the muddy, rancid shore toward the Aubinian palace and the unknowing prince within it, covering her mouth and clinging to the memory of Gil's laughter like the edges of a warm cloak.

———

Isbe has always enjoyed making her sister laugh. Just days before the report of the princes' murder, she and Aurora were making snow statues in the palace gardens. The air tasted like watered honey, a sure sign that more snow would come. Isbe was just putting the finishing touches on a sculpture of Pig, a mutt that had become a favorite of the palace guards.

You're missing something, Aurora tapped, bending down and quickly patting together a mushy lump of snow, which she placed at Snow Pig's feet.

"What is it?" Isbe asked.

A pastry he stole from the kitchens, of course.

"Let me see yours," Isbe demanded.

Aurora guided her over to the sculpture *she'd* been working on all morning and set Isbe's hand on its shoulder. Isbe gently felt for the chin and face before running her fingers over the rest of him, taking in the details Aurora had added. It was Prince Philip, again. Of course.

"Yours is missing something too," Isbe announced,

grabbing a handful of snow off a nearby hedge and patting it into a flat circle like a medallion. She used her fingernail to carve the Aubinian insignia on it: a hawk perched on a sword.

Showoff, her sister replied.

Aurora had read everything there was to know about the Aubin court, from their favored fashions to their dining customs to the castle layout itself. She'd tapped all of this information to Isbe, sometimes struggling when the details were too complex for their secret language. The spires on the towers of Aubin's palace, for example, became *roof spears.*

Now Isbe reached up and, before Aurora could stop her, rearranged Prince Philip's face so that his tongue was sticking out. Aurora laughed, and then, out of nowhere, pegged her with a snowball. And that spelled the end for Philip and Pig, as Isbe screamed and Aurora laughed and both got covered in snow until Councilman Maximilien spotted them from a window and ordered them inside.

———

Then, the cold air on her bare hands and cheeks had made Isbe feel alive and happy. Now, though, her legs tremble uncontrollably and she falls to the ground. Unable to shake the chill from her bones, or her mind, she gets onto her hands and knees in the icy mud and sewage, and crawls.

17

Malfleur,
the Last Remaining Faerie Queen

From above, the LaMorte Territories appear to be on fire. Thick smoke from the underground furnaces hovers over the valley villages, obscuring the bustle and toil of thoroughfares, the icily flowing mountain rivers, and the gnarled black trees common to the region, making it seem instead as though the mountain range, white capped and tapering into grays and purples like the belly of a dove, is magically rising out of dark clouds.

Malfleur pulls her lynx cloak tighter around her shoulders. The cold is harshest just before dawn. Ever after all these years, she still hasn't gotten used to it.

She knows the rumors. That the LaMorte Territories are scattered and disorganized, a patchwork of contentious tribes loosely held together through shared customs—and shared fears. They say that the fiefdoms suffer under her iron-fisted rule, due in particular to a lack of young mothers, since so many girls of a certain age are forced to pay their tithe to the queen, after which their youth and beauty shrivel.

But from her perch atop the bastion tower of Blackthorn, at the very peak of Mount Briar, Malfleur sees a different picture, a fluid series of gasps and pangs: the coy shape-shifting of the clouds, white in the white sky. The suicidal streak of a falcon on the hunt—all silver and light—disappearing into the smoke as though plunging into a shadowed sea. And beneath it all, the hiss of the furnaces.

It had been an incredible feat both of magic and invention, a way to make the infertile soils of the steepest slopes pliant, a way to make the harrowing crags and cliffs habitable—underground kilns that boil water day and night, transforming this once barren region into one that is wet enough to bear life and grow.

The idea had come to her from the lips of a bard. He spoke of the burning flame of the heart, its own kind of hell. She had to have him executed, for obvious reasons; words of such beauty can only breed discontent, persuading the people to dream of things they can never have.

His death had nothing to do with the fact that he reminded her of someone. Someone she knew long ago.

After having the bard cut in little pieces, she fed him to her white panther, to see whether the taste of poetry was bitter or sweet. But the panther told her the man tasted just as all creatures do: like the fear of death.

In the end there'd been nothing left but bones and hair . . . and the lingering effect of his words on her mind. *Its own kind of hell.*

Now her kingdom is prospering like never before, all because of the furnaces, like infernal, burning hearts. But this, of course, is not enough for Malfleur. If anything, the accomplishment tastes ashen and caustic as the air itself.

People mistake her. Though her tithe may be youth, it is not vanity that motivates her. What is beauty—impeccable skin and eyes so blazing dark they make men weep—without power? No, what Malfleur has sought for more than a century, and what she seeks still, cannot be counted in the heartbreaking arch of an eyebrow or the catlike dance of bone and muscle across the back. Malfleur has traveled the world, studied the nuances of magic in realms near and far. It is self-evident: magic is a force of the *mind*, not the body. And she is still far from perfecting hers. She needs more time—and *that* is why she continues to tithe youth.

But she's getting closer. Her powers are ever increasing. Her army is robust and expanding. Her experiments on human-animal language acquisition are beginning to flourish, though there was a setback a few weeks ago, when a large flock of starlings escaped midtesting, in a cloud of terrified flaps and screams.

As if in response to this thought, the muzzled albino panther standing beside Malfleur on the stone lookout—the queen's most successful experiment so far—stretches, her fine shoulder blades like miniature mountains that sink back into snow-colored fur.

"Your day ends as mine begins," Malfleur says to the creature. She has often thought of training herself to become nocturnal like a leopard or lynx, but she's always loved to sleep in the night. It was one thing she and her sister had in common. Belcoeur was addicted to dreaming, while Malfleur craves the opposite—the thick, black hours in which her mind, and her magic, are an undisturbed blank.

The panther licks the back of her paw through the straps of her leather muzzle, then turns to the queen. "Like leaves," she says in a velvet purr. She lifts her front paws onto the parapet. "Like leaves in wind in rain in fall in . . . *restless.* I want . . . river. I want . . . rush. I want . . ."

"You are hungry, my girl," Malfleur replies. "I can fix that."

"No. No fix. I am not hungry for flesh. I am hungry for . . ." The panther sniffs the air. "I am hungry for . . ."

"There is still a tower full of pine martens and minks for you."

The panther chuffs, and the queen hears a feral frustration in the sound. "I am hungry for *hungry for.*"

Malfleur looks at the animal's slitted eyes. "You are hungry for *hunger,*" she corrects, finally understanding. The creature has grown complacent after days kept by the queen's side.

"I must hunt." The panther lets out a low, ravenous moan, ripped through with thunder. The sound gives

Malfleur a chill, reminding her why she keeps her pet muzzled while at the palace.

"So hunt," Malfleur answers. "I release you."

"But there is disease," the animal says, licking the back of her other paw, then wiping it across her chin, where the leather binds to its chains. She is cleaning a thin wound, torn jaggedly along her jawbone. "I chase. I do not scavenge. You think I am no different than a jackal or a wolf? The world must run from me, not lie in wait. I do not eat disease."

"Disease?"

"The sleeping sickness," the panther says, beginning to pace in a circle. "It spreads. It starts with the girl with the sun hair—"

"The princess."

"But it comes. It comes closer. It ends when we are all . . . fallen. I do not eat rotten fruit fallen from tree. Then I too become . . . rotten flesh. Food for flies. *Food for flies.*" The panther spits the words in a series of guttural hisses.

The queen too is disturbed by word of the sleeping sickness. Some of her citizens believe her to be its cause. But she would never claim this disease. Her curse was meant only to kill an otherwise harmless princess. She had nothing against the child. It was what the child represented that bothered her: yet another human heir to a kingdom that would have been, in her time, faerie ruled. It was meant to punish the pompous King Henri and his petty wife and the ridiculous council parading about the palace that was once her own family's. It was meant to restore fear to the hearts of

158

complacent Delucians. Of the fae too, who no longer seemed to believe in their own powers or, more importantly, in hers.

But she had made a mistake by bringing the spinning wheel into the curse. It was a careless, bitter jab on her part, referring simply to a bad memory from her childhood. Curses have a way of unearthing little needles from the curser's past; and she should have been more careful.

And then Violette interfered, like some puffed-up orange ostrich. It is never advisable to amend a curse. Magic does unnerving things when perverted by other magic, even—or perhaps especially—when great magic is impeded and altered by a lesser magic. The princess, Malfleur is certain, was saved by Violette, in that she fell sleep and didn't die. But neither the curse nor its amendment should have resulted in a *contagion* of sleep.

She can picture what the panther has seen: fields of once-slumbering sheep, now ravaged by wolves. Wagon horses and their passengers toppled and snoring themselves to a frozen death at the side of a road.

"But if the borders are full of such easy prey," she says now to her pet, "then how did you come upon that impressive scar?"

"This," the wildcat says, arching her neck so that her bloodied cheek catches the just-cresting sun, "came from no animal. It was the . . . claws of the vines."

"Claws of the . . . you mean *thorns*." Her magic has its limits. She could give the beast the language of a human but couldn't make it think like one.

"Purple flowers grow around the palace of Deluce. They smell like ladies' mouths. Too sweet. They are spreading. Leaves like mouths hiding fangs. Like mouths . . ." Here the panther lets out a great yawn, the chains of her muzzle clanging, her own fangs glinting.

Malfleur is far too intelligent to believe in coincidences.

She squints across her kingdom, and the ripples of dark smoke against the bright sky become inked words on the fine vellum pages of a storybook. The caw of the hunting falcon becomes the call of a girl's voice from another room. She's in the small cottage where they used to summer, a century ago now. "Don't start it without me!" her twin sister cries, even though they have read the book every night since she can remember. They are getting too old for stories. She flips to the back and sees that Belcoeur has placed violets—their mother's favorite—in between the pages to press and dry. She fingers them, and they turn to dust in her palm.

Malfleur blinks, and the childhood memory too turns to ash, blown away on the wind.

It cannot be. Her sister cannot have returned after all these years.

But the lush purple flowers, the thorn-ridden vines, the stories of a sleep so deep it cannot be penetrated—these tell a different story, and Malfleur shudders.

She'd never wanted her sister to die. She'd wanted her to live and suffer, the way *she* had for so many years. But maybe she should have killed her when she could.

Malfleur knows that timing is everything. It cannot

be coincidence that a way into—and out of—Sommeil has apparently surfaced, causing those vines to leak out, at the very same time that her curse on the Delucian princess took effect. The irony is like the sting of a hornet; it smarts and swells and worsens.

This is the danger of a faerie curse. Once loosed into the world, a curse will find its way into being . . . but *how* it does its work is a mystery, even to the curser. It knits events together invisibly.

The spinning wheel.

The symbol Malfleur had chosen to represent her twin's betrayal, and upon which her curse was based. Could it be, all this time, that the spindle contained its own power? Had Belcoeur enchanted it and left behind that final symbol *as a way back*?

Well. If the Night Faerie is rising, the queen knows what she must do. She must march. Before the disease spreads any farther. Before her sister's power can corrupt her own.

For, as far as Malfleur sees it, only one of them may exist in this world.

"My pet," the queen says. "I have another job for you."

But the creature does not reply. Beside her, the white panther has curled into herself, her breath coming in bursts of white steam against the black of the muzzle. She is asleep.

18

Isabelle

Coughing and sputtering, Isbe finally reaches an opening in the village walls that rises just inches over the freezing, wretched water, letting air whistle through and beneath it. She doesn't know how long she's been traveling, mostly on all fours, along the sewage route. The castle village is farther inland than she thought. It's been more than a full day, and there's a dull burn in her stomach and throat.

Holding her breath, she goes under.

She emerges on the other side of the wall and gags. Then she crawls along the inside of the wall, away from the stream, until she finds a frozen puddle. She pulls back her hand and then, with a trembling fist, slams hard into the puddle, cracking its surface. Beneath it is clean rainwater, which she hungrily splashes over her face, gulping handfuls of it down, until she can no longer take the added injury of cold on cold.

Her legs are so chilled she's not sure if she can stand again, but she manages to wobble to her feet. Now that she's moved several yards from the stream, she is able to take in other smells beyond its putrid odor. She detects the smoke of a blacksmith and fumbles toward it, leaving the safety of the wall. All she can think of right now is fire. Warmth. Day has fully broken, and she can hear the bustle of peasants pushing carts and herding animals. Someone is bound to spot her soon and realize she is out of place.

Several times she trips and falls—on a wooden crate, a low stone wall, other items she's too distressed to recognize. She's too numb to feel the pain of blooming bruises along her shins and arms. A rooster crows at her.

She bangs her fists along the outer walls of the blacksmith's shop until she finds the door, a sour burning smell puffing out from its corners.

The door swings open, and she falls forward into the smoke and heat.

———

"'Ee's *not* dead!" a young boy exclaims sometime later. For a moment, Isbe is sure it's Piers, Gil's nephew. But as she comes to, she realizes the voice bears a distinctly Aubinian accent. *That's right*. She found the blacksmith's hut. This must be the smith's son. "But 'ee canna see me!" the boy adds.

Another boy comes over. "'Ee's got a demon a' some kine. Let's get Da."

"Wait, no," Isbe says, sitting up dizzily on the dirt floor. It's not the first time someone has seen the way her eyes wander, sightless, and believed her to be possessed by an evil spirit. "Don't go to your father. I'm . . . I . . ." *Think, Isbe.* She recalls the stories Gil and Roul used to love to scare her with when they were kids. "I'm a messenger from across the sea. I have news of . . ." She lowers her voice to a whisper. "The murder of the princes. I have . . . I got business with the palace. But a, er, a *pirate,* 'ee took my ship. Now I need you boys' help."

"You seen pirates!" one of them hollers.

"How ca' *we* help?" asks the other.

"Was dem princes killed by the pirates too?" asks the first.

"Shhh," Isbe says, doing her best to seem conspiratorial. "The . . . dem pirates could come back for us."

"For us?" One of the boys—he can hardly be older than five or six—begins to whimper.

She turns to face the older-sounding one. "I jus' need two things. First is a cloak. 'Ave you got a clean cloak for me?"

He darts away and returns, placing a heavy woolen blanket into her palms.

"This will do," Isbe says, wrapping it around her shoulders.

"What's t' other thing?" the younger boy asks.

"Hand me a stick or a fork—anything like that—and I'll show you," Isbe says.

One of the boys places a rustic tool into her hands. She's not sure what it is. She bends over and tries to draw in the hard dirt of the floor, carving the image from memory. The castle's main gates are at the eastern wall. The tallest tower is the northeast one, which overlooks the sea in the distance. And the servants' quarters are clustered along the northern-most wing, which gets the harshest winds and is thus less coveted by the royal family and its guests.

She points to a notch she has just drawn in that wall. "I need you to take me here. In secret."

She lets the boys study the messy drawing in the dirt for a full minute or two before rubbing it away with her sleeve.

"Will you tell us more about da pirate?"

"Yessir," Isbe promises. "I'll tell ya all about 'im . . . on the way."

Shimmying through the peasants' pantry window is not the hard part. Though the main gates to the palace are well protected, the peasants' pantry is easily accessible from the outside. It would not be fitting for farmers to have to deliver grain from the granary to the kitchens via the front entrance, which is reserved for militia, merchants, and visiting nobility.

And of course, there's no way she'd pass for any of the above. She has to hide behind a sack of wheat for the better part of the day, knowing the palace is heavily guarded and that sneaking about in full light is a bad idea. She remains curled in the blacksmith's wool blanket, trying to warm up. Weary as her body feels, she's far too nervous to sleep.

But navigating the northern wing and finding passage to the palace wall walks along the roof that evening is not the hard part either. By testing, listening, and pausing, she is able to make her way to the turret she recalls from her snow-sculpting sessions with her sister. This is far safer than wandering the halls themselves, where she's bound to knock over something fragile, creating a distraction, or walk straight into a servant who might report her to the guards.

No, the hard part is guessing which of the chambers belongs to the youngest prince. At the news of his elder two brothers' deaths, would William have moved up into their likely more plush and comfortable rooms, or remained in his own? She knows that royals are always considering such advantages and what they signify. Then again, Aubin is not as enamored of luxuries as Deluce is. The Aubinians are known for being a more austere people.

How she wishes she were with Gil, and that they were entering the castle the way they'd initially planned—as merchants offering goods to the master of trade.

How she wishes, for that matter, that Aurora had never fallen sick with sleep.

How she wishes, above all, that the faeries were not such a vengeful and self-serving breed, because it is Binks's fault that Gil and Isbe have been separated, she's certain. It's Violette's fault she lost her sight at the age of two. And it's

Malfleur's fault that a curse was put on Aurora in the first place.

But wishing, she reminds herself, does not produce results.

Her arms shaking from exhaustion, she scampers down over the edge of the parapet and finds footing. Quickly, before she can think how foolishly dangerous this is, she inches along the wall until her foot hits an oriel. The window doesn't open easily. It takes several kicks before she is able to enter with a loud, shattering crack. She almost loses her grip, and gasps. The wool blanket falls from her shoulders, into the open wind. Then she swings herself the rest of the way through the broken glass and into the room.

She catches her breath. Thankfully, no one else seems to be in the room at the moment, or surely there would be hollering and she'd have been apprehended by now, and dragged to the dungeons. She has thrown caution away as easily as she lost her borrowed "cloak," and by this point she's hardly even thinking straight.

Isbe realizes her hand is bleeding, but there's no time to worry. She gropes for something to hold on to—the room must be sparsely appointed, as it is difficult to find anything. She ends up yanking a drape off a large chair in the process, probably leaving a bloody handprint. This must be Edward's or Philip's room—why else would the furniture be covered?

She crashes into a table next, banging her hip hard. This is a disaster. In her hurry to find the door, she smashes an object that sounds valuable as it breaks. A servant is bound to have heard. She can only have a few seconds left before someone discovers her.

Ah. The door. She exits and runs her hands along walls oddly bare of tapestries, down a hallway, her mind racing, not even caring that she might be tracing blood. How is she to find William? Will he believe her story? Will he even remember who she is? She notices a faint fragrance coming from every direction, citrusy and fresh, as though the windows have been purposefully kept open—so different from the sweet floral musks preferred by the Delucian palace.

"You there!" a female voice calls in a thick Aubinian accent. Probably a servant. She's been spotted. The voice is about fifty paces away—likely at the very end of the long hall.

Isbe doesn't turn around.

"Stop!" the woman behind her cries.

She pushes open another door and stumbles into a room, slamming the door closed behind her.

Then she is roughly shoved down, and the air is knocked out of her.

Someone is pinning her arms to the floor. He smells of fresh sweat masked by lime soap.

"State your purpose if you want to live," the young man says. His voice is quiet, a tree in the wind, but his grip on Isbe's arms is tense. She feels the vibration in his entire body and recognizes it: fear.

"It would . . . be easier . . . to . . . state my—" she huffs out, finally giving up.

The man rolls off her, taking his exotic lime-soap smell with him. Isbe heaves a deep breath.

There's a rapid knock on the door, and a woman's breathless voice comes through, the same servant who tried to stop Isbe moments ago. "An intruder, my lord!"

"I have it well in hand, Elise," he calls through the closed door. "You may return to your duties. Now tell me," he demands, turning his voice back toward Isbe, "the name of the person so bold as to enter the chambers of the prince without invitation. And in your condition," he adds.

"I have been blind for sixteen years. I am quite capable of getting around in my *condition*," Isbe declares, sitting up with effort.

"Actually, I didn't mean *that*," he says, less roughly. "I meant your . . . well, the disarray of your attire, the hideous stench emanating from you . . ." He lifts her hand and then drops it again. "The fingers nearly blue from cold. And there's the haphazardly shorn hair . . ." He sucks in a breath. "Gods help me—are you a *woman?*"

Insulted, Isbe pushes a stray clump of soggy hair out of her face, feeling something wet streak her forehead. Blood, most likely. Then she remembers what she must look and smell like, her hair having been hacked short with a knife, and having sailed the open sea, nearly died, and then tunneled into the castle village via its sewage system before bloodying her hand from a broken window. She crosses her arms over her chest. "How'd you figure it out?"

"Your frame is much too small to be a man's, your voice

too high, your lips too delicate." He is still sitting beside her on the cold marble floor, and she can feel the weight of his gaze on her, more intense than the weight of his body had been.

"I fooled the entire ship of sailors who brought me to your shores." She feels a zing of pride when she says this aloud.

"And let me guess—you paid your way aboard this ship."

"*Yes*, but—" She stops. Could he be right? Were they just playing along, pretending to believe she was a boy and that Gil was her brother? Would the captain have simply given passage to anyone carrying the right amount of gold coins? Humiliation sweeps through her, heating her cheeks. "Well." She swallows. "Since you asked my name, it's Isabelle. Daughter to the late King Henri of Deluce."

The man emits a sound that resembles a choke and a snort.

"What?"

He makes the sound again. It is, she's horrified to realize, a laugh.

"I've been through far too much to be made fun of now," she says, trying to steady the slight tremor in her voice. She begins to stand, hoping her weakened legs won't wobble.

"I'm sorry," he says, his cloak giving a low, velvety swish across the floor as he stands too. "I'm not making fun of you. I just . . ."

There it is again, the laugh. She glowers.

He clears his throat. "So, Isabelle of Deluce, if that really is who you are. What *did* cause you to go through so much just to seek admittance to the prince? Did the Delucian council send you? Because it certainly wouldn't appear so. And how did you possibly get across our borders? They've been closed to travelers from Deluce for the past week, ever since news spread here of the—"

"Sleeping sickness, I know. I have my ways," she answers, not willing just now to explain that she nearly drowned and was saved, only to be unceremoniously dumped on an abandoned and reeking dock miles from the palace. "And I will only explain why I am here to the prince himself. Please prove to me that you are in fact William of Aubin."

"*I* must prove my identity to *you*?" he asks with faint amusement. "I could have you sent to the dungeons for the rest of your life for trespassing."

"Give me your hand," Isbe demands.

She hears him hesitate, clearly taken aback by the forwardness of her request. But then, gently, he picks up her right hand and places it on his palm. She moves her fingers over his, feeling the strength and sturdiness of his hand before running her fingertips over his rings until she finds what she's searching for—the royal Aubinian signet.

Satisfied, she turns her face toward his. "It *is* you."

"How *did* you get in here?" he asks, sounding sincerely curious. "The palace is quite well defended. If my castle guard is sleeping on the job, they'll be hearing about it soon enough. You've embarrassed a family—and a nation— known for our caution."

"I've lived in a palace all my life. I know my way around."

"Well, you've made quite an impression."

She's not sure what to think of the comment, but once again she feels the weight of his gaze, and it makes her uncomfortable. She clears her throat. "We need to talk. I'm here to seek your . . . well." She hesitates, realizing she should have planned her speech better. "My kingdom needs your help. I—*I* need your help. You have to come with me back to Deluce. At once. Now, in fact. We should leave today."

"Travel to Deluce? With you? That's ridiculous."

"It's not ridiculous! I . . . we—this is an emergency. Deluce is desperate. You're our only hope at the moment."

William sighs. "I'm very sorry, Isabelle. Really, I am. The sleeping sickness sounds terrifying. I hate that Aubin has had to close its borders, but we can't afford a crippling plague when times are hard enough as it is. I really am very sorry indeed, but I don't see what I could possibly do to help."

"Sorry indeed? Don't be an idiot, William. Don't act like you don't know that *both* our kingdoms are in danger. And *I'm* very sorry for the loss of your older brothers—" She feels a little bit bad about spitting out that last part. "But the responsibility to do the right thing for Aubin lies in *your* hands now. I hope you don't intend to let your kingdom fall to Malfleur."

"Ah, so this is a political visit."

"What else would it be? I'm not here for a hot cup of tea!"

"No," the prince says, that gentle swaying-tree sound back in his voice. "You certainly are not."

"I'm here to talk about how our countries can help each other in a time of great peril. The threat of Malfleur is *real*, no matter how much you'd like to deny it."

"I don't deny it," he says, pacing. "Aubin has long suspected Queen Malfleur's dissatisfaction with the LaMorte Territories. We've been anticipating a move on her part for years. But that doesn't mean I'll help Deluce."

This surprises Isbe. Her impression, both from the palace as well as her brief time in the country at Roul's home, has left her believing that the majority of people doubt Malfleur will ever organize. And certainly most of them don't know what Isbe knows.

"If you agree with me that the faerie queen is a true threat, then how can you conscionably refuse to help? Who do you think will be next if Deluce falls? Once she has all our gold and our caverns of wine, what do you think she'll come for? The sunny shores of Aubin, that's what."

"Perhaps," William says. "But unlike Deluce, we have weapons. We're prepared for war. Deluce, on the other hand, is fattened with wealth and pride, lazy, ignorant, and massively divided by infighting. Your people are unhappy, your military wildly disorganized, and now a devastating disease is sweeping through the aristocracy, beginning at the very top. An alliance would be imprudent at best, and more likely doomed."

Isbe feels as though she has been punched in the jaw.

She is floored by this account of her kingdom. The sting of his assessment is made worse by the faint taste of truth in it.

She blinks rapidly, trying to regain her composure. She needs to try a new tactic. "Malfleur's people *killed your brothers*. Isn't that enough to incite vengeance?"

"That portrait of the situation is only one view."

"What do you mean?" Isbe feels her face getting hot with frustration.

"We have every reason to suspect that Deluce, and not LaMorte, is responsible for the murder of my brothers," William says, his words hard as stone on stone.

"But—I—*why?*"

"Because your kingdom doesn't *want* this alliance any more than ours does. If you really think your royal council is acting in the general interests of the populace, then you are wrong. It seems I know what the Delucian peasantry wants more than *you* do, Isabelle. They are sick of seeing the lavish waste of the upper classes while they work and suffer."

She swallows hard. "And Aubin's peasants are living in luxury, I suppose?" she asks, sweeping her arms around to indicate the decadence of the room, though even as she does, she realizes that from what she's observed so far, this palace is in fact far less furnished, decorated, and perfumed than the Delucian palace.

"No," William admits. "But we lead by example. We have strict regulations that all nobility must adhere to. We make public accounting of all our taxations. Our kingdom

174

is lean and efficient. Our expenses go toward weapons and military, not superfluous indulgences."

"But . . . but . . . Deluce is constantly exporting goods to Aubin."

"Oils, metals, essentials. Not spices or silks."

She can't argue with him—she doesn't know enough about Delucian trade to assess whether what he says is accurate. "Even if you're right, you're still not going to be able to save yourselves from Malfleur, if the information I have is true."

"And what information is that?"

"The sleeping sickness is the work of the *fae*. Dark faerie magic, William. Meant to cripple us just as Malfleur launches her plot to overtake us. And that means closing the borders won't help. The sickness is not a typical disease of nature, but the result of a *curse*. It will come for you too, all of you. Unless we work together to stop it."

"And how do you propose we do that?" He seems to be really listening now.

"I know how to undo the curse," she says.

"Hmm," he says—it's his thinking noise, she realizes. "A faerie curse. You must realize how this sounds. The fae have been dormant for decades. Most could not abide by the laws laid down by my father's father and have long since left Aubin . . . those that haven't died out, that is. I've never heard of one having the power to curse a nation and cause a disease."

"You have to belie—"

"That said," the prince goes on, cutting her off. "If what you say *is* true . . ."

"It is. I know it is. Malfleur cursed Aurora, my sister, to die on her sixteenth birthday. Then the faerie duchess Violette amended the curse, saying she wouldn't die but would fall into a deep sleep, only to be awakened by true love. As far as I can gather, my father and his wife made every attempt to cover it up, and the Delucian council is complicit in hiding it. They saw it as an irredeemable scandal, one they clearly wanted to keep hidden from the people and, even more importantly, from Aubin. And now almost everyone in attendance at her christening is dead or asleep. But Violette said true love would awaken Aurora. And that's where you come in."

"You think I'm Aurora's true love?"

"I think you *can* be. I don't know much about the fae except that their curses are not always as literal as they seem. And I have to try. I *have* to try. If you come help me, and if you succeed in awakening my sister, it will send a signal to Malfleur that we *can* stand against her magic."

The prince is quiet for a moment. "But what if we can't?"

"So you do believe me, then?" Isbe asks, relief flooding her, bringing in a new wave of energy.

"Hmm," he says.

"Let me ask you something," Isbe says softly. "If you had a chance to bring back your brothers, would you try?"

His laugh this time is curt and hard, a door slamming. "The answer to that is complicated. My brothers . . . they weren't very kind."

Isbe doesn't know how to respond to that. It's not at all what she was expecting him to say. All the hope she felt moments ago shrivels like a dried leaf. He doesn't believe in faerie magic. He doesn't believe the sleeping sickness is a curse, or that he could possibly play a role in undoing it. He isn't going to help. She's come all this way—she's lost Gil and risked her own life, and for what?

Her mouth feels dry. She licks her lips. They are chapped, and sting. Her whole face is chapped, in fact, her skin stretched dry from the salt and the freezing wind. Her body aches—she's still cold, and wet, and horribly reeking— and her hand stings from her cut. Her head hurts. Despair pushes down on her, making it difficult to stay upright. She needs a chair. Why is there no chair? She sways slightly, trying to think, trying to figure out how to save this. But she can't think. Not anymore. Gilbert is gone. Aurora is asleep—maybe forever. And Deluce, just as the prince said, is doomed.

"Isabelle, I do believe that Malfleur intends to go to war, and that our kingdoms are mutually endangered. Though her soldiers, if they mean to take the Delucian palace, will first have to survive the sickness, which may in fact buy us some time. Still, I will hear no further political entreaties until you have done one thing for me."

Isbe swallows. "And what is that?" She's been through so much, she's afraid this last request will be the one that kills her.

"For the love of all things decent, I insist you have a bath."

———

It is late now. She is alone. The night guard is quiet enough that she can hear the scampering of mice in the corners of the halls, the fluttering of bats in the courtyard, the lone coo of an owl searching the dark, its hunger as yet unsatisfied. She can hear, almost, the settling of sheets around sleeping bodies, the scuttling of the palace baker preparing for the next day's meals, the hum of snores. And even more faintly, more impossibly, comes the sweet voice from her mother dreams, twisting the lyrics of the rose lullaby like vines around her heart.

The prince informed only Elise, one of his most trusted servants, to draw and heat the water and to provide fresh clothes before leaving Isbe to disrobe. No one else knows of her presence. Hundreds of fresh cuts and scrapes cry out silently as Isbe lowers her sore, tender limbs into the bath through a cloud of citrus-scented steam, but gradually the chill begins to recede from her bones. Her nakedness makes her feel even more alone, and she sinks lower, until the water comes up to her chin and ears, to the tips of her shorn hair.

This bath is going to make her smell like William.

She clutches her wounded palm and thinks of the prince's premonition about Malfleur. Thinks of how readily he said it: *war*.

The word moves through Isbe with a tremor. She spent much of her youth spying on military drills and has always fantasized about fighting for a cause.

Maybe even dying for one.

Gilbert always said she was crazy to want that.

The heat seeps into her, thawing and unlocking feelings she doesn't want unlocked. She can't think about Gil. Not now.

She holds her breath and goes under. Beneath the surface, her ears ring, and she is back on the ship, crossing the sea, listening to the high whine of the harpoon's taut rope just before it snapped, remembering the hope that flew into her even as she was tossed into the frothing waves. She thinks of the clamor of the men as they grabbed for spears, as they flung their weapons wildly at the majestic, crying beast, wanting the giant body for its blubbery, pungent oil and the high value they could charge for its tusk. It pierces her chest, sharp as the tusk itself: the unfairness that one life must sometimes be sacrificed to save another.

She comes up gasping, her hair dripping warm, soapy water down her shoulders.

If this is what it means to be a true princess—making difficult decisions that could risk uncountable lives—she's gladder than ever that she isn't one.

19

Aurora

I *don't remember*, Queen Belcoeur had said in a whisper that wormed into Aurora's chest and made it ache with cold. It was real. It had to have been. It *means* something, she's sure.

Aurora slips out the Blackthorn gate, closing it with a quiet creak behind her. She doesn't want to wake anyone. But especially not Heath. He looked so young when she'd stared down at his sleeping form a few minutes ago, lying on the rug beside the smoking orange embers that had been the small fire in his study. And faraway too, like she was looking not at him, but at a reflection of him in a body of water—wavering, rippling. She didn't want to lie to him. Somehow this—taking his maps and notes and sneaking out while he sleeps—seemed better.

So, she thinks as she makes her way across the dewy fields, *the queen is too mad to have any answers.* Madness is not uncommon among the fae. Two hundred years ago, the North Faerie had been an expert chess player and a brilliant scholar of astronomy and philosophy, before her mind began to play chess with itself and left her frail, blithering, and wild-eyed. A great tragedy, considering her tithe had been logic. By the time she was murdered, she had long since lost her powers and her ability to rule, except in name.

But maybe Aurora can help Belcoeur remember why she made this place, and for whom she has been waiting all these years. For someone to free her?

Aurora has laid awake night after night thinking about the profound sadness—even *fear*—she heard in the queen's voice. The way out of here is not, she senses, a logical one at all, but an emotional one.

The clue she keeps clinging to is the image of the hand-woven cottage, with the steaming teacup in the window—that, and the distinct sense Aurora had when viewing the tapestries that every scene was in some way a representation of a piece of the real world. There must be some reason behind Belcoeur's choices. If Sommeil is a warped version of her world, then perhaps, Aurora thinks, the answer to how to get out lies in understanding the differences between the two.

For the first time, Aurora realizes that being an outsider could mean she, unlike the others here, *can* unravel this mystery. And besides, she knows she won't be able to look Heath in the eyes again until she has proven herself to him.

Though the night fell rapidly, dawn now approaches with an agonizing slowness, the white lip of the horizon quivering. Aurora focuses on that pale line in the distance. Even though it's risky, even though it means heading back alone into the Borderlands, she has decided to look for the cottage again. If Belcoeur was expecting someone to arrive there, it must be important.

If she were home, she knows, Isbe would scold her for going so far without her.

She misses arguing with Isbe.

She misses everything about Isbe.

She can hardly think, she misses her so much.

The land is barren, everything parched, trees reaching naked branches up into the sky, where one by one the stars sacrifice themselves to the coming day. Abandoned farmhouses dot her peripheral vision, rotten wood silvered in the faint glow of dawn. Aurora can't shake the feeling that *everything* here shifts or blinks or wanes, just slightly, when she's not looking directly at it.

And then she's entering the forest, which still contains the last sigh of night, musky and chill. Aurora pulls her hood back over her head. She does *not* like nighttime in Sommeil. It reminds her too much of childhood, when darkness meant the end of playtime and the beginning of dreams—haunting, changeable. When she'd sometimes hear the coughing of plague victims even from her high tower room, and wake the next morning to find more of the palace staff had been carted off with the dawn. The night here is thick as a wool cloak that once belonged to her mother—it almost *smells* like the cloak too, and the floral perfume the queen loved to wear. It is the smell of sadness and smallness and fear.

She finds the wall—or rather, it finds *her*. One moment mist seems to knit the trees together; then it's as if the fog has solidified to stone in all directions. She takes a deep breath and begins to move along the wall, wondering how she'll find the rift, especially if the rift is always in a different place. The challenge seems nearly impossible.

And yet Heath finds his way through it every single day.

She pulls out his scrawled pages of maps and charts. But try as she might, she can't interpret them. Restless, she refolds them and resigns herself to inching along the wall, using her hands to feel for variations. Once again she feels the *essence* of the stones, but their story has no beginning, middle, and end. It's more like a song, a sequence of dark, swirling emotions on a continuous loop. It scares her, this vastness, this trappedness.

She pulls her hands away, tempted to turn around and race back to Blackthorn. But then she thinks of the disappointment in Heath's eyes during their argument, and she knows she can't. *Someone* needs to solve the mystery of this place. What if she really is the only one who can piece it together?

Besides, she can't risk never returning home to see her sister or to meet the prince of Aubin or to unify the kingdoms against Malfleur. Her whole life is back in Deluce, and she needs to be where her life is.

She begins to sing to herself, surprised by how soothing it is to hear her own voice echoed back to her as she runs her fingers over bumps and cracks and sections of stone so smooth they seem to whisper of peace. The rose lullaby comes to her as she walks.

> *One night reviled,*
> *Before break of morn,*
> *Amid the roses wild,*
> *All tangled in thorns,*
> *The shadow and the child*
> *Together were born.*

> *The bright sun did spin,*
> *The moon swallowed day,*
> *When one her dear twin*
> *Forever did slay.*

As the lyrics leave her lips, something changes beneath her hands. The wall begins to soften, to give. Could she have found the rift so soon? She stops singing, and the wall is once again impenetrable. She backtracks but can't find the spot again. She stares at the stones for a second, and then something occurs to her. She tries singing the lullaby again.

And the wall *bends* inward, rippling like a body of water.

She sings louder, and as she does she steps forward, and forward . . . and *through*.

———

At first, the Borderlands do not appear threatening, and she wonders if Heath has overstated their dangers. The sun breaks open, lighting up a thousand shades of green in the canopy above her. Birds dart between branches, chirruping. Fresh pinecones crunch beneath her shoes.

After several steps, Aurora turns quickly—but the wall is still visible. She breathes out in relief, then gets an idea. She pulls the necklace of rubies and pearls out of her cloak pocket. One by one, she removes the jewels. She bends down and leaves one at the base of a tree. Then she moves deeper into the forest. Every ten feet or so, she lays down another, leaving a glimmering trail. As long as there's enough light to see by, she'll be able to trace her way back to the wall.

But by the time she comes to the end of the necklace, she has seen no variation in the woods, and no sign of the location of the cottage. She once again unfolds Heath's maps, and stares at them in confusion. Should she go back or continue on without a trail to retrace?

She turns in a circle, surveying the area. The idea of moving in the wrong direction makes her pulse spike with nervousness. She walks a few more paces, thinking there might be a clearing ahead. Yes—just there, through the thicket . . . she picks up her pace, trying to outrace the fear that lurks just behind her, threatening to break like a wave over her head. But panic begins to seize her chest, and she's reminded of losing her way in Deluce and stumbling upon the cottage, and then the spinning wheel that transported her here to Sommeil in the first place. She's suddenly dizzy with the idea that it could happen again, that she may be doomed to fall through one strange version of the world into another and another and another, like a series of marred reflections, until there's no longer any hope of finding herself.

There is no clearing; it had been a trick of the light.

The worry is a whorl of wind in her ears, a stir of leaves overhead, a shivering. She is a child again—so very afraid of the many things she cannot understand. Of the things she'll never be able to say.

Aurora grabs on to the bark of a tree, the fear making it hard to breathe. She wants to cry. She wants to be held. She wants to be saved.

But no one is here to save her.

She takes a heaving breath. *Isbe,* she taps into the side of the tree, in their old language, in her truest language. *I can't do this alone.*

Another wind snakes through the branches, rustling the leaves. A twig snaps.

And Aurora knows: she's *not* alone.

She blinks into the brush, which stirs again.

A set of eyes emerges, several carriage lengths away. And pointed white-gray ears.

Wolf.

Her heart lurches into her throat. She can't move. It's not

common, she knows, for wolves to stalk in broad daylight. Then again, if there's little game, perhaps they too are starving, drawn out of their natural habits by the smell of flesh.

Aurora trembles and backs up slightly. In response, the wolf makes a jerky movement, as though about to leap from the underbrush. She freezes again, trying to recall what to do in the presence of wild predators. But all she can think of is the romance of Ulrica, abandoned as a baby in a wolf's den, where she was raised for sixteen years before the valiant and dashing Prince Bertram discovered her and made her his wife. Ulrica could never sleep in the luxury of the palace; she would lope into the mountains, howling. One night, the prince followed his love and watched her transform into a wolf in the pale glow of the moon. He cried out in shock; then his love turned on him and sank her fangs into his neck.

Aurora looks at the wolf's eyes. And then she turns and runs.

Sprinting through the forest, she hears the wolf tracking her, gaining on her. Her pulse is nearly deafening; her breath burns in her chest. The forest is too dense—she can't dodge the low-hanging branches quickly enough. She swears she can feel the heat of the animal's breath at her heels now. It's too late, she'll never outrun—

She trips over a tree's roots and flies forward onto her hands and knees, a startled sob of pain bursting from her throat. Quickly she rolls to her side, ready to greet death face-to-face, when a blur of brown dives across the corner of her vision.

A young male deer in its prime.

The hart bounds high through the trees—the most graceful thing she's ever witnessed.

And then the wolf lunges—

And the deer is struck down.

Aurora scrambles up even as the wolf bends over its writhing prey, so close to her she could almost touch it, can even feel the steam leaking from the deer's wound.

The beautiful hart struggles, whimpering, kicking its legs as the wolf leans in to the animal, tearing at its belly. There is blood streaking its body, covering the wolf's mouth messily, reminding her of the vivid lip color the Night Faerie wore. Tears sting Aurora's face. She runs.

———

She can't be sure how long she has been running when, out of nowhere, she reaches the cottage. She bursts inside, panting, then slams the door and falls to the floor to catch her breath.

She made it. She lost the necklace, has no idea how to get back to Blackthorn, and is still deeply shaken from watching the wolf attack the deer, moments before it would have attacked *her*. But somehow she made it here, to the place where Belcoeur left out tea in anticipation of someone coming—though Aurora, apparently, was not the person the queen had been expecting.

She pushes herself back to her feet again, and finds the room with the table set for tea. She touches the fluffy-looking sugar; an insect scuttles out of the bowl. She shudders and pulls away, knocking over the teacup. Scalding water flies at her, and she sucks in a breath, stumbling backward. She understands now why the palace cooks at home always forbade her from coming near their boiling pots.

Aurora's also certain, now, that Belcoeur's tapestries somehow depict—or even control—Sommeil. The way the image of the steam over the teacup had seemed to waver . . . it must have been the queen's way of making sure the actual tea would remain hot.

But still, who was the tea left for—and why?

Aurora continues to wander through the cottage. Though much seems to change—the location of doors and windows—the little chair she'd noticed the first time is still in the parlor room, facing the wall as it had before. It looks like a spot someone would send a child in trouble to sit for hours as punishment, she realizes.

Curious, she approaches the chair, noticing grooves in the wall just above it. She bends down to look closer. Someone has etched words into the wood. Much of it is barely legible, caked in dust. A scattering of initials, perhaps, and code words. One entire phrase she's able to piece together, a limerick. *The secret boy—we almost kissed—he won my jewel— in a game of whist!*

The words seem to ooze in and out of the wood, sometimes more prominent, then fading again. It gives Aurora a horrible feeling of uncertainty.

The secret boy? This was a childhood crush.

Her mind reels with the simplicity of it. Could the queen

have been waiting all these years for a lover to come rescue her?

And the reference to the jewel: this reminds her of the necklace, and the pearl that somehow unlocked one of the enchantments on the forbidden wing at Blackthorn. Why would a piece of jewelry have been so important to the queen that it would, effectively, cut through her magic? If Belcoeur had created this whole world and everything in it, why would she have created a necklace that could do such a thing?

But Belcoeur *didn't* create everything. She didn't create Heath, or Wren, or any of the other living peasants. They were all descended from the original servants who worked for the queen. They are just as real as Aurora.

Something tingles in her chest. It's the feeling of discovery, of things slotting together like the strands of warp and weft on a loom. Her heart races. The tingling sparks into flame. Maybe the *necklace* came from the real world. Maybe in that sense, the object itself is immune to the power of the queen's dreams. The rose lullaby too comes from her world. And when she sang its lyrics, the wall opened for her.

She's not sure what it means, but she has become certain of one thing: the key to getting out of Sommeil is not going to lie in any pattern, or any place you could mark on a map. It is going to lie in a *story*. A true story about Belcoeur and her secret love.

The one to whom she lost her jewel . . .

The missing bead on the necklace, Aurora guesses.

No one knows romances better than Aurora does.

Energized by this revelation, she moves back through the room toward the door with little difficulty . . . until she steps outside.

The forest is still, but Aurora has the oddest sensation that everything has rearranged itself. She thinks of her discovery: items from the real world can shatter the spell of Sommeil, can see their way through the illusions. Shouldn't Aurora herself then be able to see clearly, to shake the cloudiness from her mind, to navigate the changing landscape? She tries to concentrate, but the velvety strangeness of the air itself continues to ebb and flow within her, infecting her thoughts. Of course it makes a peculiar sort of sense that *objects* might be impervious to illusions in a way that people are not. People are susceptible. *She* is susceptible.

She takes a deep breath, and begins singing the rose lullaby again. It seems to help. The trees don't move. No wolves appear. She steps into the woods as confidently as she can.

After only a few repetitions, she sees a parting of the trees, and between them, a steep riverbed. A harsh, rocky cliff juts out, dropping down about thirty or forty feet into a dried-up ravine. Perhaps she can climb to the top for a better vantage point.

As she hurries toward it, she can almost hear the former waterfall in its heavy silence, a dull and constant roar. Sickly moss still clings to some of the stones, indicating the stream that once flowed freely here. Aurora can picture what it must have looked like, water tumbling over the ledge and sparkling in the sun. One of the boulders looks distinctly like a man's face. Her heart leaps. It looks just like the one she and Isbe named for its odd shape years and years ago, in the stream that runs just past the cattle pastures beyond the palace of Deluce. *Nose Rock!*

She runs toward the riverbed.

This is no different from climbing the palace towers with Isbe, she tells herself as she reaches the rocks and looks for a foothold. For a moment, she could swear she hears Isbe's voice calling out to her from far away. *Hurry, Aurora!* she's saying. *Before they find us!* In her memory, she and Isbe are on the roof, searching for a spot to hide from angry council members. Aurora is both nervous about getting in trouble and filled with Isbe's contagious joy.

But this isn't a game.

Her heart beats hard in her ribs as she reaches hand over hand, beginning to climb.

20

Belcoeur,
the Night Faerie

"Someone's coming, Sweet Pea!" The queen bursts into the throne room, her heart full of crows' wings beating, beating. *"Sweet Pea?"* Belcoeur nearly trips over the lace of her floor-length gown as she turns a full circle. Her crown weighs heavy on her head. Has her Sweet Pea gone off? Another one vanished? She drops to her knees, searching. She would pray, but the fae don't believe in such things.

There you are. Relief is a burst of sunshine in her chest. She can breathe again as she retrieves Sweet Pea from beneath the throne, running her fingers along its hand-carved name. The hairbrush—her favorite, for its silver filigree and gentle teeth—must have fallen. But what is this, caught in its furry mouth? The queen extracts a large clump of thin white strands, like frayed threads, or giant cobwebs.

"Sweet Pea," she whispers, horrified. "What have you eaten?"

She'll have to have everything cleaned. The castle must be spotless.

"We must be *ready*. Someone is coming, haven't I told you?" She calls for the courier, who scurries in. "Have there been no deliveries?" she demands.

"Your Majesty, no . . . ," he replies helplessly.

She stares at him hard, watching his hairy ears twitch and his tiny hands tremble. Then he tucks his head and scampers away. Belcoeur is certain she sees the tail of a mouse darting through the doorway behind him. She shudders. Things are slipping, slipping between the cracks, like a stream eddying helplessly through moss-damp rocks. She can't help but fear she has forgotten some important detail.

She hastens to her hall of tapestries and walks up and down its length, studying her creations, looking for an answer. She pauses next to an image of a little riverbed bent over a ledge, where a rock juts out, noselike, over the rest. Why has the river gone dry? That's not how it should be. That's not, she's certain, what her visitor would want. All of her dreams . . . ready to be dashed in an instant if things don't go precisely as planned.

Her pulse stutters: a broken metronome. It's wrong. All wrong. She has made some vital mistake! Desperately, she reaches out and claws at the tapestry. Her nails snag.

The ravine becomes an angry gash, revealing a wide flow of loose, unwoven blues and grays.

The miniature silk river pours forth.

It floods.

21

Aurora

One minute she was clambering across the parched ravine. Then all at once the stream came alive, spurting over the ledge above, forming a real waterfall, its current so strong it swept Aurora instantly off her feet and sent her swirling into an ever-deepening, ever-quickening whirlpool, swishing downriver, faster, faster.

She kicks her legs and flaps her arms, trying to keep her head above water, thinking of fair Alcyone, who fell in love with the morning star—and in her grief, drowned. Aurora had adored that story, back when it had only been one of many myths to read and savor. Before she understood what it might really feel like to lose someone.

The river engulfs her; she feels its longing, its loss . . .

and the truth about Sommeil flows through her, clear and crisp as the river. Even as Aurora moves with the current, she is buoyed by this new certainty: Belcoeur isn't trapped here at all, but she retreated to this place, both of solace and loneliness, not unlike Aurora's own tower room back in Deluce. Aurora remembers the starling, the one that possessed dark faerie magic and could speak . . . the one that taunted her for being a caged bird.

She's been so blind. To think she was a prisoner of circumstances, that it was her lack of voice, a jealous faerie bargain, that held her back all these years. Really, it has always been her own obedience—her desire to please, to do everything right, to follow instead of lead—that has stopped her from truly living.

The thought urges her to kick harder, with more confidence. She is not just swimming toward safety now but away from her former, meeker self. She can almost hear the wail of the old Aurora, weak and scared, carried downstream, far away.

She has finally made it to the shore when she hears a distant sound. There *is* someone wailing. She looks back to the river, madly rushing on its course. There's someone else out there—a little girl.

She can hear her crying.

She can hear her screaming.

Aurora races downstream along the muddy banks. A young girl is thrashing and struggling in the waves. Without thinking, Aurora plunges back into the cold water and drags the little girl to shore by the collar of her blue dress, one arm wrapped under her armpits.

By the time she pulls her up onto the riverbank, she's shaking and exhausted. But the girl, who can only be around five or six years old, seems oddly unfazed.

The child stands up, smiling. "Roses are red. Violets are blue. Children behave and so should you," she says, her hands on her hips, her eyes black and blazing. She's apparently unaware that she's drenched, her dark, shoulder-length hair tangled and wet.

"Where's your mother?" Aurora asks, catching her breath. "You shouldn't be playing by the river all alone."

"I'm looking for violets!" the girl declares. "Roses are red. Violets are—"

"Do you live at Blackthorn? What's your name?"

The girl shrugs. "Daisy? Daisy! I need *violets*." The girl clasps her hands together. "Violets for the tea party. Violets are blue. Children behave and so should *you*."

She begins to skip ahead, then turns back, as if remembering Aurora is there. "You will help me, right? I can't go home without the flowers."

"Daisy?" Aurora says. That must be the girl's name. "You need to tell me where you live so I can bring you home."

The girl cocks her head, blinking. "Violets are blue. Roses are red. Evil will reign when the faeries are dead."

Aurora shivers, even though the sun is burning hard, drying her off. "You like rhymes?"

198

The girl nods. "I'm the best at puzzles. Will you help me?"

Aurora bends down so she's at her level. "How can I help you? Do you live near here?"

The girl's eyes wander, as though she's trying to remember. "I think so. . . ."

"Why don't you show me which way you came? Your mother must be so worried."

"My mother?" She barks out a surprised laugh. "Will you help me find violets? We *must* have violets for the tea party. Tea is black. Milk is white. Naughty children are thrashed at night." Now there are tears in the girl's eyes. "You're not going to leave, are you? Please don't leave me!" She grabs on to Aurora's hands. "I'll never find them in time." Even through her tears, her voice drops low. "The tea party will be *ruined*." Suddenly the girl runs ahead, darting into the woods.

Aurora's pulse hammers. "Daisy! Come back here!" She starts to run after her. "Daisy? Slow down!" She stops running and turns in a full circle, trying to get her bearings. The river has disappeared. Her neck feels hot. "Daisy!" she calls out.

Then she hears the girl muttering to herself and heaves a sigh of relief as her head bobs back into view—she'd been crawling through tall grass nearby.

"Daisy Daisy Daisy," the little girl says to herself. "Where's Daisy?"

"You're Daisy," Aurora says, though anxiety rustles back up through her chest.

"*You're* Daisy," the girl repeats. Then her face changes. "No. Daisy is baking the cherry tarts. Peach for a pudding. Cherry for a tart. Nothing tastes sweet to a broken heart."

Belcoeur too had spoken of cherry tarts. "Are you Daisy or not?"

The girl looks at her. "I'm Marigold!"

Aurora sighs. Either the girl is being purposefully defiant, or just playing some sort of game. *Or*—

Of course . . . the girl is an Impression. Like Heath told her about.

Beside her, Marigold—if that is the girl's name—has been plucking wildflowers and knotting them into a small crown, discarding the buds that displeased her. "There," she says happily, putting the finishing touches on it and then placing the crown on her head. "Now *I* am the queen and you must obey me!" she exclaims, then bends forward, giggling.

Aurora feels a chill. It looks like the girl is, somehow . . . *flickering*.

She blinks, and shakes her head. Once again, the child is solid before her.

"Marigold is naughty," the girl says. "*Daisy* is nice. For goodness does not strike the same nest twice."

Once again, her rhyme sends a shiver through Aurora. All of her limericks have a dark side. "Goodness doesn't strike the same nest twice. . . . What does that mean exactly?"

Marigold looks up at her, and once again, her face seems to flutter, like a moth's wings against a lantern—white, light, white, light, white, light. It must be a trick of the sun setting behind the trees, but it leaves an unsettling feeling in Aurora's gut. "One night so mild," the girl responds, "before break of morn, amid the roses wild, all tangled in thorns, the shadow and the child together were born."

One night so mild. "It's the rose lullaby," Aurora says . . . but the way it starts is *One night reviled.* "Where did you learn that?"

Marigold shrugs again. "I didn't learn it. We made it up."

"You—but—" Aurora stares at her. Everyone knows the lullaby is about Malfleur and Belcoeur. *The shadow and the child* . . . Who *is* this girl? "Marigold," she says, squatting down. She wraps her hands around the girl's arms, gently but firmly. "Do you . . . do you have a sister?"

Marigold cocks her head and thinks for a second. Then she nods. But as she nods, she once again begins to change, morph, *fade*—like a flame guttering. Even her arms seem like they are turning into ether under Aurora's touch. She yanks her fingers away, unexpectedly scalded. Her fingertips have been burned pink.

"Marigold," she blurts out, startled. But the girl is ghosting into nothingness before her eyes. "Marigold!"

"Daisy Daisy Daisy," the girl sings, her voice faltering. "Daisy is as Daisy does."

"Who *are* you?"

"Mari's a falcon, Daisy's a dove. One of us is flying high, high above," the girl says, pointing to the sky.

Aurora squints up and sees a bird careering through amber ribbons of light and shadow. Night is approaching hungrily, rising up from the horizon like a dark tide. The bird darts into it, consumed.

When Aurora turns back, the girl has vanished.

On the ground where she stood lies the floral crown.

22

Isabelle

Isbe's good mood has soured quickly. She actually felt restored after her much-needed bath and having slept in a bed just as thick and soft as the ones in the palace where she grew up, even if her dreams were marred by a haunting melody equal parts whale song and lullaby. Even if she'd been up half the night contemplating how best to convince the prince to help her.

She'd slept in his private guest quarters and been awakened by Elise. When she inquired about the prince, however, the maid told her that he'd gone for an early ride. "He enjoys getting out while the sun is just rising," the woman had said fondly.

Off on a *riding* excursion? When they've only just agreed

that the safety of both their kingdoms is at stake?

That was more than an hour ago. Isbe is still pacing and exploring the room, tense as an arbalest about to loose its bolt, when the maid returns again and clears her throat. Isbe whips around to face her.

"The prince has asked that you wait for him in the music chamber," she announces. She leads Isbe down a corridor, then up a wide, winding staircase to a room flooded with the warmth of sunlight from every direction. A tower room, then.

Curious, Isbe feels her way around the room after the maid leaves her there. She wonders if the prince himself is fond of playing instruments.

Her fingers trace over the keys of a clavichord. Her sister knows how to play both the clavichord and harpsichord beautifully. Isbe, on the other hand, never had the patience for it, though she enjoys listening. Maybe this is a sign that William *will* make the perfect husband for Aurora. Maybe her plan will work.

"Do you believe in natural talent?" the prince asks, entering the room on a draft of fresh air. He smells like lime and saddle. The latter reminds her of Gilbert.

Isbe turns toward him. "I believe in a lack thereof."

He laughs his curt laugh. "Exactly. I'd like to think we aren't born one way or another—that one can become accomplished at anything with enough practice. But that has not been the case with me and stringed instruments, despite devoting many hours a week to the cause."

So perhaps he won't be wooing Aurora by song any time soon, she thinks.

"It's as though my hands are somehow too . . . literal," he explains, his footsteps on the marble floor echoing closer. "I can play the notes, in roughly the correct rhythm, but the music lacks . . . whatever it is that makes music enjoyable."

"Flow. Ease," Isbe replies, recalling the many times her sister has played, and the way the music transported her. "The feeling that the sound has sprung up spontaneously from some natural source."

"Precisely. Let me show you something," he says, offering her his arm.

Isbe allows the prince to guide her to a corner of the room and seat her in a chair facing a small round table. She puts out her hands to feel what's on the surface. There are small items arranged like a chess set, made from something smooth and cold—possibly ivory. *Narwhal tusk,* she thinks.

"It's a model," William explains. He sits on the other side of the table and places her hands delicately on one piece at a time.

"These are our warships. This is our cavalry." The objects are beautifully and intricately carved. Each rider has a horse and each horse has a mane that blows slightly differently in an invisible breeze.

"Did you make these?" she asks in wonder.

"I did. And *this,*" he adds. "This is something I've been

working on." He guides her hand over a small item, oblong and angled.

"What is it?"

"A cannon. But not just any cannon. This one contains missiles filled with oil. It's more dangerous, but more effective, because it spreads fire more rapidly across enemy lines."

She runs her fingers over the model. "It's cracked," she notices.

"Philip wasn't impressed by the idea. He said oil was too expensive."

Isbe imagines the prince's older brother throwing the cannon models on the floor in derision as she moves her hand back to the warships, feeling the delicacy with which their sails were carved, wondering what William is getting at. . . .

"Isabelle of Deluce, I'll do my best to help you and your sister."

"Wait. What?"

"Even if she doesn't awaken," William goes on, "we can certainly arrange for a marriage announcement—no one will have to know the difference. Aubin is almost as good as Deluce at covering up a scandal."

The idea that Aurora may never recover causes Isbe's guts to twist. But this is *good* news. He will help her. "Why? What made you decide?"

William sighs. "I do know what it's like to lose a sibling, Isabelle. Even one not as beloved as yours is to you. I've lost two. It's like a lantern sputtering out in a dark tunnel. There are times when I think about how I'm going to lead Aubin into a brighter future, and I am overwhelmed by the impossibility of it." He pauses. "You know, I used to love looking at the stars at night. I used to think they were put there to guide us. Now I know they are just watching and winking, mute observers, bemused by our failures and our loss."

She has never heard anyone talk this way before. Of stars and of loss. How can the man who sculpted such meticulous objects out of ivory, who speaks so rhapsodically about the night sky, be the same man who rudely knocked her to the floor when he first saw her—the man who deeply insulted her kingdom and its people?

She never spent much time thinking about the personalities of the Aubinian princes. Most of her and Aurora's gossip had been about their looks and reputations. But she's beginning to feel that William is contradictory and strange. With his velvet cloak. With his smell of lime. With his swaying-tree voice and his slamming-door laugh. But he has a heart—he must, for he seems moved by her desire to save Aurora. Moved enough to help.

"So you'll come with me to Deluce, and you'll help me establish the alliance," Isbe says carefully.

"I will. But there are conditions," he adds.

"Which are?"

"We need your oil."

His statement lands heavy as a boulder. So it *isn't* empathy that's convinced him. His decision is tactical: he wants Delucian oil for his fancy cannon design.

Anticipating her next question, he goes on: "Like I said, we're an efficient country. We've spent all of our money on warships, not on whaling vessels. We could accrue our own sources of oil—but not as quickly as we would need, if we are to implement these weapons in time."

Isbe swallows. She imagines the narwhal that narrowly freed itself from the harpoon, spinning through the darkness of the North Sea, its tusk pointing the way like a glowing sword, the bloody wound in its shoulder reddening the waters as it dives. And she knows there are far larger, far greater beasts of the sea that have died and must die in order to provide all of Deluce's oil.

But then she thinks of Gil, promising his luck away to Binks for information. For *her*.

"What's your answer, then?" the prince asks. "Shall we stand on the same side of this war?"

Isbe takes a breath, then holds out her hand for him to shake. "You have a deal."

———

She had almost forgotten what it feels like to enter or exit through an actual door. Isbe turns her face to the sun now, blinking, taking in its distant warmth. The new cloak William gave her smells fresh and clean, like the winter air that whispers along the bare part of her neck as she allows the prince to lead her, arm in arm, through the palace gates.

When William told her over a breakfast of warm bread, salted fish, and bubbling, runny eggs, that it would be a danger to travel under his banner—that he'd be a moving target after the death of his brothers—she suggested they dress as peasants and journey as husband and wife.

But the prince dismissed the idea. "The ports are still closed. If I issue an order to reopen them, it will draw attention to our departure. We must take the land route, which is easily a week's journey. And what with fears of the sickness, it's likely no inn will accept us along the way. Luckily—"

"I have an idea," they both said at the same time.

He let her go first.

Isbe's idea was to travel by way of the trade route along the river, and then cross the South Sea at the land bridge, using the convent at Isolé as a safe haven before making the rest of the journey through Deluce. She didn't mention to him why she thought of Isolé—that it was the very place to which the Delucian council had planned to send her on the eve of Aurora's wedding. She knows nothing about it other than that it must be trusted by the council and therefore is likely safe.

As for William's idea, he mentioned only that last night the ideal mode of travel occurred to him, and that he would show her in person.

Now, as he leads her across the palace grounds and into the castle village, a church bell gongs six times. They move past the church, where she hears the whinnying of two horses, and the shuffle of leather straps and buckles. A carriage.

Surely he isn't suggesting they take a royal carriage! She turns to him and he explains. "I was thinking about the death of Edward and Philip. That's what gave me the idea to travel as they did."

"But they were killed!" Isbe blurts out.

"Exactly," William says.

There's a silence while Isbe tries to make out what he is telling her. Pigeons flutter out of the bell tower above them, cooing. "Travel as they did . . . ," she says slowly, and then swallows, putting it together. "In a . . ."

William puts his hand on her back, a kind of affirmative pat. "Hearse," he finishes.

She has to admit, he's clever. No one will think to interfere with the small wooden construct, its horses draped in black, a casket in place of a passenger seat behind the driver's perch.

Then again, it means they are going to have to lie down together in a coffin.

"We'll make preparations, and leave tomorrow," he says.

———

The next day the wind carries an angry bite to it. Isbe shivers as she and William make their way back to the church at sunset. The old, gravel-voiced wagoner—one whom the prince claims they can trust with their lives—greets them gruffly and without fanfare. It's clear from his tone that he thinks what they're doing is a terrible idea. Isbe wonders just how much William has offered him to take this risk. Or perhaps he has no choice.

It takes a few minutes to get into position in the contained space, and Isbe almost laughs when William has to get out and try again with his cloak untangled. Luckily the coffin is lined in velvet and is, of course, as yet unused. There is no smell of death and decay, only cedar and pine. It is like a small enclosed bed, and not altogether uncomfortable, although it is nearly impossible to shift around without jostling each other. The driver leaves the lid open a few fingers' width. It's enough to allow for a thin strip of moonlight and fresh air without anyone seeing in.

Isbe hears the driver whip his horses, and soon they are trotting along the pitted road. After only a few minutes of their heads banging together on the small velvet pillow, William suggests Isbe slide down somewhat so that her face is near his chest.

And then, the very long and very awkward silence begins.

———

"I think we're at the river road," the prince mutters into her ear sometime later, startling Isbe, who had been nearly asleep. "The road feels bumpier here."

She scrunches her brow for a moment. "No, not yet."

"No, I think we are. I hear the current."

Isbe shakes her head, which causes her cheek to brush William's doublet. "That's a loose terret. The reins are rubbing against one of the horses' harnesses."

"How can you—" he begins to ask, but stops himself.

"I'll let you know when we're near the river," Isbe assures him. She'll smell it.

William fidgets and shifts. It must make him uneasy, not being able to see where they're headed. A thought strikes her, and she accidentally snorts.

"Are you laughing at me, Isabelle?" he asks. "I confess I'm not an expert on the susurrus of loose carriage gear."

Now Isbe actually does laugh. She's never heard anyone use the word *susurrus*. "No, I just had a thought that amused me."

"Which is? Do entertain me. We have a long journey ahead."

"I was thinking that people are so very dependent on light—either the sun, or oil for their lanterns, or candles. Without it, they have no idea where they're going. But I *live* like that, and well, I'm not saying it's better, but one could argue that it's a more honest way to be."

"More honest?"

"More true to life. Because we're all stumbling through darkness, really. None of us knows where we're heading. Not in the bigger picture anyway."

"You're quite the philosopher, Miss Isabelle of Deluce."

She could swear she feels his smile through the growing warmth of his chest near her cheek. She smiles back into him, wondering if he can feel it too.

"So tell me," he says. "Is your sister philosophical as well?"

Right. This is all for Aurora. She's not here to make interesting conversation. Isbe thinks for a minute. "She is thoughtful and intelligent. She taught herself to read."

"Really," the prince replies, sounding impressed.

"Well, there wasn't much else to do at the palace all these

years," Isbe says automatically. "But yes, she reads very well. Less for the ideas in it, more for the . . . stories." She can't bring herself to say *romance*. It is somehow too uncomfortable a word to say to a near stranger, especially one with whom she happens to be sharing a coffin. "Aurora is . . ." How to explain it? "She's a quiet person."

"I suppose it's commendable for a woman to be soft-spoken," William says, a bit of distance in his voice.

The comment annoys her. "I suppose. But Aurora isn't soft-spoken. She is silent."

"She doesn't speak at all?"

Isbe squirms. "She will make you a good wife," she says. That's what the entire point of this journey is, after all. William must fall in love with Aurora. "My sister can convey worlds to you in a single look. She is creative and joyful, patient and kind, and you must have heard rumors of her beauty."

"Anyone can be beautiful," the prince says. An odd comment.

"Not like her."

"Well, I look forward to seeing her, then."

"Aurora is more than just sweetness of face and temperament," Isbe says, growing frustrated with the way William's remarks seem removed, formal, as though they're discussing a prize horse to be traded. "You don't know her like I do, but one day you will. She sees into the heart of things. She always knew what I needed, even before I did."

"And what is it you need?" he asks, his voice again

reminding her of a tree in wind, shaking leaves loose inside her.

His question feels somehow too personal. "What I need is to save my sister."

"So you've said."

So they are understood. *Good.*

Silence comes again, but this time it's a little less awkward, and she begins to relax into the jostling ride, the scent of velvet and wood and lime soap that wraps around them, the faint thud of the prince's heart in her ears. . . .

———

Isbe always liked the erratic rhythm of Freckles's hooves, and now their sound fills her mind, bringing her back to the summer day three years ago when she snuck out on the unruly mare, only to get thrown in the mud. She remembers rinsing herself off in the little country stream, and once again, the memory washes over her: Gilbert teasing her, the two of them pushing each other playfully. Falling on top of him. His hand in her hair. His lips finding hers. Tingles running through her body, the water rushing all around them, crisp and cold, as they kissed and kissed and—

"That," she hears William say, pulling Isbe back into the present, "is the sound of the river."

A warm blush spreads through her neck and face, and she's overcome with the humiliation of having relived those intimate memories in such close quarters with someone else. What if William can somehow sense the nature of her thoughts?

But just as quickly, her embarrassment falls away, replaced by a tension in her chest. *Gil.* She doesn't know where he is, doesn't know if he's even alive. She's supposed to be saving the person closest to her—her sister—and yet she's lost the only other person she has ever loved.

Loved.

She did love him. *Does* love him. It's a love that's both romantic and familial at the same time, friendship mixed with trust mixed with *knowing.* All that, and the desire to feel his hard, calloused hands on her skin again—or even just to have him near, his soft scent of horses and hay, his calmness. That worn-river-stone smoothness of familiarity . . .

Is this what it feels like for a heart to break? She's not sure. She doesn't feel broken, only heavy—aching and sad and a little bit sick. He might be dead.

He might have died without knowing that this was how she felt.

"Isabelle?" William's voice is a rough whisper.

She nods against his chest. "Yes," she whispers back. "We've reached the river."

23

Violette,
a Faerie Duchess of Remarkable Bearing
According to Her Selves

One is never really alone with a mirror. Add a second mirror facing the first, and one's company multiplies infinitely. So many versions of oneself, seen from so many angles. This is truth. This is happiness. Violette pities anyone with fewer than forty-two mirrors in her bedroom, two hundred and forty-seven in her grand hall, and sixty-three in her water closet. She even has five of them on her ceiling over the bed so that when she wakes in the night with the candles still burning, as she has done just now, the million and one insects of loneliness lurking in the shadows can't touch her.

Violette has memorized every inch of herself, from the wavy hair as glossy as a ruby in sunlight, to the eyelashes as long and elegant as spiders' legs, to the lips as perfectly pursed as a taut bow just before the kill. And yet . . .

Violette marvels at the new and wonderful things she is still learning about herself, qualities she never knew were there, never even thought possible. Like the curse or, rather, its amendment. Proof that her power is indeed enough to counter Malfleur's. The spindle. The girl's birthday. A princess asleep. It has all occurred as it was outlined sixteen years ago.

The only catch is the sleeping sickness. It was never meant to infect others.

For a fleeting moment, Violette fears she has done something wrong. Hadn't Belcoeur, before she vanished, brought the golden spinning wheel to Violette and asked that she keep it safe? She should never have agreed in the first place. It had given her a bad feeling all along, even before the princess was born. It had been important to Belcoeur, obviously, or she wouldn't have asked, and Violette had felt the burden and the sadness of its presence. It had become a symbol of loss.

Decades later, after the child's christening, she didn't like the object of a curse being so close to her all the time, staring at her like a big dumb animal, majestic and silent and hungry. She resented being asked to keep so many secrets for others, when she had so many of her own to tend to. That was why she'd finally decided to get rid of it. But it couldn't be burned or melted or destroyed. So eventually she'd simply stowed the cumbersome thing away in one of those abandoned cottages in the royal forest. At the time, it hadn't seemed particularly foolish; what had seemed foolish would have been to believe that a faerie curse could still come true. Everyone knew how far the fae had fallen, even then.

Or maybe they hadn't. And maybe Violette hadn't—*hasn't*—either.

Surely it's not too grandiose a notion to think she might now save the kingdom. It cannot be hyperbolic to assume she, Violette, is both the source and answer to all this madness. She probably should do something about it. Try another curse reversal, perhaps.

Yes, she really ought to get out and let the world marvel.

She tucks her fluffy covers up to her chin, watching intently as her double mimics her in the mirror directly above. She is pleased to see that this, her most favored reflection, has paid such dutiful attention.

She begins to drift off again. It cannot be paranoia to assume that the night is full of the sightless and the angry—people who've had their vision robbed by Violette herself. Can it?

She looks up, staring into her own eyes between each heavy blink, her face *almost* unfamiliar in the waning, wavering lamplight. What was it she was pondering?

Oh, right. The sleeping sickness, and how to end it.

Then again, she thinks, perhaps it's not such a good idea to get involved after all. Going out and saving the kingdom would require interacting with *other people* . . . seeing not just their appearances but through to their hidden fears, their anger, their twisted, thwarted insides. And she's had about enough of that for one lifetime.

With that decision made, she closes her eyes.

Infinite reflections close their eyes too.

PART

IV

DARKNESS DID WIN

24

Isabelle

"We're here," says the old driver, lifting the lid of the coffin.

As she sits up, Isbe can tell that they have pulled off the side of the road into the shadow of some pine trees, hopefully hidden from any passersby. Not that there are any. They seem to be in the middle of nowhere. Isbe shivers. They haven't heard a passing cart or rider in many hours. But they have safely crossed the border into Deluce, even if they are in the most remote part of the kingdom.

They have been traveling the river road for several days. At one point they drove right through a village where a riot had broken out after pro-LaMorte mercenaries showed up and demanded recruits, on pain of death. Isbe had practically held her breath until they'd cleared the area, and barely exhaled until they reached the land bridge connecting Aubin and Deluce through the small, neutral territory of Corraine.

Even here, there's been little reprieve from the murmurings of Malfleur's rise. They say she hears everything. They say her defectors have been found stabbed in their beds.

William helps Isbe out of the hearse, and as her shoes touch the dewy grass, her legs wobble, leaden and numb.

"This is Isolé, where I leave you," the driver says hurriedly. The waver in his voice betrays his regret in having aided in their secret plan. He is gone almost before the prince has a chance to slide a purse of coins into his hand with a quiet clink.

"What does it look like?" Isbe asks.

William takes her shoulders and turns her. "Up a hill," he says. "Surrounded by a high stone wall and rows of cypress."

Isbe has always imagined cypress trees like thick furry soldiers, stiff and orderly.

"The sky is a wash of variegated white fog," the prince goes on, his voice moving closer to her ear, "like cows' milk once it has begun to separate. Still, you can see the sun just about to set through the tops of the stone archways in the cloister, and—"

"William," Isbe says. "I didn't realize you could be so . . . descriptive."

"You don't realize very much about me at all, Isabelle."

There's no note of sarcasm in his response. He is simply stating fact.

"Perhaps not." She wants to reach out and read his facial expression with her hands, like she would with Gil or Aurora, but she refrains. She had asked him if she could do so before, and he had refused her, without saying why. Instead, she marches up the incline in the direction he has pointed her, clenching and opening her palms as she walks, left to imagine the high ridge of his cheekbones, his serious mouth.

———

Isolé. The desolate convent where the council had intended to deposit Isbe. She tries to imagine a life of seclusion: nursing the sick, giving alms to the poor, spending hours in silent prayer. It's possible she never would have seen Aurora again—she's sure that's what the council wanted.

As she makes her way up the hill beside William, she hears women's voices chanting—evening vespers, the last prayers before sundown. She hears something else too: the ding of metal on earth. Shovels, or pickaxes.

They enter through the cemetery, which smells of solemnity. Sage and skunk.

"Sisters," the prince says in polite deference.

The dull metal clanging stops. They must be digging a grave, Isbe realizes. There are two or three of them at most.

"'Tis it you need?" one of the nuns asks. "Sick calls commence at seven in the morning."

"We're seeking temporary asylum here."

There's a silence, during which Isbe figures the nuns are taking in their appearance. She can hardly fathom her own, even in the clean cloak and traveling dress William procured for her. Her hair no longer comes down farther than her chin. She has gotten even skinnier in the past few weeks. She probably looks like a ghost. And William beside her, said to be both tall and handsome with the dark skin common of the Aubinians, must provide a stark contrast.

"Aren't any free beds in the dorter," one of them whispers, "and now's not a good ti—"

"Hsst, Sister Katherine," a second nun interrupts. Her voice is a thin hiss, and Isbe pictures the pointed face and sharp, pronged tongue of a snake. "It is not for us to say. Sister Agnes will summon Reverend Mother Hildegarde. She will make the decision about what to do with our visitors."

"Yes, Sister Genevieve," says a third, quieter than the other two. "Please," she says to Isbe and William with a rabbitlike sniff, "follow me."

They follow Sister Agnes through the graveyard, into the cloisters, and then into a building that the sister tells them is the calefactory. "Only warm spot in all of the convent," she explains, stoking the big fire, whose heat sparks out, penetrating the entire space.

Isbe is grateful for the warmth as she and William sit down on a long, narrow bench beside the roaring flames while Sister Agnes leaves to find the prioress. She knows the calefactory is likely the only room other than the kitchen in which a fire is allowed. The sisters favor a life of deprivation.

As if responding to her thoughts, William mutters: "I've never understood the absolutism of religious practices. What sort of higher power would create fire in the first place, only to ask that his worshippers all but forego it?"

Isbe nods. "It sounds exactly like the kind of thing a selfish dictator would do—or one of the fae."

"It would be both blasphemous and deeply unwise," says a booming female voice behind them, "to compare our heavenly father to a corrupt faerie."

"Reverend Mother," William says, standing quickly.

Isbe follows suit. "We only meant that—"

"I don't care what you meant, daughter. If history teaches us anything," Mother Hildegarde says, "it's that the intentions behind our statements matter far less than the way they're interpreted." Her presence is commanding; her voice fills the room, as pervasive as the heat of the flames. "Men have warred and died for centuries over the interpretation of a few words."

"But of course," William says with immaculate manners.

"In answer to your question," the prioress continues, "I'd love to heat the dorter and refectory, but we can only afford the maintenance of a single fire. My women are too busy for chopping firewood." Pride reverberates from her voice like the echo of an empty wine barrel. A woman nearly as wide as she is tall, Isbe guesses.

"Perhaps we may be of service to you, in exchange for shelter and protection from the elements," the prince says.

"We have a long journey ahead of us."

"Here," the prioress says, handing them each a bucket. "You may as well make yourselves useful while we talk. The water must be boiled and prepared for the laundry."

Isbe can almost feel William tense in response to the demeaning task. Then again, the reverend mother doesn't know he's a prince. They take the buckets and place them on a rack over the flames. Sister Agnes returns with a cart full of dirty linens, and then the prioress dismisses her so that they are once again alone in the calefactory.

While William and Isbe awkwardly attempt to wash the clothes, the prioress questions them about where they've come from and where they're going.

"Reverend Mother," Isbe says, "we were driven from our village by supporters of Malfleur. We are traveling north to see my sister." That part, at least, is true.

"Your sister?"

"She's . . . she's at the Delucian palace." Again, it's the truth, even if Isbe is gambling on the fact that the prioress will *interpret* her words to mean that her sister is employed by the palace, not its royal heir.

"You're planning to head straight toward the sleeping sickness."

"We don't have any other options," William replies.

"So will you house us tonight?" Isbe asks, feeling anxious as she wrings out a cloth. She wishes she could see the reverend mother's face.

The prioress is quiet for a moment. Finally she answers.

"Yes, but you must do me a favor."

"Anything," William quickly says. "We are happy to perform any other chores you may wish."

"You must bring a message to the palace for me. The council has failed on a promise."

"I'm sorry?" Isbe asks, confused.

"Sixteen years ago, when I was still chief minister to King Henri, he and I came to an agreement."

Isbe stands there in astonished silence, a drenched sheet heavy and dripping from her raw hands. The prioress was once on the king's council, and during Isbe's lifetime? How did she not know this?

"Perhaps hard to believe now," the prioress says, obviously in answer to Isbe's stunned expression. "But at one time his highness had many female advisers."

Her father had many female advisers? This is news to Isbe. She knows only that he had many *mistresses*. But quite a bit changed after her father married Queen Amélie and Aurora was born.

The prioress continues speaking. "I was to accept his bastard daughter upon the eve of the wedding of Princess Aurora, in exchange for a healthy sum to fund my orphanage. It was a fair enough arrangement, but years have gone by, the princess has succumbed to disease, the young woman I was expecting never arrived, nor did the money. Now our granary is empty, and we are up to twenty-four orphan girls here at the convent, all of them lacking proper winter clothing, food, and supplies. One of the girls, Josette, only six years old, is suffering from pneumonia. I fear she won't live to see spring. Still, my requests have fallen on deaf—or should I say sleeping—ears. I ask only for what was promised me."

Now Isbe's mind reels. The king had promised to send his bastard daughter here. *She* is the bastard daughter. Isbe had no idea that the council had been intending not just to send her away, but to deliver much-needed finances to help the lives of orphans! She hadn't even realized Isolé housed orphans at all.

Guilt prickles her throat and becomes a wrenching pain as she swallows it down into her gut. If she hadn't run off with Gilbert, if she had instead followed through with the council's plan for her, would these twenty-four orphans be better off? Would little Josette have a better chance of surviving?

She's tempted to say something—to admit her identity, to claim responsibility, to vow, at least, that once the curse has been reversed, once Aurora is healthy and restored to power, Isbe will do everything she can to make sure Hildegarde gets the support she has sought from the palace.

But she knows she can't say any of this. With royals dying and Malfleur on the rise, it simply isn't safe to reveal her identity, even if she *is* merely a bastard. More importantly, she isn't in any position to make hollow promises. She doesn't know what will happen when she reaches her sister. *If* she reaches her . . .

She must be gawking, because the prince nudges her in

the ribs with his elbow. "As you wish, Mother," he says.

"Yes." Isbe stumbles and turns her face down, hoping to disguise her discomfort. "As . . . as you wish."

———

William is instructed to sleep alone in a tiny guest room off the scriptorium, which, it turns out, is really an impressive library. Isbe, on the other hand, is given a straw mat on the floor of the calefactory, alongside the orphan girls, who come flooding into the room silently after their supper, the hurried patter of their little shoes the only indication of their size and number. There's not a single whisper or giggle among them. Isbe marvels at how well-behaved they are; it's like a room full of young Auroras.

Though they've put out the fire for the night, the room is comparatively cozy, and Isbe is grateful to be crowded in on all sides by the warm bodies and soft snores of the girls.

But still she can't sleep. When she tries, she dreams of Gil, of his hands holding her against the rocking rail of the ship, his body so close to hers, sheltering her from the worst of the freezing, violent wind, his kiss—so sudden, so unexplained . . . and then his name wants to dislodge itself from her chest and fly out, calling for him.

It's not very late. The sisters all go to bed almost as soon as the sun sets and get up well before it rises for early prayer. Isbe lies there, trapped in the tomb of her dark thoughts. Every way she turns, there's an invisible wall pushing in on her. She can't get Mother Hildegarde's voice out of her head. She can't stop thinking about her father. How he banned all his mistresses from the royal court . . . around the same time that the prioress claims to have struck a deal with him.

Is it possible the prioress had been *more* than just an adviser to the king? The thought causes heat to boil in her stomach, bubbling up into Isbe's head. Was Hildegarde one of her father's mistresses?

And then the shadow of that question looms behind it: could Hildegarde in fact be . . . Isbe's *mother*?

She tosses on her mat. The notion is staggering. It stands to reason that her mother, whoever she was, would have preferred her child to be raised in the palace, and why else would the chief minister have wanted her to be sent here once she was of age? What other value could a bastard half princess have for the reverend mother?

Something about it doesn't *feel* right to Isbe, though. Hildegarde's voice, she realizes, is not the one from her mother dreams. The voice that sings the rose lullaby to Isbe in her sleep is softer, sweeter, more wavering. Still, should she trust the hazy convictions of a dream over the logic of the facts? If there's any chance the reverend mother is the same woman who birthed Isbe and left her all those years ago, she *has* to know. But she can't simply ask Hildegarde without drawing suspicion.

Isbe sits up. She must investigate. She must discover the truth.

Carefully she extricates herself from the group of sleeping girls and slips out of the calefactory into the courtyard, where she stops, trying to get her bearings. She wants to start in the scriptorium. She will have to awaken William so he can assist in reading the stored scrolls and letters. If what Hildegarde says is true, then there must be correspondence between Isolé and the palace, and if that's the case, then surely one of the letters might hint at the true nature of the prioress's relationship to the king and maybe, even, to *her*.

The air echoing through the cloisters is crisp and cold. Wind whistles faintly through the dense needles of the cypresses, braiding threads of their woodsy odor across the dusk. On nights like this, Isbe is reminded that she's inhaling the breath of ancient history, of those who lived and built civilizations and died out long ago . . . and this is the same air that will be breathed by the great unimaginable tribes of the future.

She once told Aurora that there is a scent of *almostness*. Well, there's a scent of *alwaysness* too.

There will always be winters.

There will always be loneliness.

She moves quietly in the direction of the scriptorium, passing the refectory where they ate their meager supper of tough mutton and dry bread, and steps through a narrow stone doorway. She realizes this is not the scriptorium but the infirmary when the heavy herbal scent of medicine hits her nostrils. An older nun is snoring loudly in a corner, a sound like a wagon that has come off its wheel.

Isbe is about to duck out when she remembers something.

"Josette?" she whispers.

There's a stirring. "Yes?" comes the voice of a young girl.

Isbe slowly makes her way toward that voice, careful not to bang into any of the other beds and awaken the snoring nun. She kneels down beside Josette's bed and takes the girl's hand. It is icy cold.

Josette coughs. "What is it? Are you one of the travelers?"

"I am," Isbe tells her. She wants to say more, but she can't tell her that it's her fault the convent is owed money, that it might be her fault Josette hasn't gotten better care.

"And are you really going all the way to the palace?" There's awe in the girl's voice.

"Yes."

"But aren't you afraid of the sickness? Or the evil faerie queen?" she whispers.

"I suppose I should be," Isbe replies, realizing it's true.

"You remind me of Mother Hildegarde," Josette whispers.

Her words send a shiver down Isbe's spine. "Tell me about her."

"Reverend Mother knows about everything. She is said to have *visions*. I have seen her roll through fire and come away unburned." Josette's whispers get more excited with every detail. "She has stood in freezing water in the winter for hours and not caught even a chill. She sometimes goes away for days, and we discover she has been meditating all that time within a tomb under the ground."

"What stories!" Isbe says with a smile.

"They aren't stories. It is all true. There is something special about Mother Hildegarde. Like you."

"There's nothing special about me."

"Yes," Josette says simply. "There is. I heard Sister Agnes whispering that you arrived here in a hearse. Is it true? Have you come from . . ." The girl's voice drops lower. "The other side?"

"No," Isbe whispers, a mixture of laughter and sadness bubbling in her throat.

"Are you dead?"

"Not that I know of."

Josette coughs again. "I've read stories of the dead coming back."

"You know how to read?" Isbe asks, startled.

"Of course!" she cries, a little too loudly. Then, more quietly, she goes on. "Mother Hildegarde teaches all of us to read, and to write too. She is very . . . political."

Isbe stifles a smile.

Josette doesn't seem to notice. "Are you afraid to die?"

Isbe thinks for a minute. "I suppose I am. But I'm more afraid of all I have to do before then."

"Me too," Josette says.

"Then you'd better get your sleep." She leans over and kisses Josette's forehead.

"What was that for?" the girl asks.

"You remind me of someone too," Isbe whispers.

William is not as easy to awaken. She has to physically shake him before he comes to with a startled intake of breath.

"I was dreaming," he explains. "It was so real. I dreamed you had no sister, that *you* were the princess of Deluce but were pretending not to be. That you had invented the idea of the sleeping sickness as a cover so no one would find out you had fled the palace in search of adventure."

Isbe doesn't know what to say to that at first. "I assure you, I'm not clever enough to have invented any of it. It's all too serious and all too real."

"I realize that. It was only a dream," William replies, though he seems to be saying so as much for his own benefit as for hers. "It's just . . ."

"What?"

"Nothing. Never mind."

"No, tell me what you were going to say," she presses.

"I can't shake the feeling, Isabelle, that there's something you haven't told me."

"You think I'm lying to you?" Isbe asks, truly surprised.

"Maybe not," William answers. "I just have a sense that there's more to you than I yet know."

"Well, of course there is. We've only known each other a short time."

They pause for a moment, their breath coming and going and neither one saying anything.

Then William grabs her hands. "I should have done this

before, when you first asked me." He guides her palms to his face.

The gesture is startling, but Isbe eagerly seizes the opportunity to scan his expression, to memorize his features, to fully take him in. Her fingers dance lightly across his full lips—much more pronounced than Gilbert's. His eyes are big and widely spaced. He has a prominent forehead. A regal forehead. His skin is smooth . . . except for a slight scar along his jaw.

"Like I mentioned," he whispers, by way of explanation, "my brothers weren't very nice."

They sit there in the unlit guest quarters, a room hardly larger than a closet, Isbe taking in what he has said, and not said.

Finally she breaks the silence. "You're probably wondering why I woke you."

She hurriedly explains that she needs him to scan through the convent's stored documents, and to her relief, he readily agrees to help. "I won't be falling back to sleep anytime soon anyway," he says. She can't help but wonder if it's more than that—maybe *he's* the one who longs to pretend he's someone else. Maybe he's the one who was looking for a reason to flee from his life in search of more.

They spend awhile carefully combing through stacks of correspondence in the scriptorium—a room that tickles her lips with the taste of dust and worn hides—but fail to find any letters from the Delucian court.

Isbe is beginning to feel frustrated. "Let's try another

tactic. Perhaps there's something about Mother Hildegarde herself that we can dig up. About her past, before she came to Isolé."

"What is it, exactly, that you're hoping to uncover?" the prince asks.

"It's like I told you. I have reason to believe the prioress knows secrets relating to the late king, my father. Secrets that she might decide to hold over the palace in the future." It's not a complete lie, but Isbe isn't about to reveal the whole truth. The fact that she doesn't know her own mother's identity is humiliating and private. It doesn't concern William in the slightest.

"Well, I've found something interesting. It doesn't pertain to King Henri per se, though," he says, handing her a piece of folded vellum.

"What does it say?"

"It's a . . . well . . . a sort of medical—or metaphysical—analysis."

"Of?"

"Of Mother Hildegarde."

"Read it to me," she demands, quickly biting her lip in an attempt to hold in her impatience.

William mutters to himself as he reads, sharing the highlights. "It seems a doctor was summoned to bear witness to the mother's miraculous capabilities. Withstanding extreme circumstances, handling fire while exhibiting no bodily harm, fasting for many days without visible effect, that sort of thing."

"And?"

"Well, it seems the doctor decided that the prioress displays an inability to experience pain. He concludes here that this is a viable explanation of the miracles . . . and that it's also most likely she is barren."

"Mother Hildegarde is barren? Are you sure?"

She hears William folding and unfolding the vellum. "I'm not sure of anything. I'm only reading to you what I see here. The doctor believed her to be incapable either of feeling pain or of bearing children, that's what it says."

"It's true," says someone from the doorway. It takes Isbe a second to place the asplike voice.

"Sister Genevieve."

"Everyone knows Mother Hildegarde couldn't have children of her own before she came here," she says. Isbe has the impression that each of the nun's statements is another fly lapped up by a forked tongue. "It's one of the reasons she entered the fold and began taking in orphans. She was married once, before, you know."

Isbe swallows. "We didn't mean to pry, we were only . . ." But she can't think of a proper excuse. She shifts her weight, wondering if the nun is going to report them to the reverend mother and have them thrown out into the cold.

Instead, Sister Genevieve says, "It's all right. Visitors are often intensely curious about Mother Hildegarde. She is quite extraordinary. However, if you have any questions, you may ask them of her directly, during daylight hours."

"We're sorry to have disturbed you," William says. "We

didn't think anyone would be awake at this hour," he adds.

There is the briefest of pauses before Sister Genevieve replies. "I happened to have heard a noise and needed to check that an animal had not gotten into the granary. We've had a problem with rodents." She clears her throat lightly. "It would be my pleasure to escort you back to your sleeping quarters now," she says, calmly but firmly.

Isbe steps toward her, and Genevieve holds out her thin arm to guide her.

———

It's only once Isbe is back among the sleeping orphans, lying on her mat and drifting off to sleep, that she pinpoints what has been bothering her since Sister Genevieve discovered her and William in the scriptorium. Certain oddities.

First, Genevieve had appeared silently, unaccompanied by the faint crackle of a lantern's burning wick. *Though perhaps that's not so peculiar. Maybe the nuns are taught to conserve oil.*

Second, she had claimed to be checking the granary for rats, but didn't Mother Hildegarde explicitly say their granary was empty? Still, it's possible the prioress had been exaggerating.

However, the third peculiarity is what has Isbe quite convinced that the sister, despite her divine oath of truth, was lying: the scent on the nun's hands. They smelled like fresh dirt. Like rust. And like blood.

25

Aurora

"Marigold?" But the girl really is gone, and Aurora's voice, disembodied, echoes through the woods.

The sun has set; darkness has risen. The night surrounds Aurora now, throbs with that same anticipation it always has, making her yearn for Isabelle. For home. For Heath. For everything to be different than it is. For something to begin. For something that she has already, inexplicably, lost.

A hand clamps down on her shoulder. "A beauty like you shouldn't be wandering the night alone."

Aurora turns around and makes out the figure emerging from the darkness. "Heath?" She sighs in relief. He's just as breathless as she is. "How did you find me?"

"My notes were missing. It wasn't hard to guess where

you'd gone. I heard the waterfall. I feared . . ." He clears his throat. "I followed the river downstream and then I saw the trail. And that's when I really got worried."

"The trail?"

"Of scattered flowers. You met Marigold, didn't you?"

She nods, swallowing hard. "She disappeared."

"She only exists in daylight," he explains, as if it were the most natural thing. "Lucky for you," he adds, his expression clouding over. "What were you doing out here anyway? I told you not to come back to the Borderlands. You could have died. I'm surprised she didn't try to drown you."

Aurora shakes her head. "She was helpless. She's just a little girl!"

"I have more than once come upon one of these lying on the ground near the cliffs' edge," he says, holding up the flower wreath, "only to discover the bloodied mess of some poor fellow smashed into the rocks below."

A shiver runs up Aurora's neck. But she will not be scolded, not for the bravest thing she has ever done: saving someone's life. "Well, she *didn't* hurt me. In fact, she may have *helped* me." Her confidence begins to return. The cottage . . . the words in the wood . . . the clues. "Heath, I think I've learned something new about the queen—"

A powerful, angry *crack* ricochets around them, cutting her off.

"A storm is coming," he says. "We need to get back to Blackthorn. *Now.*" He starts off, into a dense knot of trees and branches.

"Heath!" she says, surprised by how good it feels to shout, as though the thunder has crept inside her throat and become part of her.

He turns. "What?"

"We should go *this* way," she says, and begins to run. Let him follow her this time.

The sky fractures as she enters a clearing, and rain gushes down, instantly drenching her. She blinks against the heavy rain, taking in the massive bruise of sky above, swollen and torn through with lightning. She tries to listen to her heart, to the rose lullaby that lives inside her, an internal compass. Heath catches up to her, and neither of them says anything. The sudden storm brews powerfully around them. When lightning flashes again, it lights up the entire woods, and Aurora gets a good look at Heath's face. He's staring at her in wonder. Gone are the concern, the skepticism, the sickening disappointment she swore she saw in his eyes during the past few days. He has not, she realizes quickly, underestimated her . . . but she has underestimated herself.

She breathes deeply—the musky wet forest smells of Sommeil lure her one way, but there's a voice, an urge, lower, beneath that call, a message of truth cutting through the dreaminess of the storm. Once again, she knows which direction to go. She can *feel* the way back to the wall, back to Blackthorn, back to the queen.

The wind tears past Aurora, nearly knocking her over as she leads Heath through a thick cluster of trees. The rain pounds down on her face, blurring her vision as they push deeper into the aching, pulsing blackness of the forest. Thunder rages. The storm is moving swiftly. If it keeps heading this way, they could easily be struck.

The wall flashes before her; its gray stones shine in the lightning.

Then Aurora *is* lightning as she and Heath hurtle across the illusion. Pushing through the wall feels different this time. She doesn't need to sing or even *think* the lullaby . . . she only needs to be, immutably, Aurora. Instead of trapped in the wall's coldness, she feels only euphoria—a shot of pure joy—at her ability to fly to the other side unharmed.

The meadows of the Blackthorn estate open up before her, and she runs not from the storm and not to safety but for the easy pleasure of her body moving through space and time. A laugh bursts out of her chest, carrying Aurora's new aliveness in its wild sound. She is powerful.

She is free.

At the next bang of thunder, Heath grabs her hand and they cover the rest of the distance to the castle together.

———

Inside, Heath lights a lantern and Aurora sees that they have come through a side entrance, into a gallery. The room is drafty, cool, and empty, the walls lined in paintings, with a few sculptures on pedestals scattered throughout the space. She has wandered through here before, but only in passing.

They stand facing each other, water droplets softly plinking to the floor. A raindrop runs down Aurora's brow and cheek, trickling into the corner of her lips. Heath runs his hand through his hair, which is dark with rain. He seems at a loss for words, a half smile tugging at his mouth—caught, probably, between reprimanding her and something else. The electricity of the storm has followed them, and Aurora shivers, wanting to touch his dripping cloak, his collar, his chin—to let the lightning shock within her travel out. But she doesn't.

"We should get you dried off," he says. A puddle is rapidly forming around both their feet. "Storms are reckless creatures," he adds. "We could have been killed."

Aurora nods but remains wordless.

She steps away from Heath, trying to catch her breath, to remind herself of the important discoveries she made today at the cottage.

Rain beats against the shutters, and her eyes start to focus in the dim light. A giant painting looms before her. It's a large portrait of a young man on a horse. The man is handsome, with wide shoulders and a straight back. His light brown hair is cropped at his shoulders, and a thin beard outlines his square jaw, more filled in than Heath's faint stubble but not the full beard of an older man. He appears to be around their age, and on his head sits a very simple crown: an oddly familiar circlet of gold, worn low on the forehead, no jewels.

She hadn't really noticed the painting before . . . but then again, she hadn't been looking for signs of a thwarted romance until now. Her mind swirls with questions; something about the lush painting has captivated her attention.

"Charles Blackthorn." She's startled from her thoughts by Heath's voice, warm and close to her neck. "People say he went mad over a woman."

"Charles?"

Heath nods. "I didn't want to tell you, but that's why the tower room was empty before you came. People avoid it—they think it's haunted. They say his ghost comes back, looking for his one true love."

His one true love. And then she remembers: she saw the letters *CB* carved with a childlike scrawl among the other initials on the walls of the cottage in the Borderlands.

Could this be the love story she's seeking, the reason for Belcoeur's madness? Could Charles be the visitor Belcoeur believes she is waiting for? If so, and if he really did die many years ago, then the queen will be waiting forever . . . which means there's a chance they really won't ever escape Sommeil.

Though "escape" is no longer the word she would use— that would imply a desire to leave all of it behind.

"Luckily, I don't believe in ghosts," Heath goes on. "Or true love, for that matter."

Aurora balks. "You don't believe in true love? That's ridiculous!"

"Is it? What proof do you have that it exists?" he asks. He seems to be leaning in closer to her.

"I—it isn't something to be *proven*." She's breathing slowly. His closeness is making her unsteady. "It's just something you feel," she says, thinking of the many epic tales of love she has read. "And when you feel it, you know."

He tilts his head, smirking just a little. "Sounds like the stuff of stories."

"Well, what evidence do you have that it *doesn't* exist?" she challenges. This heady mix of frustration and determination is beginning to feel familiar, and not in a bad way. She finds she likes that he contradicts her, that he's willing to debate, that he expects her to argue her side. And that, with her newfound voice, she *can*.

Now his face is so near she can feel his breath. "Just that I've never felt it before. That kind of love involves choice— or it should. And that's something I've never had. You can't have choice if you don't have freedom."

"Then I hope that changes," Aurora whispers. "Everyone deserves true love."

"I'm not so sure I agree. I've heard of people doing terrible things in the name of true love. Wouldn't want to end up like old Blackthorn, mad and alone."

"But if you don't believe in love, then you *will* end up alone." She blinks as her words settle into the narrow gap between their bodies. His lips seem to loom before hers, heart shaped and soft looking, even as they quiver into a smile.

"Maybe so," he whispers back, lifting his hand to touch her face. He brushes a strand of wet hair off her cheek. As his fingers make contact with her skin, she shivers.

He leans back slightly, and she remembers she's still drenched. Thunder crashes beyond the walls and rain pounds the roof, heavy and whooshing, as though an entire ocean has opened up in the sky.

"Let me build a fire," Heath suggests. "You must be cold."

But he doesn't move to the hearth. He stands there, staring at her, his lips slightly parted. Plenty of men have gazed at Aurora with something akin to hunger, but none of them *knew* her; none of them could.

"You . . ." He shakes his head, his long hair swinging in front of his eyes. "You make me *want* things." He licks his lower lip nervously. She stares at his mouth, horrified at the fire that instantly rages through her.

"You make me want to believe in other worlds," he goes on. "In other possibilities. And I should hate you for that," he says, though there's a smile still trying to cut across the stricken look on his face.

She swallows. "I'm sorry." Like everything about Sommeil, his words leave her tingly with dissatisfaction, with the fear that she will *never* be satisfied, never get what she wants, even if she doesn't know what that is. Or perhaps *because* she doesn't know.

"Don't be."

His voice is so quiet she almost doesn't hear him, but something begins to rise within her, tightening around her lungs like vines. She always thought love would come to her just as it did in the romances she read: full-blown and over-powering. Absolute and unquestioning.

What's happening to her now is nothing like that. It's tremulous, curious, speckled with dangers and uncertainties.

"I . . . I . . ." But he can't seem to finish what he was going to say.

She puts her hand on his shoulder, a small gesture but infinitely bold—bigger, even, than when she touched the spinning wheel and its sting changed her forever.

He seems to know this. He takes her hand and lifts it to his lips. He kisses her knuckles softly, hesitantly. His lips linger on her skin, sending currents of warmth through her arm and down her entire body. She feels light-headed as he tugs her closer to him, until his lips graze her ear, his breath tickling her neck. "Aurora."

An aching desire leaps up in her like flames in a breeze. Her lips catch the stubble on his chin, the high ridge of his cheekbone—still wet from the rain—then find their way to his mouth. She feels his surprised inhale, the way something clicks into place as his body goes firm and urgent against hers and he begins to kiss her back.

She is falling—into the divide between before and after. Her world is changing again, no longer simply with the miracle of touch but this new discovery of how touch can have *meaning*. She feels the kiss everywhere: a tingling ache in her fingertips, a sigh against the backs of her knees—the kiss she didn't realize she'd been waiting for, ever since meeting Heath, even when he had a dagger pointed at her throat.

Her *first* kiss.

The word "oh" drifts into the air around them as if on a swirl of fog.

Aurora pulls away, enough to take a breath.

"Oh." A soft voice. Not hers, and not Heath's either.

She turns. *Wren.* The girl stands framed in the entrance to the gallery, her face pale, her fingers clenched together. "Forgive me," she says, backing away. And then she's gone.

26

Isabelle

Reverend Mother Hildegarde keeps Isbe and William busy for most of the morning. It turns out there are many grueling chores to be done and too few hands to do them all. But Isbe hasn't stopped wondering about Sister Genevieve's appearance last night, that uncanny scent of blood and dirt and rust. She keeps imagining different scenarios: Sister Genevieve cutting her arm on a gardening hoe as she tends to vegetables, for example. Or perhaps Sister Genevieve discovering a rat in the granary and killing it with the sharp end of a pickax. Surely there are any number of possible explanations for her being out so late. . . .

And for her tending to the granary despite what the prioress said about it being empty.

Still, Isbe knows a lying voice when she hears one.

Finally, during a break for the nuns to have their midday meal, she finds a moment to pull William aside. They pass the dorter, the refectory, and the bell tower, turning the corner through the cloisters and moving across the graveyard to the granary at the far side of the complex. William throws open the double doors to the large grain storage room, and Isbe holds her breath.

"So . . . it *is* empty, then," she says after a pause.

"Quite so. Hardly even a trace of wheat on the stone floor," William confirms. "It looks as though the floors have been recently swept, in fact."

"Perhaps to keep the vermin away," Isbe says, thinking. She's, truth be told, a little disappointed, though she's not sure what sort of secret she thought she'd discover.

They decide to return to the refectory, hoping to catch a scrap of bread before the meal has been cleared. But upon passing once again through the graveyard, its scent of sage and cypress and new-turned dirt gives Isbe pause. She pulls back on William's arm, and they stop out in the open. She can feel the sun on her wrists and face.

"Is there another fresh grave?" she asks.

William hesitates, scanning the area. "Possibly."

"Weren't the sisters digging one just yesterday when we arrived? Is it the same plot?"

"I'm not sure."

Isbe sighs, frustrated. She knows she should let go of the apprehensive nag in the back of her mind, but it's like a piece of snagged cloth that won't come loose.

William clears his throat. "Isabelle, what are you really after here? Why are you so curious about Hildegarde and the others?"

She shakes her head, feeling a lump of annoyance lodge in her throat. She doesn't want to explain it to him. And yet the words begin to form of their own accord. "She knew the king, my father."

"Sure, but what's in that? Many people knew the king well, I can only assume."

"I thought she might be . . ." Her voice is a ragged whisper. "I thought perhaps she might know something about who my mother was. Just take me to the fresh grave. Please."

She hears William sigh quietly, as though he's attempting to hide it. "Very well," he says, leading her there.

She kneels down in the soft earth. She is not very accustomed to praying. She closes her eyes because that's what one is supposed to do. She puts her hands together, and her head down. She knows she needs to stop trying to find answers. This journey isn't about her, or finding out who her mother was. This is about saving Aurora—her sister, her closest friend, the person who knows her better than anyone in the world. The only person, in fact, who has ever cared about what happens to Isbe.

Failing her is not an option.

Isbe places her palms into the earth. Whatever soul is buried here, Isbe hopes he or she is in peace. She gives the damp ground one final pat and is about to get to her feet when she reconsiders. There had been a touch of something cold, something hard. . . .

She pats the earth near the grave again, then pushes aside loose dirt. "William," she gasps. "There's something under here . . . there's . . ." She begins eagerly moving clumps of dirt aside with both hands. She feels metal. She feels . . . a *handle*.

She lifts her hand, dirt now caked into her fingernails. She is holding a dagger.

"Now that *is* odd," the prince says, kneeling beside her.

She runs her fingers rapidly over the hilt, feeling the careful carvings in the wood. "William, it's not just any bodkin. It's got an insignia imprinted on it. It's . . ." A hawk perched on a sword . . .

"The Aubinian seal." The prince's voice has gone cold as the blade in her hand.

"How would this have gotten here? Why would it be buried in the ground like this?" Isbe's fingers tremble with a mix of excitement and dread.

William is quiet beside her, but she can feel his tension. Finally he lifts her by the elbow and says, "We need to leave here, now."

"But—"

"My brothers," he chokes out. "They were traveling with a large retinue to overlook stores of Aubinian weapons proffered to the Delucian council."

"And they were ambushed—"

"At Tristesse Pass, not far from here. Come on, we have

nothing to stay for anyhow." His voice is urgent. "No one is by. We can slip away unnoticed if we hurry."

Her pulse hammers in her ears. William's right. For all they know, his brothers' killers could still be lurking nearby, protected by locals and perhaps even by the convent itself.

They have to leave now, and quickly.

But even as they flee the courtyard in broad daylight and head for the road into the nearest village, the foolish part of Isbe—her curiosity—thinks they ought to have stayed to learn more. She can hardly imagine Hildegarde harboring murderers! Still, she feels William's wariness as they make their way toward town, and it begins to infect her as well, starting out as a tension in her hands and wrists, evolving into a stiffness in her chest.

As they enter the village in search of horses to take them the rest of the way, they find it eerily quiet. Even in winter, there should be peasants herding goats to market, traders hawking wares, people going about their daily business with a coarse and noisy obliviousness. Instead, the tension, Isbe realizes, is not just within her but outside of her too, in the lack of busy voices and grunts and—

"Where is everyone?" she whispers to William. She clutches the Aubinian dagger, which she has shoved into her belt, hiding the seal beneath a fold of her dress. "Something isn't right."

No sooner are the words out of her mouth than a man's deep voice barks out, "Halt, in the name of Queen Malfleur."

———

Isbe always thought that her death would have some sort of meaning or bravery to it. Maybe she'd take a dramatic fall from a wild horse. Maybe she'd throw herself before a drawn rapier at some profound and important moment. Maybe she'd lose her mind and run naked through a frozen field, hollering until her last breath turned to frost.

But now she fears her death will be swift and unremarkable. There's no doubt the soldiers intend to kill her and the prince. She and William are currently sitting back to back on the floor of a recently abandoned manor, tied together by the wrists. The lord who once governed over the village from this very manor is still where the soldiers left him: hanging, dead and bloodied, from the front gates of his own estate, winter flies ravenous at his eye sockets. Isbe didn't even need William's gruesome, whispered description to envision it. She got all the information she required from the stench as they were shoved past, before being dragged roughly inside, thrown to the floor, and bound.

The soldiers who apprehended them are just beyond a closed door, arguing in gruff murmurs.

Perhaps it is stubbornness alone that's keeping her from succumbing to complete panic. That and the lingering question blazing through her brain like fire: *How did the soldiers discover their identities?* It's not like the visages of Deluce's bastard half princess or even Aubin's youngest and thus, until recently, least important prince are well known across the land. Neither of their faces has made it onto any stamps or coins. The mercenaries did find the dagger Isbe was carrying, bearing the royal insignia, but that alone would not be proof of anything.

Perhaps they make an unusual pair: William, with his noble bearing and the smooth dark skin of a highborn Aubinian, and Isbe, with her sightless eyes and raggedly shorn locks. But the soldiers didn't just capture them because they're unusual. They specifically referred to Isbe and William as "the ones we've been looking for."

Isbe can hear their muffled argument through the door, even now. One word emerges from the rest, ringing out like the toll of a bell: "ransom."

William's body goes alert against hers. He has heard it too.

Which is perhaps why neither of them is all that shocked when, a short while later, a couple of the soldiers burst back into the room and, instead of threatening them with violence, simply corral them toward a covered wagon. By now it is getting late, and Isbe can feel the chill as the winter sun begins to sink below the horizon. She's heaved up onto the back of the wagon and hears the swish of leather and clanking of metal rings as a horse is harnessed.

So. She will not be making her journey to the afterlife today.

She will be making the journey, instead, to LaMorte. Presumably to become a pawn in the faerie queen's game.

She thinks of the models William carved. The miniature knights, the ships, and the cannon; how they reminded her of elaborate chess pieces. For some reason, even though she should be thinking about ways to escape, or to die nobly if they're tortured for information, she instead thinks how wondrous it must feel to turn an unyielding mass of ivory or marble into an object that seems to breathe. So different from one of her silly snow statues. She thinks, uncontrollably and irrationally, of William's hands.

A bell peals in the distance—probably all the way from the convent, signaling evening vespers once again. The nuns will be going about their divine offices, pews lined with their devout postures and solemn faces, the prioress probably wondering, meanwhile, where her new visitors have gone.

"Isabelle," William whispers now. It's the first thing he's dared to utter since their capture, and her name itself sounds forbidden to her, foreign. *Isabelle* is a stranger, a woman being held hostage in a war that's only just beginning, her role in it uncertain and out of her hands. Isbe is not that woman.

"Isabelle," he repeats, more urgently. "If we're parted, or . . . if I don't get another chance to tell you this . . ." He wraps his hand around hers and squeezes it.

She feels a small, unexpected shock, like a piece of flint sparking in her chest. A wish, maybe.

But nothing ever comes of wishing, Isbe reminds herself.

He doesn't get to finish his sentence.

Instead, there is a loud swishing rush of wind, like a flock of enormous birds converging nearby. Isbe and William simultaneously tense. There's the startled cry of one soldier, followed quickly by a gargling gasp, as though his partner is choking on his own spit. Then a few swift swipes of fabric through the air, the thump of a skull coming into contact with a rock, and two thuds.

There's a breathy voice, unpeeling the dark like a snake shedding its skin: "Hurry up before the rest of 'em come out."

Isbe knows that voice.

It's Sister Genevieve.

———

Isbe shuffles along the dirt road that leads out of the village, under the hasty cover of the spare habit Sister Genevieve gave her. William too is wearing one. Under different circumstances, the disguise might be comical. As it is, the reality of the situation has begun to sink in. They were nearly killed. Nearly shipped off as bait in a larger conflict. She hadn't been afraid—hadn't allowed herself to be—but now her body won't stop shaking.

"Where are you leading us?" William asks.

Sister Genevieve—and Sister Katherine—are guiding them rapidly through the darkened countryside.

"Somewhere 'ats a bit more fit than where we found ya," Sister Katherine replies.

Isbe's mind is reeling. "But why, how, when . . ." She doesn't even know where to begin. The shock of being rescued by the nuns has yet to fade. "What did you do to the soldiers?"

"Knocked out, but they'll be comin' to shortly," Sister Katherine explains, a note of pride in her voice.

William is obviously just as baffled as Isbe is. "Those men were twice your size."

"She keeps us in good shape, Mother Hilde—"

"Sister Katherine!" Genevieve whispers.

Sister Katherine huffs. "*You* were the one who insisted on rescuing 'em. Said it weren't fair to sell 'em off like a pound o' lambs' meat at market."

"Sell us off?" William asks. Isbe hears the knife's edge in his voice. She is feeling something similar too, down in her gut, like she's been stabbed.

Sister Genevieve sighs. "I suppose you may as well know the truth. The prioress felt we could garner much-needed funds by offering you two up to the enemy. And she was right—we did get a healthy sum."

The invisible knife in Isbe's gut twists. Mother Hildegarde gave them away. "But how did she know who we are?"

Sister Genevieve snorts. "We had our suspicions from the start. Catching you snooping around in the scriptorium didn't help. But it was really Hildegarde herself who recognized you, Isabelle."

"Said you got the same look as your mother," Sister Katherine adds.

Isbe gasps, a strangled sound. "She knew my mother? What did she say?"

"Only that much and nothin' more," says Katherine.

"No need to slow down. We've still got a long way to go and back before morning lauds, or we'll be missed," Sister Genevieve says, pulling Isbe along by the elbow.

"So the prioress has been, what? Training you to defend yourselves against soldiers," William says, something like stunned amusement in his voice.

"'Mong other things," says Katherine.

And then it occurs to Isbe. "Last night—the granary. You weren't checking for vermin at all, were you?"

Sister Genevieve answers. "We were practicing. Every night a group of us stays awake, learning our stances, exercising our skills, handling new weapons. Granary's the perfect spot—big enough, empty enough, and the thick walls hide any sound."

It all begins to unfold in Isbe's mind. "You keep the weapons buried in the graveyard during the day."

There's a silence. "Yes," Katherine answers, clearly impressed that she has pieced it together. "Can't risk anyone discoverin' we're in possession of stolen royal weapons."

Stolen. Isbe feels a flood of victory. She was right about one thing: the convent was not harboring or protecting William's brothers' murderers—they were hiding the weapons and the weapons only. And Hildegarde may have betrayed them, but it was in the interest of supporting a convent full of orphan girls, educating them about the world, and training them to be able to protect themselves in the event of war. The surprise of it is quickly replaced by awe. Isbe would rather be betrayed a thousand times by such a woman than allied to one less brave and interesting.

"We're almost there now," Katherine says.

"Why *are* you helping us?" Isbe asks quietly.

"Because," Sister Genevieve says. "If you really are who Mother Hildegarde says you are, and you plan to seal an alliance between Aubin and Deluce against Malfleur, then we might consider you two our only hope."

Sister Katherine murmurs in agreement. "Only thing more evil than the faerie queen of LaMorte is her dead sister. Nothin' was ever as bad as the Night Faerie, a' course."

Sister Genevieve ignores her comment. "But you two will have to somehow survive the sickness and the mounting presence of LaMorte soldiers. It's said they're immune to it—those beaks they wear protect them somehow—which means for all we know they've already got plans to seize the palace. Time is of the essence. You'll never do it without help."

"And so you're leading us to . . . ," William begins.

"The Veiled Road, a' course," Katherine answers.

"Veiled Road?" Isbe asks.

"It's a safe route through the kingdom," Genevieve explains.

"Mostly servants in noble houses an' the like," Sister Katherine adds, "willin' to help each other out in the case of a military takeo'er."

Isbe marvels and thrills at the idea of the Veiled Road, delighting to imagine the council's shock if they were to find out how organized some parts of the serfdom really are. At the same time, this information is only further proof of what William told her back in Aubin—that Deluce's aristocracy is famous for not understanding the lives and needs of its own peasants. It's something that really needs to change if Deluce is ever to become the kind of nation that can truly defend itself and respond to the needs of the people. A kingdom divided is a kingdom doomed—that much is obvious. Certainly it is obvious to Malfleur.

Isbe's heart rate picks up again as she reminds herself of the urgency of her journey. She needs to awaken Aurora, undoing the curse and giving a sign to Malfleur that her country is not as weak as it seems. But then what?

Then they will have to defend themselves, with the help of William's armies.

They will have to fight.

27

Malfleur,
the Last Faerie Queen

Mountain folk hold a very different view of hunting than plains folk do. Though she resisted at first, the queen has come to learn the nature of the LaMorte people over time, and even to admire their savage, survivalist ways. Still, she hadn't realized how much she missed the more civilized hunting rituals she grew up with—the rhythmic mass of horses moving in unison across wide fields and then the blur of mottled leaves as they cantered through the royal forest. The hounds' zealous barks, echoing under the metallic arc of dawn. The rapid pounding of hooves reverberating through her entire being until she felt herself to be both an intrinsic part of the living landscape and its master, its god.

The queen digs her heels into her stallion's side and leans

forward, savoring the wind in her hair as she races across the greenest valley in the territories. It has been a long time since she has been out on a hunt like this. For a moment, she can almost forget that her kingdom is on the brink of war—a war of her own creation.

She hears her cousin Almandine catching up to her now as they head back to the castle, empty-handed.

"Did you invite me out here after all these years simply to show off your superior riding form?" her cousin asks with a smirk. Her courser's hooves splash across wet mud. "Or to gauge the likelihood of my support for your campaign?"

Neither, Malfleur thinks as she takes in Almandine's impeccable posture, her body almost an extension of the animal's. She's tall for a woman; tall for a faerie too. And unlike most of their other remaining relatives, she has kept up her appearance over the last century, though her hair always has the look of someone who has only recently gotten out of bed.

Yes, Almandine remains one of the prettiest and most self-possessed of the lesser nobility. If Malfleur *were* to desire the company of other fae, she might in fact choose Almandine over the likes of Claudine or Binks, or that blithering Violette.

"Aren't I allowed a visit every once in a while, for nostalgia's sake?" the queen asks.

Almandine shrugs, trotting ahead. Perhaps she even believes Malfleur. After all, a joy in the sports of hunting and hawking *was*, in fact, one of the few things Malfleur and

Almandine used to have in common when they were much younger, though for different reasons. While Malfleur took pleasure in the art of the chase, Almandine was drawn to the athleticism of riding—and the ample opportunities a hunting party afforded for drinking and flirtation, of course.

But this morning, Malfleur didn't have any real intention of capturing prey—at least, not the type to be caught with a bow and arrow.

She has her eye on a far more elusive prize.

She and Almandine approach Blackthorn, their entourage trailing behind. From this angle, it rises up before them regal and full of old-fashioned elegance, unlike the palace in Deluce. Once her childhood home, the Delucian palace now bears almost no resemblance to what it looked like then. King Henri, along with the string of mortal monarchs that came before him over the past hundred or so years, made continual updates to the architecture and interior—paintings that once depicted the faerie histories were replaced with giant portraits of human kings, with their thick beards and rolling stomachs—until the place began to reek of excess and bombast.

You'd never know that a couple of little faerie twins, Malfleur and Belcoeur, used to run through those very halls, laughing and carving notes to each other in the walls. You'd never know there used to be dozens of hidden passages connecting various rooms to form a sort of secret maze throughout the castle. Now, as far as Malfleur knows, their entrances have all been filled in with cheap plaster.

But ever since Malfleur assumed control of the LaMorte Territories all those years ago, she has taken great pains to keep Blackthorn's original beauty intact.

"I never knew you were the sentimental type," Almandine comments, one eyebrow arched smartly as they enter the main hall, where an array of her favorite treats—including distilled mulberry gin—have been laid out. "You really haven't changed this place a bit, even after all these years." She turns to the queen, her amethyst eyes sparkling like the crystal cordial glasses on the tray. "You remember the very first time we were here together, don't you?" She gives a double clap. "*What* a party that was."

Malfleur removes her riding gloves slowly, remembering. A great number of faerie families had been invited up to Blackthorn during the height of hunting season. Back then the fae and the human nobility were much chummier than they are today. She and Belcoeur had come along, though since they were only thirteen years old at the time, their mother tried to forbid them from socializing in the evenings. Of course Malfleur had never been one to obey rules.

"As I recall," she says now, filling Almandine's glass with a generous pour, "you gambled away all of your clothing in a particularly naughty game of whist." Almandine has always been known for her promiscuity. She has even converted her home to mimic a Roman bathhouse, though it's hardly an improvement over a common brothel.

"And *you*, in typical fashion, managed to give up only a single pearl from your necklace," Almandine recounts. "You always were a coy one."

Now Malfleur returns her smile. She remembers how they'd established the rules of their little game—for every trick taken, the player could demand that any other player in the game remove one article of his or her attire. Many of the young men—more seasoned at card games than the women—had focused their attentions on Almandine from the start, who found herself half naked by the third round, precisely because she inevitably chose materialism over modesty, far more willing to give up her fur-collared cape and gown than her jewels.

Malfleur remembers staring in shock at her older cousin, who sat on the arm of a chair, just a lacy chemise slipping off one shoulder, an emerald ring the size of a ram's eye on her thumb knuckle, and her delicate wrist piled high with glinting bracelets as she twisted her hair and laughed with an easy, open mouth.

But when the dashing fifteen-year-old Charles Blackthorn won a hand, he turned instead to Malfleur. She reached up to touch her necklace—the only accessory she wore—then hesitated. The necklace, in fact, belonged to her mother. She'd stolen it before sneaking out of the guest quarters that night. She'd be in terrible trouble if her mother found it missing. Still, her pride prevented her from undoing even a button from her gown. And so she cleverly unthreaded the necklace, removed a single pearl from its string, and handed the pearl to him. The other men in the game laughed at her stunt and pounded Charles on the back, wishing him better luck next time.

Later that night, Charles spotted her as she was sneaking back to the rooms where her sister and parents lay sleeping. He stopped her in the dim-lit hall and took the pearl from his pocket, offering it to her between his fingers. "I would hate for your necklace to remain incomplete."

She stared up at him and replied, "The *night* would be incomplete if you don't keep it. It would mean I had not played fair, had not kept my word."

Charles grinned. "I admire a girl who keeps her word." The way he gazed at her, it was as though he didn't even see the puckered white scar that streaked across her left eyelid, part of her brow and upper cheek. A burn that hadn't healed—and never would.

"So keep the pearl, as a reminder that I am that kind of girl."

He took a step closer and leaned down to her height. "I *will* keep it, then." He held the pearl to his lips and kissed it, which sent a shiver down the young Malfleur's spine, before he replaced it safely in his chest pocket. "You have my word," he said.

It hadn't been until almost a year later, when they were summering at their family's cottage, that Malfleur's mother finally noticed there was something wrong with the necklace, and called Malfleur to her angrily, demanding to know what she'd done. She grabbed her daughter's wrist, hard, and made her watch as she threw the necklace into the blazing hearth, stating that it had been irreparably ruined by her whorish, thieving paws.

Malfleur began to defend herself, fury and humiliation causing the magic in her veins to boil, when Belcoeur
appeared and took the blame, claiming she had borrowed
the necklace to try it on and that she had snagged it, clum-
sily, when she'd gone out to pluck roses from the garden.
Belcoeur was always doing things like that—emerging
angelically at just the right time to stand up for her twin.

Back then, her sister's sweetness had frustrated Malfleur,
as though Belcoeur was purposefully reminding everyone
that she was the kinder, better, more beautiful one. It was
only later that Malfleur began to suspect her sister's intentions
weren't so innocent, began to realize that Belcoeur was like
a shadow—always just to Malfleur's side, smiling benignly,
waiting to inherit the light as soon as her sister left it.

After all, no one could ever compete with Malfleur's
magic—or challenge it—except for Belcoeur.

———

Almandine has traveled with a retinue of her favorite servants, and as she tips back her third glass of mulberry gin,
one of them is rubbing her bare feet with oil—a tall, golden-
skinned man with shoulder muscles that bulge through his
livery. She moans softly, her eyelids half lowered.

"My dear," Malfleur says, hiding her disgust. The memories have given her an unexpected pain in her stomach.
"Have another glass."

Almandine grins drowsily and accepts.

"Tell me." The queen sits back down in her claw-foot chair and stares at her cousin. "Have you ever considered a different tithe?" She keeps her voice casual.

Almandine's heavy eyelids flutter open slowly. "I . . . whatever do you mean?"

"Never mind," Malfleur answers quickly. She expected her cousin's confusion. Faerie tithing is quite simple—it's an unspoken bargain between two people. A willingness, a desire. Whatever the faerie desires most is what he or she tithes. In Almandine's case, it's a sense of touch. In Malfleur's, it's youth, beauty, *time*. Tithes rarely change because the fae don't change. Their core desires remain the same forever, defining who they are.

Or so Malfleur thought, until she began her experiments.

Almandine shakes her head. "You're an odd one, my dear. I've never doubted that. You and your puzzles." She instructs the servant to massage her neck next. "Speaking of puzzles, I do wonder how you really intend to take over the Delucian throne when the kingdom is ravaged by this, this . . . sleeping sickness. Do you know anything about it?"

Malfleur can't tell whether Almandine is testing her.

"After all," her cousin goes on. "How will your own troops survive? Isn't it interesting how a curse has come both to devastate the palace and protect it?"

Now the queen is certain—she's *definitely* goading her.

But Malfleur isn't easily ruffled. "That's simple,

sweetheart. I figured out how to create a resistance to the sickness! The same way anyone would—by first understanding the cause."

Almandine once again looks baffled . . . and a little curious. "Do share."

Malfleur retrieves a set of wrapped sketches drawn up by her minister of war and begins unrolling them on the table beside her cousin. She watches in satisfaction as Almandine gapes at the black, beaklike masks she has devised for her soldiers.

Almandine shivers. "I confess I don't understand. . . ." She hesitates. "But I see why everyone believes what they believe about you."

"Which is?"

Almandine looks at her and murmurs: "That you are evil."

"Is that so?" Malfleur keeps her tone neutral. "I suppose we'll see about that, won't we?" She can tell by the way Almandine stiffens that she has succeeded in unnerving her. "Wait here." She pushes out of her chair and makes her way to the dressing chamber in the east hall.

She tilts the mirror toward her, its surface dinged and scratched from the panther's attempts to attack its own reflection. Malfleur smooths her riding dress and then touches her face, which, thanks to her tithe, is almost as youthful as it had been when she was only thirteen, when she first met Charles Blackthorn—despite the mottled scar across one eye, the one she's known for, the one she'd had since early childhood. And yet an entirely different person looks back at her. Gone is the innocence that once brightened her eyes. Now they are dark and hard like polished onyx.

She takes in a slow breath. She can't believe Almandine thinks she actually invited her here to gain her support. No. Almandine, like nearly all of her kind, has proved herself worthless over the past century.

The once glorious race of the fae has burned down to just a few glowing embers.

But if today goes as planned, it will be the beginning of a whole new era. It will mean she's on the brink of a greater power than any faerie in the history of the known world has ever possessed. For the fae have only ever tithed from humans. In that way they've always depended on the race that has been slowly, for many centuries, displacing them. But Malfleur has been practicing, learning to tithe more than just youth and beauty. And now, she hopes, she has mastered the greatest feat ever: tithing *magic*.

She has failed before. Aimed too high. Sometimes when she closes her eyes at night, Malfleur still sees the Red Throne . . . and the blood of the North Faerie staining her hands.

That had been an accident. The goal was never to kill the other faeries, not exactly. Only to take what was most important to them.

After she succeeds with Almandine, there'll be no stopping her. Soon no one will be able to match her power.

Not even Belcoeur.

28

Isabelle

Isbe used to enjoy teasing her sister for her notions about love and marriage and, of course, the princes of Aubin. She always thought romance was a cloudy concept, like the steam over a pot of boiling stew—it smells of hearty ingredients, it warms the senses . . . but ultimately it dissolves. It won't satisfy you and certainly won't keep you alive. The soup of life is something else: it's the things you do to build up who you are—exploration of the world and of your own mind. The important thing, then, is the soup. But like steam, romantic love in and of itself has no survivalist function. It's just the excuse rich people use so they can marry and procreate and continue their lineages; so they can go on perpetuating the belief that their families deserve to live in giant, fully staffed palaces while every other family is forced to cling to any crust of bread they can get their hands on.

There are many things Isbe *used* to believe.

But similes elude her now. All she can fathom currently is the proximity of Prince William's very literal, semi-unclothed body. Which is, now that she thinks about it, coated in completely nonmetaphorical steam.

That's because they happen to be hiding out in a stone-walled sauna, deep in the cellars of the faerie Almandine's estate, where a servant insisted they'd be least likely to be discovered. They're sitting on benches on opposite walls facing each other, and William's doublet is currently lying discarded somewhere. They were told nearly an hour ago to wait here for Annette, the head housemaid, who was supposed to come for them and show them to a safe room to sleep for the day, before commencing their travels.

"Perhaps we could at least remove a few of the rocks," Isbe mutters now. The sauna is heated with hot stones from a fire that are then dunked in water, creating the steam that heats up the enclosed space. She's glad for once that she chopped off her hair—at least she doesn't have to feel it sticking wetly to her skin. Then again, the shorter locks make her feel more vulnerable too. More exposed.

"You heard what they said," William replies. The mistress of the house likes everything maintained, apparently. She'd notice if the servants didn't keep the sauna heated throughout the day and night. "Still, I suppose it's a bit unfair for you."

"Why for me?"

"Well, I don't need to worry about modesty. I could be sitting here naked and you'd never know." There's a bit of laughter in his tone, though his words make her feel even *more* overheated.

"It *is* unfair," she admits. "I have a feeling if I were to undress, you might notice."

"I'm sorry to admit it, but I definitely would."

If there was any doubt before, Isbe is fairly certain now that the prince is flirting with her. They are, in fact, flirting *with each other*. This has been happening more and more recently. Their conversations will stray from political strategy to philosophical musings to quick-fire banter without her realizing how they got there.

"Anyway," she says now. "It doesn't matter. It's women who are taught to be modest, not men. You can do pretty much whatever you want without impunity."

"Now that I disagree with," William responds.

"Really? Imagine my surprise. You *never* disagree with me," she says. "But do tell. For what action would you, as a man, risk censure?"

"For one thing, I can't play the harpsichord in public. I would definitely receive censure for *that*."

She laughs. Sometimes it startles her the way William makes her laugh, even though they are on a potentially deadly mission. She *shouldn't* be happy, she tells herself. Not when her sister may not survive the sickness. Not when their country is being invaded by the forces of an evil faerie queen. Not when she is stuck in a morbidly hot chamber with a distractingly interesting prince who does not belong to her, and never can, and never will.

Then again, she's heard peasants laugh openly and freely even during the cold of winter, when their bones practically protrude from their thin shifts. She's heard a dying orphan squeal with secret glee. Happiness is funny like that. It's not bound to circumstance.

She adjusts her dress, feeling how it clings to her, wishing she could just rip it off her body like she might have done when she was a child playing in the stream with Gilbert.

Gilbert. There's another source of painful confusion. How can she feel what she's feeling now in the presence of William and still know in her heart that she has never cared for any boy the way she cares for Gil? It's possible she may never know for sure whether he survived, may live in half mourning until the day she dies.

The playfulness evaporates from her heart, replaced with a tightness: guilt for joking about a *harpsichord*, let alone with Prince William, the man she is bringing home for her sister to marry. She fidgets, the heat starting to go to her head. It's definitely hot in here . . . but she and William have become accustomed to hiding out in unusual places over the last week, ever since their rescue by Sisters Genevieve and Katherine. The two nuns had left them at a crossroads that night, just before dawn, with explicit directions to the first stop on the Veiled Road, though Sister Genevieve warned that if they didn't arrive before sunup, they'd be as good as dead. Malfleur's mercenaries in Isolé would by then have redoubled their efforts to locate Isbe and William, who wouldn't stand a chance on their own in broad daylight.

And so for nearly a week they've been traveling like this, under the cover of night, from house to house along the Veiled Road, ushered in by servants who, increasingly, seem to have heard about them and their plans. Despite the fact that they previously understood the alliance to be deeply unpleasant to most of the serfdom, it turns out that the story of the bastard princess of Deluce and the third prince of Aubin has reached—and inspired—many throughout the land.

Many people no longer see Malfleur as a trumped-up threat invented by the council, but a real looming danger, thanks to her gruesome mercenaries raiding so many villages along the western and southern borders, threatening serfs, and killing nobles. And while the sleeping council is still out of favor among the masses, it seems many of the serving class are willing to look on an alliance with renewed optimism. It's incredible, really, how terror can change the tides of a kingdom.

Which is how Isbe and William have come to find themselves in yet another secret chamber within the estate of a very rich noblewoman—and a faerie, at that. They were surprised at first to learn that Almandine's home was a stop on the Veiled Road. They had, perhaps naively, assumed that much of the faerie population supported Malfleur, if for no other reason than the fact that they feared her retaliation if they didn't. Then again, Almandine herself might simply have no knowledge that her servants are part of the anti-LaMorte resistance.

Beads of sweat drip down Isbe's back.

"In all seriousness, Isabelle," William says quietly; he seems to have noticed her mood darkening. "I may have many privileges, as a royal, and as a male. But I am not free to do whatever I would wish. I am not free, for example, to choose whom I marry—or to marry for love."

The silence after his words is heavy. "I'm not sure what you mean," Isbe finally responds. "You agreed to come with me. You agreed to marry Aurora. For the alliance. That was absolutely your choice. And . . ." She takes a breath, finding herself sick to her stomach to have to repeat this once again. "You *will* fall in love with her when you see her."

And then the two of them will have the true love that is destined to undo the curse. This is the wild hope, like a hand in the dark, to which Isbe has been clinging ever since she and Gilbert left Binks's study, which seems like it occurred in a former lifetime but was actually less than a fortnight ago.

William hesitates before responding. Isbe realizes that every time he pauses, every time he takes a breath, she unconsciously holds hers in, waiting. And when his words come, they rush to her, convincing and taut as a harpoon's line, their point snagging her in the heart and pulling, pulling. . . . "Tell me something else about her," William says.

Isbe leans against the wall, its cool, damp marble providing small relief to the overwhelming heat.

She can't help it. She doesn't want to talk about Aurora—not in this moment, not when she can feel the intensity of the prince's gaze on her skin; not when the steam is wrapping itself around her senses, making her emotions slick and difficult to hold in, like if she lets her guard down for even a second, some secret truth may slip out that she'll forever regret.

And yet the details pour out of her—because some parts of us never change. Some facts are inalterable. You cannot crack open Isbe's heart without releasing the purest form of love she knows: her love for her sister.

She tells him about her favorite childhood memories, their secret language, the hidden passageway connecting their bedrooms, the snow sculptures and the games of make-believe, the stories they told each other, the tricks they played on the stuffiest of council members.

She even tells him some of the darker memories: how Queen Amélie used to scorn Isbe, sometimes refused to let her sit at the dinner table with the rest of the royal family, slapped her hands and face when she disobeyed her nurses, and found elaborate—almost hilarious—ways to place blame on her for absolutely everything, from the grand hall getting too drafty in winter to the beets being stewed too long, to King Henri withholding his affection from her (because, the queen argued, Isabelle reminded him of his former love—an absurd claim, when everyone knew he had countless flings, all meaningless and disposable, prior to marrying the queen).

And how, amid all this, Aurora would sneak Isbe treats

from the kitchen when she was sent to bed without supper, or bring thick feather-stuffed blankets from her room when the frigid air coming off the strait snuck under the doorframe and chilled her bones. Though she couldn't stand up for Isbe by speaking, Aurora found countless ways big and small to remind Isbe that she *did* matter. Whatever happened, however hard things got, Isbe always knew that Aurora was there for her.

Isbe doesn't notice the wetness at the corner of her eyes until she feels the heat of the sauna increase as William leans closer, his fingers grazing her cheek, wiping a tear away.

"Isabelle," he says softly.

And just as quickly, she is shot forward from the past into the *now*. The memories burn off, and she can only think of how close the prince is, how steady and calm his voice is, how his fingers dance across her skin—not at all in the awkward, mechanical way he claims to play the harpsichord, but freely, as though he's reading her expression the way she has read Gilbert's and Aurora's for years. He has moved to sit beside her on the same bench, and she's uncomfortably aware of the fact that he is bare-chested. This man who teases her but also takes her so seriously . . .

This man who calls her by her full name.

This man who somehow blots out all reason, who makes her almost forget all of the impossible walls between them: Aurora. Gilbert. Status and rank and her formerly stalwart loathing for all things romantic. Not to mention the fate of both their kingdoms.

This prince who is not hers to fall for.

"Yes?" she says, to fill the space between them. She realizes now why she is always in such suspense when he speaks. It's because he never finished saying what he wanted to tell her back when they were captured by Malfleur's soldiers and thrown into the carriage bound for LaMorte. In the days that have passed since, he hasn't brought it up.

"What if there's another way to establish the alliance?" he asks hoarsely.

"Another way?"

"Please." He puts his hand on her shoulder. "Don't pretend to misunderstand me."

"Pretend . . . I'm sorry . . . what?"

"Your sister may or may not awaken."

She doesn't like his tone, so weighty all of a sudden. The air around her feels thick. It's hard to breathe. "She *will*. We have to try."

"There are no guarantees. She may not wake up."

"Stop saying that. You don't think I know that?" The heat of the tiny room envelops her, rising up from within to choke her. "Giving up on Aurora is not an option. Not for me." Her throat is so tight she's not sure if she can continue speaking.

"I'm not saying I want to give up!" He lets go of her shoulder.

"Then what *are* you saying?"

"I want the alliance, like you do. We have agreed it's mutually beneficial." *Mutually beneficial.* Why does the phrase sting so much? The words ring cold in her ears like a piece of silverware that has clattered to the floor.

She swallows back her discomfort. "Yes. We have agreed." Emphasis on agreed. He doesn't seem like someone who would go back on his word, which is why she's finding this turn in the conversation so perplexing.

"Well, this journey has allowed me to do some thinking since then."

No. If he backs out now, she's not sure what she'll do. She'll scream. She'll explode. She'll find the closest poniard and rip open his throat. Well, maybe not that. But she certainly wouldn't be afraid to point its blade meaningfully at his neck.

He clears his throat. "And I've realized that I no longer want to marry Aurora."

"You don't . . . you don't want to marry my sister? But that's the whole point. How else can we undo the curse? How else do we convince the kingdoms? How else do we send a powerful enough message to Malfleur?"

"I'm not trying to talk politics."

"What?" Now he really has her confused, and she's beginning to think the sauna steam has melted her mind into little more than a puddle.

"Isabelle!" he says, exasperated. He grabs her hand. "My marital interests lie elsewhere now. Have you not considered it?"

Has she not considered it. Considered it. Considered . . . what? She feels nauseated.

"Let me rephrase that," he adds quickly. "*Will* you consider it?"

"Will I consider . . ."

"Being my wife."

She chokes and leans forward, coughing. Her eyes water. She must have inhaled saliva. She must have also lost her hearing. She coughs again, and the coughing turns into a delirious sound that can only be described as deranged laughter.

"You think I'm joking?"

"No—I—" She breathes. "I got confused. I thought you were—"

"Proposing to you? I was. Trying to, at least."

"*What?*" she blurts out, cheeks burning. "If that's your idea of a proposal, then you should stick to playing the harpsichord." She clears her throat, immediately regretting her reaction.

"I'm serious. I take it, however, that you are not interested."

"Not interested?" She shakes her head, unable to process the wild mix of emotions—she's elated and shocked and terrified. Confused and mortified and overwhelmed. All she can do is focus on his words. "What I'm interested in," she says slowly, trying to make him understand, trying to make *herself* understand. "What I'm interested in doesn't matter."

Why does she feel so choked up? It's the truth, anyway. The firmest thing she can hang on to. This journey isn't about her. It's about the kingdom. About her sister. About William, even, but not about her.

"Is that a no?" His voice has gotten quieter, his grip on her hands less certain. Now he lets them go, and she feels something inside her, something carefully constructed, beginning to splinter.

It's a struggle to speak. The word *no* seems so heavy, so final. She shakes her head. "You're marrying my sister."

William slides away from her on the bench. "I see."

Isbe wants to cry, or maybe to scream. "Apparently you don't."

How can she explain why his idea is so impossible? It just *is*. Aurora is the one to be wed. Aurora is the beautiful one, the crown princess, whose title matters—who matters, *period*. Prince William choosing Isbe would be laughable. No one would take it seriously. Isbe lives on the sidelines. Isbe stays in the shadows. Isbe *is* the shadow. Aurora is the light. These facts are as natural to her as the knowledge that the sun rises in the morning and sinks at night. Some things just are the way they are. It may not be fair, but she has learned to accept it, learned to live with it, learned not to want things she can't have, because wanting those things hurts too much.

"I'm sorry, really. I didn't mean to upset you," he says.

"Well, you *have*," she responds, the hurt—and the fear of that hurt—curling into a tight ball in her throat. "I really wish you hadn't said such a foolish thing. It wasn't thoughtful of you at all."

"It didn't occur to me that you'd be angry," he answers roughly.

It didn't occur to her, either. But she *is* angry. He knows so little about her, truly. He knows nothing of Gilbert, who might be dead. Gil, the person to whom she always believed she would give her heart, if she were ever to give it away.

And did William even consider what it must feel like for her to have to decline a proposal from a prince? A prince whose unexpected brashness thrills her. A prince whose bravery and steadiness have, in a very short time, become an intrinsic part of her own? A prince who is clumsy with musical instruments but swift with a weapon and full of grace when he touches marble, molding it into beauty—and too when he touches *her*. A prince who freely uses big words like variegated and susurrus. A prince who is willing to think differently than his brothers, than his countrymen, than anyone else she knows. Maybe *if* Isbe were the crown princess . . . or *if* William were not the last heir of Aubin . . . or *if* Aurora weren't in trouble . . .

But none of those things are true. She opens her mouth to remind him so, when instead, the door of the sauna is thrown open and a burst of cold air shocks her into silence.

"Not to fear. It's me, Annette," says the woman who must be the head housemaid of the estate. She speaks elegantly, without the accent of many of the peasants Isbe and William have encountered on their journey. "You can come this way. And please do hurry."

William couldn't have stood up any faster even if his breeches had caught fire. He throws his doublet back on with a hasty *thwack*.

"We're ever so flattered to be of service to you both," Annette says, leading them through an elaborate maze of servants' quarters, "and grateful for your efforts during these . . . difficult times."

As they move through Lady Almandine's estate, Annette explains that the household servants are all taught in the arts of massage and that their primary duties involve maintaining the various salt- and clear-water baths of differing temperatures. According to Annette, there is an entire room full of twigs, dedicated to "whipping the blood into a frenzy." Lady Almandine apparently also has many personal trainers who keep her well practiced in the arts of riding and fencing and dancing. And then, there are the lovers.

Isbe blushes as Annette lowers her voice, continuing to gossip about her ladyship. "Lady gets all kinds of . . . *private* visitors," she says. "Big, small, tall, short. Men, women, and some whose sex I couldn't tell you if I tried. That's why there are so many snaking halls throughout the house. Many ways for her . . . *friends* . . . to arrive and depart discreetly. It's also why we've become one of the most important junctures on the Veiled Road," she explains with pride.

"Ah," Isbe says, though the last thing she wants to hear about at the moment is the intimate life of a deranged faerie, when all she can think of is William and his proposal. He is deathly silent during their tour through the underbelly of the estate.

"Though Lady Almandine hasn't taken any visitors at all in the last week," Annette goes on, her chatter becoming white noise in Isbe's ears. "Acting strange lately, she has . . . not herself, that's for sure . . ."

Only some of the words reach Isbe. What she's really listening to is William's silence.

"No pleasure in it," Annette is saying. "None at all. Changed, that's certain."

Isbe can only assume William resents her now, maybe even hates her. Men, she knows, cannot stand to have their egos stomped on. But he *had* to be let down. He was the one in the wrong. He never should have said what he did. She can only hope the steam had gone to *his* head, like it had to hers, and that he'll come to his senses and apologize. Then they can attempt to bridge the deep rift of awkwardness that has now come between them. But given his hard, angry stomps on the marble staircase as they make their way to the safe guest quarters, she's not sure that day will come very soon.

Annette keeps talking, oblivious to the tension between her two charges. "Not since her visit to the faerie queen Malfleur," she whispers.

"I'm sorry, what about Malfleur?" Isbe asks, finally tuning in to the housemaid's voice.

"Oh, just speculation, of course. The lady went out to see her cousin in LaMorte almost a week ago for a so-called hunting trip, and we don't know if she's pledged her support for the evil queen or not. To tell the truth, none of us can get a sense of *what* really happened during that visit. Only that something has very much changed in the lady's demeanor since her return, and she won't stop muttering about long-beaked birds. Vultures."

"Disconcerting," Isbe agrees. Does this mean Almandine is pro-Malfleur? When they arrived here this morning, Isbe was full of hope. Maybe Almandine could even help them, she'd thought. If she was present at Aurora's christening, it is possible she knows something about the curse and how it works. Now it's clear that it would be far too dangerous to risk discovery.

Annette goes on to tell a horrifying story about one of their horses, who bolted a month ago only to be found days later on the side of the road, gutted by another animal—something with claws and fangs. Definitely wasn't wolves, Annette says. Possibly some sort of mountain lion or wildcat, they couldn't be sure. Meanwhile, Isbe goes back to focusing on the prince and his stubborn shroud of silence. She tries to remind herself that it doesn't matter: he can hate her now, as long as he sees through his commitment to her. As long as he falls in love with her sister, kisses Aurora awake, and seals the alliance between their kingdoms. Nothing else is important: not their friendship, if that's what they'd had up until a few moments ago.

And certainly of least importance is the way her chest feels like it's been cleaved in two by a war hammer.

Annette finally stows them away in a clean room that smells of salt and roses. Winter sunlight penetrates the room through warbled crown glass, warming her face. There is, however, only one bed. Rather than discuss the issue,

William, as he has often done these past few days, settles onto the floor. She hears the clinking buckles of his belt and boots as he tries to get comfortable, still not saying anything.

She climbs wordlessly into the bed, pulling the sheets up around her damp dress. All the heat from the sauna has fled from her body and left her feeling shivery and exhausted.

She's surprised a little while later, and a bit disappointed, to hear William's faint breathing on the floor beside the bed. He has fallen asleep. She can't fathom how that's possible. He has robbed her of that ability.

The more she lies there trying to sleep, the more awake, and restless, and *angry* she becomes. They are within riding distance of the Delucian palace at this point. The only two things stopping them from continuing the rest of their journey today are one, the fact that it's still daylight, and therefore dangerous, and two, they still aren't sure how they are going to protect themselves against the sleeping sickness. They don't know how contagious it really is—nor, more importantly, how it passes from one person to another.

Up until now, Isbe's goal has been theoretical at best. But it's about to become all too real. Either they will make it to Aurora and succeed in waking her, or they will fail. Within a day or two at most, she'll have her answer.

Her still-wet clothes cling to her, the fabric crawling over her skin like a thousand tiny ants. She tries to swallow, but her throat is parched.

She can't sleep. Doesn't want to. She'll have plenty of

time to sleep later, she thinks morbidly, if the sickness gets to her. What does it feel like, she wonders, to be trapped deep in the illness that is ravaging their country?

She's *got* to get William to her sister. She's suddenly intensely consumed with the urgency of it. She needs to see Aurora. She needs to save her. What has she been *doing*, spying on nuns and freeing a narwhal? Traipsing through the countryside and *flirting with a prince*? She's no longer angry at William. She's angry at herself. If she had just stayed the course, everything might have been different. She has to make things right.

Isbe throws back the covers. The sauna must have dehydrated her. She can't think. She needs water, badly.

She stumbles out into the hallway, which is cold and echoey. She wraps her arms around herself and tries to remember which way they came. She's pretty sure Annette pointed out where the kitchens are, but the layout of the house is unlike any other she's been to. She turns left, then takes another left, then after about forty paces she feels around for the staircase she could swear was at the end of the next corridor. . . .

She's not sure which wrong turn she has taken until it's too late. She stumbles into a vast, bright room rich with moisture and minerals. She hears a tinkling sound like a gently flowing spring. This must be one of Almandine's bathing chambers. She is about to back out, but then it occurs to her that perhaps the fountain is potable. Maybe she could just take a quick sip before finding her way back.

She takes a few steps toward the plashing fountain—and hears a gasp.

Isbe freezes in place, with no idea whether the other person in the room has spotted her.

There's another gasp, and then the sound of a woman moaning.

Isbe's ears blaze in alarm. *Oh, no.*

Has she walked in on Lady Almandine with one of her paramours? Isbe feels dizzy with humiliation and disgust. She has to get out of here somehow!

Carefully she takes one step backward, extending her hands to make sure she doesn't bump into anything and make a noise.

Almandine releases another moan. Except it's not *exactly* a moan, and certainly not one of pleasure. It's more like a groan, and a little bit like a quiet sob.

As Isbe stands there trying to figure out how to make an exit without drawing notice, it becomes obvious that these are sounds of anguish. Isbe doesn't know what to do. She would just bolt, but something keeps her rooted to the spot. She has never been at ease with people crying, and truth be told, it never occurred to her that the fae *could* cry. Maybe it isn't the lady of the house after all. It might only be a troubled servant.

"Pardon me," Isbe finds herself saying. "Can I . . . is there something I can do?"

Water swishing.

The person is *in* one of the baths.

She can't imagine the household staff freely availing themselves of the mistress's baths. Isbe swallows hard. So then it *must* be Lady Almandine.

The woman sucks in a breath. "Belcoeur?" she asks abruptly, her voice ragged and shaky. "How—" Almandine's tone changes, hardens. "Your face . . . no. Who are you?" she demands.

"Madame, I apologize, I just—"

"Have you come to help me out of my bath? Here then, fetch my robe," she commands in a husky whisper.

Isbe should really run out of the room, but part of her is riveted, tingling with curiosity. Besides, fleeing would make her seem suspicious. If the lady has mistaken Isbe for a servant, that's far preferable to her discovering the truth. "Your robe? But . . ."

"Don't be stupid. The robe, on the back of the Adonis!"

"I—where?" Isbe fumbles, trying to figure out how to explain. Lady Almandine has clearly not noticed what some find obvious—the blankness of Isbe's eyes. The way they seem to wander, unseeing. She starts to walk to her right, and the faerie huffs. "That's Apollo. The one under the *west* window."

Ah, that helps at least. Isbe moves in the opposite direction—toward the hottest, brightest part of the room, where she can sense the sun has moved past its highest point in the sky. She bangs her shins on what seems to be a large marble vase out of which a small tree sprouts, then feels around, knocking into several more plants and trees until she finds a rather large sculpture that resembles a Greek god, one arm extended—on which hangs a thick knit-silk robe. She grabs it and hurries in the direction of Almandine's voice—the lady has been muttering to herself, her voice like leather on leather.

Now, as Isbe approaches her cautiously, she makes out some of the words the faerie is saying. *Daisy is as Daisy does. Always was. Always was.* She *tsks* to herself. *I should have known. She always was.*

"I'm sorry?" Isbe asks as she approaches the vast marble pool in which the faerie has been bathing. No steam rises to greet Isbe's hands, and she realizes the water is cold. And it's the dead of winter. The woman must be freezing!

"I said I should have known!" Almandine bursts out, clearly distraught.

Isbe holds open the robe, averting her eyes out of politeness, the way Aurora taught her to do.

Lady Almandine stands up with a dripping *swoosh* and slides her arms into the robe's sleeves. Isbe can feel how disturbingly thin the faerie is, all muscle and bone—and how she seems to shudder with cold. "I should have known," the faerie repeats more quietly. "She always wanted what Daisy had."

"Who's Daisy?"

"It's what she called her sister. You look a bit like her— your face, your . . ." She trails off.

"Whose sister?"

"*Malfleur's*, of course," the faerie practically spits. "Their silly flower nicknames. But she was too jealous. Always too jealous of Belcoeur. Belcoeur, who could make even the pestilent vines that *pesked pesked pesked* the forest and stung our ankles blooooooom with sweet blossoms. Malfleur couldn't *stand* it." Almandine grabs Isbe's wrist with slender, clammy fingers. Isbe's pulse races. "I should have known. After what Belcoeur did to her."

"Let me build you a fire," Isbe says, thinking quickly, hoping to urge Almandine on. The woman is clearly rattled, but Isbe is desperate to hear more. Belcoeur kind? Beautiful? The envy of Malfleur? It runs against everything she's ever heard about the famous faerie twins. If she offers further service to the faerie, perhaps the lady will spill more details. "You are too cold."

"Am I?" she murmurs. "I hadn't noticed, I . . . It doesn't matter. I should have . . ." Her listlessness unnerves Isbe. "No wonder her sister stayed in Sommeil. I would have too. I should have *known*." That last utterance a stone plunked into a pool, its weight subsumed and silenced by the water.

"Known . . ."

"What Malfleur wanted. What she . . . what she took. What she'll *take*. From all of us." She leans closer to Isbe. *"All of us,"* she hisses.

Isbe shivers. She fears the woman may topple over and die in her presence. She sounds so weak. Her teeth are beginning to chatter. . . . "What is Sommeil?" Without thinking, Isbe places a reassuring hand on the faerie's arm.

"Don't!" Almandine screams. Her scream turns into a

hacking cry. "Don't touch me. Don't ever touch me. I can't take it. I can't—" The woman is wracked with dry, choking heaves.

Isbe has no idea what to do. She recalls from Binks's story that Almandine is the faerie whose tithe is touch. She's a known sensualist. Just like Annette said. And yet . . . earlier, the housemaid was talking about Almandine having changed since her visit to LaMorte. Muttering about giant-beaked vultures coming to consume us all.

One thing is clear: whatever happened up there in LaMorte has destroyed Almandine. Which means the faerie queen Malfleur is just as powerful—and just as merciless—as they have feared.

As Almandine's coarse weeping turns back into a low, unsteady murmuring, Isbe steps away from her and hurries to the exit. She doesn't want to hear any more. She needs to find William and get out of here.

But the faerie's words reach her even as she's fumbling for the door, and they slither around her like poisoned vines.

"They're coming. They're coming. They're coming."

29

Aurora

The storm has lasted days, and Aurora has yet to fully understand what happened: the kiss that made its mark on her, irremovable—not exactly a wound, but something that she senses will never fully heal or disappear. Her whole body still aches from it. She finds she is trembling as she lies alone in her room, unable to sleep. And yet . . . she thought she'd *know* when true love happened, like she told Heath. But there are no answers, only more questions, more unfulfilled yearnings, more *fears.*

In one instance, though, the truth has crystalized.

She was thirteen; Isbe fifteen. It was raining then too. Aurora was going through a phase of always wanting to dress her older sister up, encourage her to look and act more like a princess and less like a ruffian who happened to stumble into the palace on a stray wind. Isbe, of course, couldn't have been less interested, but that didn't stop Aurora from trying. Lately, Aurora had come to see her sister as the object of an unfolding romance, and the thought fascinated her to no end. This had come about largely due to the secret love letters they had discovered in a cracked stone just outside Isbe's bedroom wall, and which Aurora had read and interpreted to Isbe. They were never addressed to a particular person, and they weren't signed either.

The mystery lit Aurora on fire. Isbe, being blind, could not read. Nor could most women in the palace. Aurora was an exception—without a voice, she was left with long hours during which she'd taught herself the alphabet and a vocabulary of which she was very proud. As for the men, it was likely that only one of highborn blood had the skill of penmanship to write these secret letters. Several distant but not unattractive dignitaries had been visiting court for the past month, and Aurora knew it had to be one of them.

Isbe, predictably, denied the notion that any of the young men might have noticed her favorably, but it was the only explanation, and Aurora was both terrified and thrilled. What would happen if someone asked for her sister's hand in marriage? Would they be separated? She at once longed for the romantic drama to unfold and ached for things to remain the same forever.

On this one particular rainy morning, Aurora had uncovered a chest in a seldom-used visiting room in the west hall, containing lavishly embroidered hennins with long-flowing veils, bejeweled buckles, and sumptuous surcoats lined in ermine and fox, much of which had belonged to her mother, Queen Amélie. The council had ordered most of the queen's personal furnishings and possessions burned a year prior, in an effort to ward off a return of the plague that killed her. But that didn't scare Aurora. She was thrilled to discover that something of her mother's had remained intact. It was a touchy subject between the sisters: when the queen was alive, she had made it no secret that she resented Isbe's presence, a constant reminder of the king's earlier dalliances. But Aurora always felt that they would have learned to love each other, had each given the other a chance. She mourned not only the loss of her mother but the missed chance for Isbe to see her as she had.

Still, belonging to the queen or not, these garments would be perfect for Isbe to try on. Perhaps Aurora might even convince her to parade in them through the quarters where the youngest of the dignitaries was staying.

With one of the sapphire-studded tiaras still in her hand, Aurora dashed to Isbe's room to share the exciting news, shoving open the door without knocking. The sisters never knocked; more often than not they came through the hidden passageway connecting their bedrooms.

She entered and dropped the tiara in surprise. It fell to the floor with a loud clatter. Isbe was not in her room—but Gilbert was. He turned at the sound and blushed deeply. He'd gone through his growth spurt only recently and didn't yet seem to own the breadth of his shoulders. His red hair was matted and wet with rain—he'd clearly climbed in through the window, which was still open. In his hand was a folded piece of thin vellum.

Aurora stared.

It couldn't be. Gil couldn't even write, let alone afford vellum and ink! Besides, Aurora knew the two of them had become very close, but only as friends. Her sister would never entertain the affections of a stableboy, would she? It didn't make any sense.

"Aurora," Gil said quietly.

She cocked her head at him. Her expression must have been all too plain: *what are you doing?*

"I . . . please. Don't tell." He rushed one hand through his dripping hair.

Aurora's forehead crinkled.

"I know. She can't even read them. I realize how ridiculous it seems. I never meant for her to read them anyway. Not really. I have no hope that . . ."

Aurora still stared, confused.

"Roul helped me find a courier to write them out for me."

Disappointment settled into her like a low cloud, dampening all her amorous fantasies. So Isbe had been right—there *was* no foreign dignitary madly in love with her. There *was* no secret paramour. There was just *Gilbert*, the stableboy.

Indignation trumped disappointment. How dare *he* risk the injury of her sister's heart? How dare he crush Isbe's hopes? Though even as she asked herself, she knew that *she* and not Isbe was the one crushed, not by the dashed dream of love but by the unpleasantly ordinary end to the grand story she'd been concocting in her head.

And though she couldn't speak, her body language as she slammed open the door and held it wide for Gilbert said everything: *get out.*

He hurried away, and Aurora seethed, vowing not to tell Isbe what she had learned, hoping that by keeping it a secret, she was in some way keeping safe the belief that one day her sister *would* find true love—that true love did exist.

As the night fire burns down to embers in a corner of her tower room, sending up tufts of smoke as rain filters in from the chimney, Aurora realizes her error, over and over, like the echoing gong of a bell.

Gilbert helped Isbe escape in the dead of winter when the council meant to send her away. He is likely with her sister even now. He has always watched out for her when Aurora could not. It is suddenly clear as polished crystal to Aurora: Gilbert is, and always has been, in love with Isbe.

And Aurora, in expressing her silent disapproval on that embarrassing day three years ago, is likely the reason he never since acted on those feelings.

Though the dashing paramour of Aurora's thirteen-year-old imagination had never existed, someone *did* pine for her sister, did spend time and hard-earned money writing his feelings down on vellum, with no expectation of a return of affection. There was no fantasy, just a real-life boy.

Aurora had been naive then, but she isn't anymore.

And she knows too—has known since seeing the servant girl's aghast face in the gallery—that Wren is in love with Heath.

But she hasn't said anything. She has held the truth close to her, like a love letter that's never meant to be read.

Heath told her he didn't believe in true love, that he never really felt he had a choice before. Now Aurora can't help but wonder whether, if circumstances were different, he'd choose *her*.

That's nonsense, she reminds herself. She can't be with Heath. She's a princess and her kingdom needs her. She must return home to marry the third prince of Aubin.

But this fact no longer remains a fixed point in her mind. Like a firefly, when she tries to look directly at the truth, tries to reach for it, its glow blinks out, allowing the idea to swim mysteriously away, lighter than air. *Home* is not the thing she longs for. Home is a kind of death now—a coffin, walled on all sides, to which she must resign herself forever. For surely her faerie tithes will hold in the real world.

She will no longer have her voice.

She will no longer feel.

She will have to release the fantasy of—maybe, almost—falling in love with Heath.

But how can she stay? Sommeil is dying, starving. Aurora has probably broken the heart of the one girl here who has shown her the most kindness and support. And Heath himself has confessed that he *wants* to believe in love—but wanting to is not the same as believing. In truth, he has given Aurora no promise at all of his feelings or intentions.

And then there's the queen, waiting forever for the impossible return of someone she loves—of Charles Black-thorn, Aurora's almost sure—to set her free.

But that can't be the full story, Aurora realizes as she sits up in bed, her long hair tangled all around her shoulders. What is she missing?

Something must have come between Charles and Bel-coeur. Or some*one*.

30

Vulture,

a Soldier in Malfleur's Army

From where the LaMorte army stands, forming battalion after battalion of muscle and iron on the precipice of Mount Briar, Deluce's palace looks like a tiny oil painting that's been left in the rain. The fog surrounding it appears quaint, like a lady's skirt. A lady they are going to ravage and make theirs.

For a moment Vulture hears a whisper on the wind, a horse's quiet snuffle, and it makes him remember . . . what it felt like to be an *I* and not a *we*. What it felt like to see from all sides of his eyes, instead of through tight black holes. He turns his beaklike mask to the left, and sees the rest of them. The queen calls all of them Vulture. They are no longer individuals but one dark mass of masks and black cloaks, of heavy armor and impenetrable eyes.

Malfleur paces along the cliff, counting off, conveying instructions. She approaches Vulture but keeps walking without any acknowledgment. The queen has forgotten him. She has forgotten that Vulture—*this* Vulture—is special. She had required a talented groom, a skilled rider, someone familiar with destriers and coursers, their behavior, the shape of their long noses. It was he, Vulture—*this* Vulture—who was asked to design the terrifying silver muzzles worn by all of her warhorses.

They wear the beaks for protection from the sickness, which is not, he now understands, her doing—though what terrible magic created it, he cannot say. But the masks do more than just block the disease. They narrow the focus, they separate the man from the world he is riding into, from the victim he must either gain command over or kill.

And there is something deeply reassuring about the darkness within the mask. Vulture can sink back into it like a boundless sea, can let go of almost everything that once made him who he was and weighed him down. All that's left of *before* is a faint twinge. The rest is black ocean, is night sky, is anger, is flight.

But that twinge persists . . . a tiny spark within him that makes him want to go back, to flee the oil vessel in one of the smaller dinghies and look for her, rescue her, or risk death in the vast *real* ocean trying, rather than stay and face the mercenaries who bound him, who threatened him, who gave him no choice, who turned him into what he is now, into one of them. Vulture.

As Malfleur passes him by, he catches a glance of her glossy dark hair, lifted and wild in the breeze, and he sees not the queen, but *her*.

Her, falling backward into the waves alone.

Her, laughing, rebuking, arguing, rallying, racing through fields on a mare's bare back. Her, throwing her hands up to his face to feel what he felt, to change him, to leave her mark on him.

But it is pointless, he knows, to think of her.

For what would Isabelle say if she saw him now?

PART

V

BEFORE BREAK
OF MORN

31

Isabelle

I t's strange to draw near the castle village where she spent her entire life growing up. Isbe thought she would find its familiarity reassuring after their arduous journey. Instead, when William shouts to her that he can see the towers and the drawbridge in the distance, she is overcome with the distinct and uncomfortable sensation of slipping into an old, tight shoe. The smell also reminds her of old shoes, though she has come to realize that it is in fact the odor of death.

Along the road leading here—completely abandoned by travelers—she and William have stumbled upon the rotting carcasses of crows who dropped from the sky having succumbed to the sickness, presumably after feasting on sleeping mice. Even now, William points out another one wobbling awkwardly through the blue dawn, and a moment later she hears it plummet to the ground with a disturbing *thud*.

Isbe grimaces. "What else do you see?" she asks, grateful that he's at least speaking to her again. After a few icy hours, his edges seem to have melted a little.

William breathes slowly beside her. "Vines," he says. "Giant flowers—purple, lush, like big yawning mouths. Collars of thorns all around them. Vines on the castle walls. Vines on the trees and road. An overturned carriage almost entirely covered in them."

Vines. Of course they'd heard about them before . . . but she's reminded of something now. "William," she says, touching his elbow. "Almandine spoke of vines, when she was talking about Queen Malfleur. She said . . . she said something about the queen's jealousy of Belcoeur. Because Belcoeur could tame the vines. Pestilent vines, she said. Belcoeur could turn them into beautiful flowers."

"Belcoeur was killed long ago."

"That's another thing. Almandine said Belcoeur was someplace called Sommeil. Something terrible happened between the two sisters, and now Belcoeur would never return. Maybe Malfleur *didn't* slay her. What if the stories and lullabies are wrong?"

She remembers too the other version of the rose lullaby— the one she sometimes hears in her mother dreams. The one in which the twin faeries play together until nightfall, and no slaying is mentioned at all.

"What if they are?" William asks. "Does it change our mission at all?"

"I'm just thinking. What if Belcoeur is back, and these terrible, beautiful flowers are her doing?"

"Then we have an even greater foe than we thought," William concedes. "But I still don't see how this changes our plans for the alliance." He says "alliance" like the word is made out of a cold, foreign metal.

"Maybe it doesn't," Isbe agrees. She scrunches her brow, thinking. "What was Belcoeur's tithe? The nature of her magic?" She wishes Aurora were beside her. Her sister has all the faerie histories practically memorized.

"I don't know much about the fae. There's another one. . . ."

Moments later, Isbe hears yet another crow fall from the sky. She shudders. "What are you doing?" William has stopped walking, and it sounds like he is squatting down.

"There's something in its mouth," he says by way of explanation.

"Be careful. It carries the disease. It could spread . . ." The sickness has become all too real. She keeps thinking any moment she'll feel a yawn coming on, and it'll be the first sign of the end. Or worse, that William will drop to the ground beside her.

"There's something in its beak," William says, investigating. "Like blood, but it's black. No, it's . . . purple."

"Do you think . . ."

"I don't know, but I don't like it. Let's keep going."

They don't get much farther before she notices something cutting through the smell of death. Saffron. Cloves. Pepper.

"Spices," Isbe says. "A merchant cart." Like the one that drove her and Gilbert to the harbor. It's both shocking and peculiarly comforting—the idea of people going about their trade even during such terrible times.

"I thought the road was cordoned off. We haven't seen any other travelers for miles," William points out.

"True. It's strange. But there can be little other explanation for such a combination of scents." It *is* troubling, though. Why would a spice merchant be traveling this way? And why can she not hear the clop of hooves or clatter of his wagon?

"Isabelle," William says, grabbing her arm and causing her to halt in her tracks right as they are rounding a bend in the road.

"Is it . . . ," she starts.

"You were right. A spice merchant. He's . . ." William lets out a sickened moan, and Isbe has her answer—the merchant is dead. She shouldn't be surprised—they've passed bodies frozen, and even carcasses ravaged by animals from the forest—but somehow this injury, among the list of distresses they've had, stings. Could this be the very man who Binks sent to help them, not so long ago? She recalls that Gil described the man's face as hideously malformed, though he hid it behind some sort of mask worn to manage the overpowering scent of all the spices.

"William. Can you describe what he looks like?"

"Why do you want to know?"

"I may have met him before." She feels her voice break-ing. She doesn't even know the man's name. It makes no sense, not when thousands are suffering and the one person who has ever loved her may be dying. When Gil is gone, possibly for good. And yet it pains her, this minor loss in the grand scheme of things.

She hears William suck in a disgusted breath and then hold it. A moment later, he returns to her side. "His wares are scattered in the road, a rainbow of colored dusts. The man is on his side, no beard, his face sort of . . . swollen. His jowls look like a few clumps of clay that have been mashed together."

So it *is* him. It has to be. "Is he wearing a sort of mask?"

"Hmm. It looks like he *was* wearing one, but it is down around his neck like a fat noose."

She tenses. There must have been a struggle, or he had trouble breathing—something to have caused the mask to be ripped off in a hurry.

"How he even got this far from the palace is a wonder," William comments, echoing her own thoughts. How *could* he have gotten this far before succumbing, like the others who've gone to the Delucian castle and never returned?

"Perhaps he knew something—some way of avoiding the disease. But then it caught up to him." Isbe ponders. "I am worried, William. I know we must advance, but are we walking straight into our doom?"

She feels the tension in his hand, still on her arm.

Her throat gets tight. It isn't just the fear of the disease that gives her pause. If she's honest with herself, it's the conversation they had while in the steam room, deep in the cellars of Almandine's estate. Or, better put, the conversation they *haven't* had since. She still doesn't know what he's thinking—if he regrets his proposal. More importantly, she doesn't know how *she* feels. Thoughts of that awkward moment have been torturing her nonstop since they fled the mansion.

"Should we keep going?" William asks, his voice soft. "The decision is yours. I will respect whatever you choose to do."

Whatever she chooses. But what are her options? They could still back away. They could find their way to Roul's in the hope that Gilbert has returned there safely. She could hide out among the peasants as they await Malfleur's invasion. And then what? Watch as he and his children are strung up to die or conscripted into the faerie queen's army? Sit back while her kingdom is taken?

No. If she's going to die, she'll die having done the right thing. She'll die next to her sister.

"I used to sneak off with a mare called Freckles," Isbe says carefully. "No one likes to ride her because she's unruly. Impossible. She never listens. But the way she runs. Gil—my best friend Gilbert—" She pauses. This is the first time she's even mentioned Gil's existence to the prince, and saying his name aloud rattles her. "He calls the mare a bad mover," she goes on, "but it's not true. She just has her own rhythm, and William, she can go so *fast*." The memory rushes through her. "When we were tearing through woods and fields together, not far from this very spot—I felt like I was really alive. I felt like nothing we'd left behind mattered anymore. I didn't have to know where we were headed. What was important was that we were flying headfirst, like an arrow. Nothing could stop us. I never let go until she threw me."

"And has she thrown you now?" William asks quietly.

"No," she answers, hard and resolute. "No, she has not."

"All right, then," he says calmly. "Let's go."

He heads forward down the road. "Careful of that wheel—it came loose. Here you go." He helps her past the wreckage of the spice merchant's cart, and as he does, he lets out a huge sputtering sneeze. It's a ridiculous sound, coming from so commanding and serious a person.

Despite everything, she laughs.

In a sharp inhale, all the pepper and ginger in the air rises up her nostrils, and she begins coughing and sneezing too.

"No wonder he needed a mask," the prince says, catching his breath.

"Yes, no wonder."

"If only a mask could protect us from the sleeping sickness," William muses.

"Hmm," Isbe replies. "A mask . . . yes. A mask. A mask!" She stops walking and smacks him in the arm. "William, you're brilliant!"

"Are you mocking me?"

"No!" The sincerity of his question—the *hurt* in it—sends a shock through her. He's still upset over the proposal . . . over her rejection. *Because that's what it was,* she realizes. "Despite what you might think of me now, I'm not callous. I think I have a theory on the sickness. What if the spice merchant made it this far from the castle *because* of his mask? It protected him somehow, but when he removed it, he died."

"So you think the disease is airborne, then," William says. "Like the scent of his spices."

"Right. Perhaps."

"Maybe carried by the breath of the birds? That could explain the crow's purple tongue, I suppose."

"The purple tongue . . . no, I have a better theory. It's—"

"The vines," they say simultaneously.

"Smelling them," he says.

"Or eating them, in the case of the birds," Isbe adds. And then, after a pause, "It's faerie magic. Either the work of Malfleur or, more likely, her not-actually-dead sister, Belcoeur. The vines carry a pestilence—like Almandine said. Some sort of poison that puts all creatures who come into contact with their scent to sleep. It explains the presence of the vines, all those flowers you described, and it explains the merchant, and the birds falling asleep midflight. William, it really is brilliant!"

"I didn't come up with it, Isabelle. You did. *You're* the brilliant one."

"Why does it feel like you're mocking *me* now?"

316

His voice is somber, and a little quiet, when he replies. "I'm not."

She shivers. No one has ever told her she was brilliant. But there's something about the way William talks . . . he makes her feel that everything she says and does matters. That he is always listening, always aware of her. That he *cares*, on some fundamental level, about her thoughts and her feelings and her actions and . . . about *her*.

Yes, he cares about her. There is no questioning it.

Suddenly she is very, very warm.

"It's worth a try, isn't it?" she says, trying to keep the smile off her face. For the first time since she heard Binks's tale, she feels driven by something other than a wild, stubborn determination. She is startled to name that thing. *Hope*.

———

Not more than an hour later, Isbe steps cautiously into the suffocating quiet of the palace courtyard with William right beside her, thick swaths of brocaded fabric from his cloak tied in layers around their mouths and noses.

The formerly bustling courtyard is now as still and cold as a tomb. Without her sense of smell, Isbe is doubly alert to the stillness—a fuzzy silence like the pause between snores. Even though she can't detect the signature briny odor of the strait, she can sense its proximity by the salty dampness on her skin.

And then, all at once, a powerful feeling of homecoming floods through her. She lets go of William's arm and begins to run.

Isbe pushes her way through closed doors and down eerily abandoned corridors. She nearly tumbles over the bodies of courtiers, some sleeping and some, she fears, already dead. She can't think about that just yet. She is home. She is home. She is *home*.

She bounds up the stairs, twenty to the landing and then four more, to the door of her sister's bower. She hears William following a few paces behind.

And then she is inside Aurora's room, and then, in an instant, beside her bed, feeling along the neatly made bedspread until she gasps, her hands coming upon her sister's, which are cold. *Too* cold. She leans forward, her heart racing, and touches Aurora's forehead. Her hair is strewn over the pillows. Someone must have carried her up here. She moves her hands to Aurora's chest and can only make out the slightest rise and fall. She gasps hard in relief, nearly choking on the heavy fabric around her face. It seems as though the sleeping sickness has somehow preserved Aurora in this state. She's alive, though deathly thin. She's alive and—

"We've made it!" she bursts out. "William? William, come here. This is her. This is *her*. Aurora." Tears sting her eyes. She finds she is shaking, torn between breaking into hysterical laughter and falling to the floor exhausted. It is hard to breathe. Hard to think. She's back. And Aurora is alive. Everything is going to be all right. They're together again.

William comes over to her, kneeling down by the bed and wrapping one arm around Isbe. Without thinking, she gives in to his slight pull, leaning against his side, trying to slow her breath, wishing she could rip off her mask and laugh, shout, kiss him.

No.

Quickly she banishes the last idea from her mind.

For several moments, both of them just sit there like that, facing Aurora's sleeping form, saying nothing.

And then she feels him take a deep breath, and when he lets it out, he says, "My future wife."

The words echo through the room like marbles scattered from a jar.

Isbe says nothing. She says nothing, and says nothing, and then says more nothing. Minutes tick by until she's convinced that they too have caught the sickness and that it is gradually numbing their throats and minds.

Finally she steels herself, stepping back into the role she has always played, the invisible armor she has had to wear every day of her life, just before entering the dining hall to meet the critical gaze of her stepmother, or undergoing another lecture by the council, or hunching beneath the blow of an angry kitchen wench's metal pot. And then, invisible armor in place, she takes that cumbersome, weighty, ever-expanding *nothing* and turns it into *something*.

"Kiss her," she commands, her chest made of iron. "It's time."

William doesn't respond. He doesn't, to her relief—or dismay, or incomprehensible regret—resist.

She holds her breath. She holds everything back, every

single feeling and thought shoved into a dark cove at the very heart of her—other than one: *wake up.*

Wake up. Wake up. Wake up.

William leans over the bed. He lifts his mask almost silently. He hesitates one more moment and then—

"Isabelle," he whispers. She realizes she's been frozen—she's not sure for how long.

"Yes?" she whispers back.

"It's not working."

"What do you mean it's not working?"

"I kissed her. She hasn't stirred. Did you . . . did you really think she would?"

Fury flies up Isbe's spine. "You aren't doing it right. You must love her. It's the kiss of true love. It's . . . she believed in it. It's—it can't be any other way." Her throat burns. Her lungs are on fire. She is going to be sick. "You are her destined husband," Isbe insists desperately. "And it's *Aurora.* She's so beautiful. She's so perfect!" Isbe shudders, her voice breaking like shattered glass.

Anger sparks and then gutters into shame, dismay, confusion. How can it not work? It has to work. Not for any logical reason, but by sheer dint of her needing it to. Of wishing it so.

But wishing never got anyone anywhere.

"I'm sorry," he murmurs, and his now-familiar, rustling-leaves voice blows through her with chilly certainty.

It didn't work.

Aurora is still asleep.

32

Aurora

Aurora drags a heavy ax through the quiet of the sleeping
castle, dew still clinging to the hem of her dress. The
morning fields had opened before her like a series of yawns,
great mouths watering with hunger, and she'd allowed them
to swallow her for hours as she wandered, searching. Since
the necklace of pearls and rubies now lay scattered throughout the Borderlands, she'd need something else, she knew,
something powerful—stronger than the rose lullaby. An
object from the real world that could break through the
queen's illusions once and for all.

And then she remembered the story Heath had told her,
of the soldiers who first tried to break out of Blackthorn,
one of them successfully forming a rift in the wall with an

ax. And so she'd scoured the estate, finally coming upon a store of tools. This ax had stood out to her as different from the others—a complex design decorated the stone head. The wood of the handle was weathered and old. It *felt* firm in her hands, definite, unlike so many other objects in Sommeil, which seemed to give just slightly when held, to take on some flavor of the person who had touched them.

As she passes through each of the now-familiar rooms and halls of Blackthorn, Aurora reminds herself that this might be the last time she sees them. She knows what she must do: she must make Belcoeur remember. She must make her realize that Charles is never going to come, and that jealousy has eroded her mind. If the queen can let go of her jealousy, she can let go of her dreams and move on. She can set Aurora free—set all of them free.

Though Aurora isn't certain who came between Charles Blackthorn and Belcoeur, she has a good guess. After all, she knows something about jealous sisters. Wasn't it the last thing she said to Isbe before her own sister fled? *Don't be jealous of me.* Aurora knows the unfairness of life better than anyone: some are born princesses, some bastards. That is how the world has always worked and will always work; those who are born blessed will be the envy of those who are not.

The musty scent of the corridor leading to the north hall clings to Aurora's senses, filling her with sadness. She feels draped in its longing like a physical weight, its stickiness like a spider's web that wants to pull her back, back, back—the walls whisper. *Stay.* They throb. *Don't hurt us,* they seem to say.

But sometimes pain is the only way.

She reaches the north hall, and the door that only recently had opened elegantly before her, inviting her closer to the queen's lair. Once again, however, the door is locked. The knob is cold and hard as bone. The castle is so quiet she can hear her breath loud in her ears.

Don't hurt us. Stay.

Aurora's arms pulse from the weight of the ax. She lifts it over her head.

And then, she swings it down.

A loud *krick-crack* ripples through the air as the stone axhead meets the wooden door, splintering it. *Pound . . . pound . . . thwack.* It takes several swings, and with each, the door shudders, cries, cracks further, and Aurora could swear she feels how it wants to heal itself closed, keeping her out. The splintering wood seems to sigh a final *stop.* She swings again, throwing all of her strength into it.

Finally the door collapses.

Her hands are raw. Her back is strained and tight. Her arms feel like lead.

She grabs a lit torch from a sconce and steps inside. The hall of tapestries. The den of fog.

Finding her way around the wing doesn't prove easy, though. There are doorways that cut right in the middle of walls that lead to twisting tunnels, each impenetrably dark, studded with mouse droppings and the occasional chilling sound of scratching or whimpering—Aurora soon finds herself disoriented. It's not just the winding passageways of the forbidden wing that have her so turned around. She has the distinct impression that the chambers have all stood up and rearranged themselves every time she emerges into a new room, like an endless maze.

And then she recalls that her own palace used to have many of these tunnels before they were blocked with plaster—all but the one connecting her room to Isbe's. *Yes.*

As quickly as the thought comes to her, she is able to slide back a wall hanging and enter another passageway, one sloped steeply upward . . . and uncomfortably familiar.

Aurora lets out the breath she didn't know she was holding as she bursts out the other side, into a tower bedroom that looks very much like her own at home.

She takes in the neatly made bed with its drooping lace canopy, the gilt mirror, and the vanity with a hairbrush lying on it, the half-woven tapestry stretched across a loom in one corner.

The room is empty but filling with the same dark fog that has followed her this far. At the foot of the bed is a trunk. She kneels before it and throws open its lid. She braces herself for more horrors—bugs or rodents or even decayed bones. But instead she finds only a heap of objects that appear to be the queen's private treasures. Across the inside of the curved lid, words have been scratched into the wood:

Everyone deserves true love.

The message sends an odd jolt down Aurora's spine. There's a rotting wedding veil, and beneath it, several old, nearly hairless dolls. Below those lie a small, flat rectangle of wood. She picks it up and turns it over. On the other side is a portrait of two little girls. Their faces look very alike, though one is sharper somehow, and has darker hair.

Marigold.

The sister with the lighter hair is holding a daisy and smiling, while Marigold is looking somewhere past the portrait artist's position.

Understanding cascades through Aurora: Marigold is an Impression of *Malfleur* as a child, one created by Belcoeur, whom her sister called Daisy. The painting—and Marigold's existence at all—indicate that Belcoeur cared deeply about her twin, despite what the stories would have had Aurora believe.

She sets down the portrait and looks to the bottom of the chest, which is covered in a dark, rusty stain. She knows what it is. Blood.

"Stop."

Aurora turns around to see—not Belcoeur but Wren, standing in the doorway wringing her hands.

"I have to do this," she says to the girl. Her voice floats out of her with an authority that surprises her. "I have to confront the queen."

"No, you don't. You could just leave it, leave us." Wren's voice has a slight warble to it, like it could break. "You've done enough damage."

They stand facing each other in the dark bedroom. "That's just it. I need to fix this. I need to go home." Aurora keeps her mind and her words focused on those truths.

"But what about Heath?" Wren asks.

Aurora shakes her head, willing the tears not to fall. "Please forgive me," she says. "I never meant for . . . I didn't know. Please don't be jealous of me."

"Jealous of you?"

"Because of the kiss—because you—"

"Aurora." Wren folds her arms across her chest. "I know Heath better than anyone. Certainly better than you. I *know* him; I know what he's like. He hasn't chosen you, and he never will." Her calm tone sends a shiver up Aurora's spine.

"But, but . . . you *love* him," Aurora says quietly, her heart still aching for the girl, and for herself, and for the impossibility of the true love in which she once believed.

"Love," Wren replies, "does not have room for jealousy. It is just a thing you know, a part of who you are forever. It's inalterable."

"But he *kissed* me," Aurora sputters. "And it's more than just that. I know it is. I can feel that it's more. It's just like what happened to the queen."

Wren cocks her head. "What do you mean?"

"Belcoeur loved Charles Blackthorn. But I think he fell for her sister, Malfleur. That's why Belcoeur made Sommeil and retreated into her world of dreams. She didn't want to have to face a life without true love," Aurora says, telling the story as if it's one she's read a thousand times in her library.

"Her jealousy is what destroyed her."

"You have it all wrong," says a raspy voice.

Both Aurora and Wren go silent. Wren pushes her way into the room beside Aurora as they both peer through the haze.

The queen now sits at the loom on the far side of the room. Aurora can't be sure how long the woman has been there, her loom softly click-clacking as she listened to their argument. It's even harder to see now. The windows are blackening—*another illusion,* Aurora thinks.

Wren turns to Aurora and then back to the queen, clearly awed. Aurora can't believe that the girl—that all the residents of Blackthorn—have lived their entire lives right beside the mad queen and have never once laid eyes on her. It's crazy to think that they've been so close to a way out all this time, but have never known it.

Then again, she realizes, perhaps *everyone* has the key to her own prison. Maybe freedom is just a matter of knowing the right story, of being brave enough to say the right words in the right order at the right time.

The old woman leans over her loom, and for a moment Aurora thinks she is weaving her own silver-white hair into the tapestry. She doesn't look up but shakes her head slightly.

"My queen?" Wren whispers, trying to wave away the haze. "What do we have wrong?"

The queen sighs. "I was never the jealous one. It was my sister who envied *me.*"

Aurora and Wren step closer, until Aurora can see the tears on the queen's face, even in the stifling dimness of the room.

"Then why are you crying?" Aurora asks gently, as though too harsh a demand might make the woman dissolve into the thick air.

"Because there's nothing sadder than someone leaving," the queen says, her voice almost childlike.

"Who left you? Was it Charles Blackthorn?"

"Aurora," Wren cautions. "Be careful. She'll trick us."

Belcoeur shakes her head. "She left. She left. But not again. Not this time. I won't be left alone again."

"*She?*" Aurora steps closer. It's getting harder to breathe in here. No matter how her eyes adjust, the air only grows thicker and blacker. Could the queen be talking about her sister? Is it possible she's been waiting all this time not for her true love but for Malfleur herself?

The queen looks up, her eyes ablaze with swirling greens and blues. "I won't be left alone again."

"Aurora!" Wren says, beginning to cough. "Run!"

Aurora feels a tug on her sleeve, but she can't move. She's fixed to the spot, staring at the loom.

"No one will leave me," Belcoeur says.

Aurora is riveted not by her words but by the breathtaking beauty of the tapestry the queen has been weaving all this time. A forest dashed with streaks of red and yellow and orange that leap toward a blackened sky.

Flames.

33

Belcoeur,
the Night Faerie

There is screaming as the residents of Blackthorn wake up to the thick clouds of ash floating over the walls of the Borderlands, toward the castle. The forest is on fire. The queen sees the two girls' bodies outlined in plumes of dark smoke as they try to run from here, run from *her.* She reaches out, clinging to the visitor's skirt.

They hate her. And she deserves to be hated, to be loathed, to be left.

"I'm sorry," she croaks quietly, though the visitor can't hear her. She chokes on the smoke. "I'm sorry," she repeats, falling to the floor as she continues to cling to the young woman's dress, holding her back.

Those two words unleash a flood of memories suppressed

for so long they make her sick with dizziness. For she *is* sorry—always has been. She's been sorry since she was seven years old, and her parents gifted her the enormous golden wheel from a distant eastern country, one that, with just a little magic, could not only spin wool into yarn but gold and silver into thread—and too, she learned, dreams. But that would come later.

Sorry, because her sister was unhappy that the spinning wheel had gone to her. Malfleur would stare at Belcoeur's fingers, their agility as they danced by the rapid flier, never once getting pricked by the sharp-ended bobbin, and Belcoeur could feel the unhappiness in her dark gaze. Belcoeur had never wanted to compete, had never believed her magic was in any way stronger than her twin's. There was an *ease* to it, true—it came to her naturally. She never studied, as Malfleur did. She never practiced. As a consequence, her magic was softer around the edges. It never quite felt like it was in her control, and she didn't mind that. But her twin did.

Though Malfleur never outright accused her, she must have held Belcoeur to blame when they discovered at a very young age that Malfleur simply couldn't dream. While Belcoeur experienced lustrously imagined, richly vivid sequences of memory, emotion, and sensation when she slept each night, Malfleur sank only into an infinite blank. It didn't take long for their parents to conclude that Belcoeur's gift—her desire, the source of all her magic—had to do with dreaming. Even without learning how to perform a tithing, Belcoeur had somehow absorbed her twin's ability to dream while they were tangled together within their mother's womb.

She had tried to make it up to Malfleur in so many ways over the years. Sometimes it felt like all she ever did was compensate for this original sin. She spun nothing with as much love as the threads she used to weave garments for her sister. And when Malfleur was caught causing mischief and sent to bed without any supper, Belcoeur always slipped her food from her own plate.

There were times when she simply couldn't protect her sister, though. She'll never forget the day they snuck out to collect flowers for their mother's birthday tea party. Malfleur had wanted to find violets—their mother's favorite—but they didn't grow in the gardens, and she had gotten lost wandering into the vast fields beyond the castle grounds. Belcoeur was forced to return alone to their mother, who was worried and upset beyond belief. Her tea party had been ruined, left out cold and untouched while she sent a search party to find Malfleur.

When they finally brought Malfleur home, Belcoeur, in her effort to make everything better, brewed her mother a fresh pot of tea, hoping they could start over and salvage the day, but by then their mother's distress had picked up speed like a summer storm and morphed into fury. Their mother, cruel as ever, grabbed the gilt cup from Belcoeur's tray and splashed still-scalding tea into Malfleur's face to teach her never to wander again. A white scar remained across her sister's eyelid and cheek—and that's when a stain of darkness,

Belcoeur is sure, began to settle into her sister's heart.

Still, Belcoeur continued to accept the blame for her sister's misdeeds as often as she convincingly could. She even came to enjoy taking her sister's place in the "punishment chair" positioned in the corner of the parlor room in their summer cottage. Her sister, during the many hours she spent supposedly atoning for the trouble she'd made, would scratch clever limericks and poems into the wall there. It became a secret way for the girls to communicate, for Belcoeur to read and decipher the messages and to feel like she was a part of Malfleur's world, even as her sister increasingly snuck away without telling her.

It hurt, the idea of Malfleur keeping secrets. Belcoeur wanted more than anything to be her twin's confidante. And so she was delighted by little phrases, such as *The secret boy—we almost kissed—he won my jewel—in a game of whist!* Belcoeur guessed what her sister was referring to: the night Malfleur had "borrowed" their mother's pearl necklace and slipped silently out of the guest quarters at Blackthorn to play cards with the older visitors.

It was only a couple years later and after several more visits with the Blackthorns, both at their castle and at hers, that Belcoeur began to suspect just which boy Malfleur had almost kissed. It was Charles Blackthorn himself. And she could see he was smitten with her by the way he seemed especially attuned to Malfleur's tenor of sarcasm, was always ready with a reply and a twinkling gaze that seemed to suggest a wink, even where there wasn't one.

When Belcoeur questioned her sister about her budding romance with Charles, Malfleur always brushed it off as a flirtation. But Belcoeur could see what her sister would not admit: that the bubbling, exciting, yearning intensity between them was mutual. They had some sort of understanding, that much was clear—even when, at sixteen, Malfleur left their father's lands to learn more about her magic and traveled for three years abroad, without offering Charles any overt promise of her affections. He would wait. That was what everyone thought.

Though Belcoeur missed her sister terribly during those three years, she took pleasure in receiving the packages Malfleur regularly sent home to her: precious knickknacks and odd inventions from all around the world, like a clock with a bird's face that popped out to chime the hour, a beautiful birdcage, a delicate silver teapot, a hairbrush and filigreed hand mirror.

She was surprised when Charles began to come around more frequently—at first to compare letters from Malfleur's travels and to marvel at the gifts she'd sent, but then, more and more often, he visited simply to talk. And the more he spoke, the more he let slip. He confessed that he *had* proposed to Malfleur, and she had rejected him outright. Though she continued to send him letters, she'd made it clear that she was more interested in her own magic than in him. And besides, Malfleur was fond of reminding him that the fae frequently outlived humans by whole lifetimes or more.

Belcoeur could see he was devastated by her sister's refusal. Which was why she did what she was always doing, whether for her sister or her mother or, in this case, Charles. She offered sweetness and consolation in uncountable small ways.

And in performing these modest acts of love, she grew to inhabit that love. She fell for Charles. His broad chest and perfect posture. His light brown hair cropped at the shoulders and almost always a bit disheveled from his latest ride. The thin beard he had newly grown, emphasizing the squareness of his jaw. The modest, simple crown he wore—a circlet of gold with no jewels. But more than these things, she loved the way he reminded her of Malfleur: his quick wit, his fiery laugh, his fiercely perceptive gaze.

She didn't mean to fall, and certainly didn't expect any reciprocity. But, same as her magic, love blossomed easily and naturally—it was beyond her control. She was helpless to stop the feeling from growing and expanding until it got to the point where the spiky, poisonous vines that often choked the trees in the royal forest would spontaneously sprout purple flowers as she walked over them.

And so it was that on the day Malfleur was to return from her travels, Charles found Belcoeur alone, head bent over a gift she was making for her twin: a dress woven from gold. It was July, so she was at the summer cottage on the outskirts of the royal forest, which afforded their father better hunting, and the Blackthorns were visiting. Having changed her mind several times about the style of the sleeves, anxious to get the dress just right, Belcoeur realized she had run out of gold thread. She had just rethreaded the bobbin and begun to tap the foot pedal, causing the great wheel to spin. As usual, she became lost in the sparkling whir of the metallic filaments through her fingers, and hardly noticed a shadow cast into the room until she heard a quiet cough and looked up. Charles Blackthorn was standing in the doorway.

"I could watch you work all day," he said, and she flushed, feeling sick with the effort of not smiling more broadly, not letting her affection have its name. He was leaning against the doorframe in his riding gear, and he seemed to be concentrating very hard.

"Are you all right?" she asked. "You seem . . . perplexed."

"Malfleur returns today," he said, as though the knowledge hadn't been tormenting her for days—and nights—both with excitement and uncertainty. She desperately wanted everything to go back to the way it had been. But a voice inside her reminded her that the love between them had been fraying invisibly for years, like the frizzy hair of a much-held doll, and one day the bald truth would be revealed. Was all love like this, she fretted—a covering, a craft, a transient softness impossible to regrow once shed?

Even as she clutched the imaginary doll harder, she wore it down to its porcelain bones.

But all she said was, "Yes. As you can see, I'm hurrying to finish her homecoming gift."

"I do see," he said, casting his glance at the single-sleeved dress hanging over the side of the wardrobe, studying it with that same expression of consternation. "It is sure to look lovely on her," he added.

"Of course," she replied awkwardly, hating the dress instantly, and hating herself.

"Then again," he said, "it would be very beautiful on *you*." And though he wasn't making eye contact with her, she understood. She panicked. She should beg him to stop talking, but she was frozen as he went on. "All it would need is a veil, and it would make a suitable wedding gown. No . . . not suitable. Stunning."

That's when he finally lifted his eyes to hers, and she shook, snagging her index finger on the tip of the bobbin. "Ow!" she cried, the end of the golden thread flying from her hands.

He ran to her—both the desired and feared effect—and without her perceiving how it had happened, he was kneeling before her, clutching her hands, kissing the injured one, then the other. He turned her hands over and kissed the inside of each wrist. His lips against the tender skin there caused her to tremble again. *Stop!* her mind shouted, but her heart leaped into her throat, and instead she breathed his name aloud. "Charles." Tears ran down her cheeks, but she didn't have the will to pull her hands back and wipe them away.

Though he was normally equipped with a variety of

clever phrases and compelling arguments, he was silent now as he slipped one hand to her bent knee and one to her damp cheek, and then, pushing her long blond hair out of her face, he took the kiss she had forbidden herself to imagine.

His lips told the story of how true his love was, that it had not been all hers but had been *theirs* for some time. His mouth was so *human* against her own, and without meaning to, she breathed in his deepest dreaming, and dreamed—right in that instant—that they were fated to be together. He pulled away, bewildered. Maybe he knew—could *feel*—that an unspoken contract had been signed, and with it, her magic had taken something from him.

Or maybe he had no idea yet. It didn't matter anyway. She felt that first sparkle of guilt, the one that caused her to glance up—and then she gasped as she realized what had happened, as she saw what had been inevitable from the start: Malfleur, still in her travel cloak, entering the room, dropping a gift of glass, which shattered like a scream.

It would have been better if Malfleur too had screamed. Anything would have been better, Belcoeur thought, than the look on her perfectly sculpted face: its scar blazing white like a star, her cheekbones high and proud, her pretty mouth—thinner than her twin's and more sharply defined—mute with comprehension.

That moment, full of such ugliness and such beauty, became a thorn wedged permanently into Belcoeur's chest. She would never breathe again without feeling the pain of it.

And still, there would be worse to come.

Her vow never to love. Her promise to shun Charles forever.

The long months of begging for forgiveness. Of being ignored over and over as Malfleur returned to her travels, leaving Belcoeur to feel as though one half of herself had died. The terror of watching her twin become darker, more remote, changed, until Belcoeur's only source of consolation was her dreams, which she had begun to collect and, using her magic, weave into elaborate tapestries where she would spend days trying to *forget, forget, forget,* only to return from them panting, air racing into her lungs like angry hornets filling her with the sting of the life she no longer wanted to live.

She called this body of her greatest work "Sommeil."

More time passed, and the wounds began to scar, the dreams a kind of salve—a salvation, really. They replaced her life, a prettier version of only the best times, while her waking existence took on the form of a blurred memory fading with each day. She had never used her magic so much as she used it then. It got so that she couldn't enter a room without sapping the power of dreaming from everyone in it.

In the sliver of twilight between waking and dreaming, she sometimes saw herself for what she had become: the type of faerie whom humans misunderstood, dreaded, abhorred.

Some nights she saw Charles again, despite her promise not to.

But she couldn't say if any of these nights, and the agonizing ecstasies they contained, were real or imagined.

There is no way to know now. Not after what happened. Not after . . .

———

Belcoeur gags on smoke, the fumes strong in her nostrils. There's the scent of old things burning:

Lace fire.

Flower fire.

Bone fire.

This young woman who struggles to free herself from her grasp is a stranger, not her sister. Her sister has not come.

And that's when the final piece of her abandoned life comes back to her. It was a short time later—less than a year after the incident—when Belcoeur began to notice a different kind of change. Her belly had grown round and hard, swirling with beginnings: the kick of a foot. The hiccup of tiny lungs. Someday soon, she realized, a child would be born.

Desperate, she wrote to her sister, begging her to understand. Begging her to forgive, so that Belcoeur might be free to love Charles again. Her wish came true when Malfleur responded.

Everyone deserves true love, my dear sister, she wrote. *And the child will know its father.*

Accompanying the letter was a magnificently carved chest—in and of itself one of the finest gifts her sister had ever sent her. With trembling hands, Belcoeur took the key that had been wrapped in the letter and used it to unlock the lid.

The first thing she saw inside the trunk was a flash of gold—the peaks of the Blackthorn crown Charles wore every day except when riding.

Then she noticed the blood. . . . And the meaning of her sister's words came crashing down like an ax.

———◆———

Belcoeur screams now as she screamed then, yanking the oversized crown she has worn for over a century off her head and throwing it to the ground before the visitor.

Her vision is blurred by tears over all she has lost—her child, her sister, her love.

For what she sees within the crown before her is the final memory, the final truth: Charles Blackthorn's severed head.

34

Isabelle

"Careful!" William's voice flies up at her from below, rough and salty in the fog.

The rope ladder sways under Isbe's feet, banging against the craggy cliffside, and for one second she imagines what it would feel like to simply let go and allow the Strait of Sorrow, a few hundred feet below, to swallow her. . . . She'd make just a small, unmemorable splash in the grand scheme of things. The image reminds her of a story Aurora once told her, about an arrogant boy named Icarus who fashioned a pair of waxen wings. He flew too close to the sun, which melted his wings; then he fell to his death in the waters below.

"Are you trying to make a point about the dangers of

excessive pride?" Isbe had asked, putting on a fake pout.

"No," her sister had replied, tapping into her hand rapidly. "I'm making a point about *wax*."

Isbe swallows hard, trying to put the memories from her mind. She can't let herself give in to this urge to mourn her sister when she's not even dead. If she starts to grieve for Aurora, for Gil, for all of them, it will mean the end. She keeps climbing down, her hands slick on the rungs.

The idea had come to her quickly. After the shock of seeing Aurora's unmoving form, they had ventured up to the wall walks to survey the surrounding land. William saw animals asleep in the barn. He saw royal banners fallen under piles of muddy sleet and snow. He saw death. He saw the vines. And, in the distance, he saw something that made even the worst of the destruction seem but a prelude: the black wave of Malfleur's army descending Mount Briar to the west.

Isbe convinced him they needed to find someplace to hide out while they came up with a new plan to lift the curse. Certainly it wasn't safe to stay put—the risk of disease was in the air, and the castle was unguarded. Nor was it wise to attempt further travel. Even the Veiled Road would be dangerous with Malfleur's organized forces now on the move. Time was ticking, and with every minute of daylight the threat of discovery grew.

The idea to find someplace upwind of the vines came first, and then the solution was natural, for there is only one thing separating the castle from the southerly winds that blow off the strait, and that's the cliff face. For years now they have housed the royal family's stores of wine—barrels and barrels of it—in caverns built directly into the sides of the cliffs. Apparently the darkness and temperature are ideal for preserving the wine's value. But they will also be ideal for eluding the dangerous fumes of the sleeping sickness and the detection of potential invaders.

The rope ladder is tricky to handle, typically used only by experienced stewards of the royal household, or on rare occasions the pantler or butler. The drop if they should fall is deadly. Next to the ladder dangles a series of pulleys and levers that convey the casks up and down as needed. The contraption clanks noisily beside Isbe, rattling her nerves.

William, who has gone before her, finally reaches out to help her into the entrance of the cavern. The blustery wind all around them drowns out her relieved sigh. She hears the scratchy snap of the flint followed by the sizzle of the lantern being lit, and the bitter cold subsides somewhat as they make their way deeper into the wine room—especially once they hang the thick velvet curtain they brought and decide it's safe to remove their masks. Isbe heaves in a huge breath, inhaling the cool musk of grapes and oaken casks.

"Isabelle." William touches her elbow, and she sucks in another breath. He still has that lime-soap smell—or maybe she's only remembering it, that not quite sweetness.

She turns to face him but takes a step back so that they are no longer touching. "You can call me Isbe, you know. That's what Aurora and Gi— That's what everyone else calls me."

343

She's not sure why she's decided to tell him her nick-name now, of all times. Maybe it's being home at last that's made her realize he needs to understand who she really is, her true role. She's the bastard. The trouble underfoot. The sister. The thorn.

"No," he replies, and a little shock moves through her—a good kind of shock. "I prefer to call you Isabelle. It's who you are to me now." He's so resolute and so certain, even if he is contradicting her wishes. . . . Maybe she doesn't mind. Maybe she's relieved, having come to savor the natural way her name rocks across his tongue and lips.

Maybe, even, he's right. She's begun to think of *herself* that way too.

"All right, then," she says, turning away to hide the heat in her cheeks. "I was just going to unpack these." She ges-tures to the small bundle of scraps they managed to forage from the pantry, navigating around the cold, snoring bodies of the local peasants who had attempted to raid it before them. "I think this should be enough to last a few days."

"A few days? How long do you intend for us to hide out here?" There's urgency in his voice.

"Just until we can decide on another way to try lifting the curse. I'm thinking we need to get into contact with the faerie duchess Violette, if we can find her. I remember Binks said—"

"Wait." William clears his throat. "Listen. I want to keep you safe. To keep *us* safe. But what we need to do right now is mobilize our troops in order to protect the kingdoms; we need weapons and a military strategy, and we can't do any of that from a wine cave."

"We can't do any of that *anyway* unless we wake up Aurora and the council," Isabelle counters, starting to feel exasperated. "We need to lift the curse first."

"There's no time for that! I agreed to come out here to the cliffs with you so we could strategize—not stick our heads in the sand. And yes, Isabelle, before you interrupt me, we *can* do it without lifting the curse." William's hands are on her shoulders. This time she doesn't pull away.

"How?" she asks.

"Simple. *You* authorize the Delucian troops to gather in my kingdom and receive my weapons. *You* coordinate the safe transfer of oil to Aubin while I send word to the chief of military back home to prepare for battle. We issue masks to anyone who needs to come within an unsafe proximity to the palace. Don't you see? We don't need your sister for any of it. Right now all we need is information we can easily dig up around the castle . . . supply stores and trade routes and—"

"So you're saying we should just leave Aurora as she is. Asleep. Forever."

"I'm saying that right now you may have to choose." He steps closer to her, still touching her. "You can try saving your sister, or you can try saving your kingdom. Neither are guarantees, but it has to be one or the other. We're at the end, Isabelle. And I need to know where you stand."

The smell of wine in the room is so strong. It must be, for it is making her feel hot, intoxicated, fuzzy. *Choose?* But she can't choose. That's not fair. That's not in her power.

"And," he goes on, stepping even closer until she can feel the heat of his body just a few fingers' breadth from her own. "If we *must* make the alliance official . . ."

His hands slide down her arms. He kneels before her. "Then accept me as your prince and rule by my side." His words are the crest of a tidal wave, and she stands there in disbelief as it torrents on. "You've shown you can do it. Through your bravery, your cleverness, your determination—some might call it stubbornness." She almost laughs. But she doesn't. She can't make a sound, can't stop the wave that is still barreling toward her. "*You* are the type of ruler who might actually inspire the people to listen. I want to do this together. With you. Marry me." The wave crashes.

Silence.

"Marry me, Isabelle," he repeats. The dazzling, shocking aftermath, lighter than air. The foam.

"But . . . I can't—"

"You can," he says. "The question is, *will* you."

She's too dizzy to stand. She can't quite believe this is happening—he's proposing . . . *again*. She gets down onto her knees as well, and he lets go of her hands so she can touch his face: the firm ridge of his cheeks, the softness of his mouth, the emotion—the *hunger*—buzzing through his skin. "William . . ." What to say? How to tell him? How to—

"*Isabelle,*" he whispers, he *insists*. Now his hands are on *her* face, on her lips, on her jaw, tilting her back slightly so that her neck is arched.

Time seems to stop, and Isabelle remembers being a child, no more than two, watching a white feather float from a down coverlet a maid was shaking out. It fell so slowly, idling back and forth on the air, she felt sure it would never land.

And then all at once she is no longer a child, and no longer waiting.

———

It is late. William is asleep beside her, what remains of his torn cloak forming a thick, soft blanket beneath them. It's the normal kind of sleep, not the sickness; she made sure to test it by waking him repeatedly until finally he growled half teasingly and kissed her until he succeeded in convincing her to stop. Now she lies awake in the darkness, touching the corner of her mouth where his first kiss landed, his lips merely brushing hers—remembering. How quickly things unspooled from there, and then his lips were parting hers and his hand was at the small of her back, pulling her up against him, and she was kissing him back. . . .

And it was different than her first kiss with Gilbert, which was wild and unexpected, clumsy and exciting and messy and sweet, like a day in the fields with Freckles, flying across the open grass, the wind tangling her hair. Escape.

With William, everything was the opposite: slow, deliberate, full of meaning. She had never felt more present in her own skin, every touch like a raindrop in a pond, rippling outward from a single spot.

But now.

She can't sleep. She's afraid that if she does, this will all go away and she'll lose what it felt like to be beautiful, to be chosen. That if she sleeps, she will dream, and in that dream she will hear her mother singing, and the song will lure her to stay asleep forever, where it's safe—or else, worse, that waking from it will shatter her.

Wind whistles along the craggy cliffs, the mouth of the strait sloshes below, and she knows she has to make a decision. William has asked her to marry him, and, although she said yes with every part of her, she did not actually *say* it.

She sits up, letting his arm slip gradually off her, and pulls on her cloak. She fumbles along the floor until she finds her mask, discarded several paces away. Then, quietly, she pushes back the thick velvet curtain and moves along the row of wine casks, barrel by barrel, counting them. By forty-eight, she has reached the lip of the cave. And though it's the most foolish, willful thing she's done in a list of very foolish and willful things, she reaches for the ladder, and climbs.

She's drawn back to Aurora's bedside as if she were sleepwalking, as if some external force has guided her there instead of the plain fact that she knows her way, knows it in her bones and in her hair and in her fingertips. She will always know her way around this castle, and she will always come back to her sister, because Aurora is intrinsic to Isabelle. She is the truest part of Isabelle. She is her heart.

She kneels, as she did before William just hours ago, and once again takes her sister's hands. "Please," she whispers.

Aurora's chest softly rises and falls. Rises and falls.

In the quiet, Isabelle can almost hear Aurora's strange, unabashed laugh. But she has the forlorn impression that Aurora is not *here*—that this Aurora is but a snow sculpture they've made, and some detail, as yet undetected, is out of place. It scares her, almost, this *other* Aurora in the place of her real sister, who is gone.

She leans down and puts her lips to Aurora's cool forehead, and kisses it, like she would sometimes do when they were little, on nights when stories of the plague frightened them, when they could hear the hacking coughs of the sick through the walls and knew that come morning, another maid or groom would be carried away from the palace on a plank, a faceless form beneath a thin white sheet. And then, they learned later when they were older, the body would be burned in a massive fire before being thrown into a shared grave.

On nights like those, Aurora would whimper and cling to Isabelle, and Isabelle felt braver because of it. But now she feels more alone than ever. Even after everything that just happened between her and William—maybe *because* of it . . . and because she still can't stop thinking about the fact that she doesn't know whether Gilbert is dead or alive . . . and that it may be her fault if he's dead . . . and that she doesn't know what she wants, other than this one thing: for Aurora to wake up.

"Please," she whispers again, her voice cracking. She's come so far. She's tried so hard. And it hasn't been enough.

Maybe, all along, she knew it wouldn't be.

Maybe all of this—her entire journey—has been a terrible, beautiful distraction from what she knew, deep down, she must do: let Aurora go.

She can't remember the last time she wept, but the tears come now, haltingly and then hard, wetting her face and rattling her whole body, causing her to gasp. She feels out of control, like a laundered garment pulled loose by the wind and flying off the line, flailing over the sides of the cliffs. She can't stop; tears drip from her cheeks and fall onto Aurora's pillow, and onto her closed eyes.

Isabelle cries, quietly and fully, solitude a weight crushing down on her.

Isabelle cries, and Aurora sleeps.

———

She's not sure how much time has passed; all she knows is that she can't cry anymore. She takes a deep, shuddering breath. *We're at the end,* William said to her. *I need to know where you stand.*

Isabelle pushes to her feet. There are still so many questions she doesn't have answers for—who to love, who her own mother is. She doesn't know what she wants. Doesn't know how to save her sister. Doesn't know how to live without her.

But she knows now what she must do.

She must say yes.

35

Aurora

A deep, breathless blackness pulses within her and around her, clogging her lungs.

"Let go of me!" Aurora screams, trying to wrench her dress from the queen's desperate clutch. "I am not who you thought." Her words twist strangely into the air, mingling with the smoke blurring her vision. After all, she isn't who *she* thought she was, either. She had been a damsel like those in the stories she'd read all her life, waiting to be rescued. Her lack of touch had not only protected her from feeling pain, but also from understanding its purpose.

The white hair of the queen flickers as Aurora finally yanks herself free and runs toward a window, heaving it open. But the outside is just as dark as the inside, and even in the heat and smoke she feels the great power of Sommeil embracing her. Its desire, its denial.

Through that tenebrosity of *want*, she sees leaping flames. Gathered shadows. Voices—many of them—are shouting. Thin silhouettes running, tripping over one another, some holding long poles, pitchforks, spears. Fleeing. Screaming.

Ashes blow through the sky, a black cloud spreading toward the castle from the wall.

The Borderlands are on fire.

No one can get out.

They will all die.

Aurora stares, momentarily hypnotized, as in one quick breath the hunger of the fire blooms and spreads. Then she is once again scrambling through the darkness of the castle's twisting passages, punctuated only by the hot flash of the flames.

She has lost Wren. She has lost the queen. Lost *herself*.

The ashes spread as the fire beyond the wall grows. It is hot, too hot. She can't think. Her hands have gone numb. It feels as though her very voice is burning away inside her throat. She coughs, she chokes, she falls.

And then she feels cold metal against her palm. She realizes her eyes were clenched against the smoke, but she forces herself to part them. They sting and water as she examines the object in her hand.

It's Belcoeur's crown. It is large, though—the size of a man's head, not a woman's. Because, Aurora realizes quickly, the queen has been wearing Charles Blackthorn's crown for all these years.

And it isn't burning. It isn't even hot, but blissfully cool.

Of course. Because it is an object from the real world. It's immune to the power of Sommeil. Immune, even, to the queen's magical fire.

She feels how heavy the crown is in her hands. There's something engraved on the inside. She squints. *True Love,* it says.

With her hand on the gold crown, she begins to breathe a little easier. The crown, she realizes, can save her. She just needs to think clearly, figure out how to save the rest of the people. She can't think in this heat, in this smoke.

She can see she has made it down to the first floor. Through the windows, people are still screaming, frenzied, racing through the grounds, attempting to break free.

The sun is still rising.

The castle is still burning.

She places the crown on her head.

The heat disappears, and she is able to gasp, sucking in fresh air. Life. *Life.* She is going to live. She has saved herself, and she will save the others too.

The light is so bright it is blazing, blinding.

Aurora blinks, still gulping, still shaking as the flames release her.

Once. Twice. And again.

The third time she opens her eyes, she figures out what has happened.

She has awoken.

Acknowledgments

In his memoir *And There Was Light*, Jacques Lusseyran writes of his blindness, "But we get nothing in this world without paying for it, and in return for all the benefits that sight brings, we are forced to give up others whose existence we don't even suspect. These were the gifts I received in such abundance." Lusseyran's often ecstatic experience of life beyond the convenience (and confines) of sight—and his notion of the world's unexpected gifts—was a huge inspiration to me in the writing of *Spindle Fire*.

I too received an abundance of gifts as I worked on this book, in the form of emotional and creative support. I want to thank Lauren Oliver, who told me that moving through a novel is like skating across a frozen lake, finding the right places to shatter the ice and plunge in. Thanks also to Kamilla Benko, for many inspirations (nuns can be cool!), and Tara Sonin—if I could tithe her romantic instincts, I would!

As always, I owe very much to the wisdom of my editor, Rosemary Brosnan, who urged me to think critically about every single sentence in this novel, and to my amazing agent, Stephen Barbara, a true partner in my career, who has championed my foray into fantasy writing—and loved many of those epic digressions I ended up cutting.

Thank you to Lyndsey Blessing, Alexis Hurley, and the entire team at Inkwell Management for sending *Spindle Fire* on its own voyage across the sea, and thank you to all the incredibly talented people at HarperTeen who've been behind this book from the start, especially Kate Jackson, Jessica MacLeish, Courtney Stevenson, Olivia Russo, and Kate Klimowicz. And thank you to Lisa Perrin for cover art that takes my breath away.

I certainly could not have written this novel with any sort of confidence had it not been for the fantastic notes from my beta readers, Marie Villaneda and Christopher Avila, from the Indiana School for the Blind and Visually Impaired, who offered wonderful advice about the character of Isabelle and how she might manage her wild journey.

I'm grateful to Jess Rothenberg, Rebecca Serle, and Leila Sales for the many hours of companionship and encouragement while I researched things like medieval convent layouts, narwhal hunting, and plague masks—or pondered what the underbelly of a dove looks like. And, of course, to my husband, Charlie, who spent many of those hours with our newborn daughter so that I could be alone with Isbe and Aurora and this crazy cast of cracked-up faeries—tracing a lifeline back to myself, even through the darkest, sleepless phases of early motherhood.

Finally: thank you, Minna, princess of the woodland creatures, my hedgehog, my beauty, my love.

A kingdom in peril. A princess awakened.

Read on for a first glimpse at the sequel to *Spindle Fire*,

WINTER GLASS

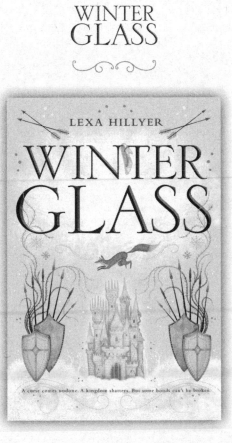

1

Malfleur,
the Last Faerie Queen

S leep is a vast and supple darkness.

But then: tiny lights, like seeds, shower across a corner of the black. Something has snagged its claws in the soft flesh of night.

———

The panther is upon her before the queen has fully awakened: the scent of flowers and meat on its breath, a feral purr rumbling at the base of its throat. The tight leather muzzle Malfleur always keeps chained over the animal's mouth has torn loose.

She does not have time to wonder how the panther—afflicted by the sleeping sickness for many weeks—woke up from its spell. With the speed of thought, her hand has found

1

the letter opener beside her bed and wrapped around its thin handle, just as the animal's fangs tear into her shoulder.

The queen cries out; pain ricochets through her body as she thrusts the letter opener in an arc over her head. It is only meant for hacking open a waxen seal, too dull to cut through the creature's skin, but never mind, for its point has found the eye. The panther roars, pulls back and flails, slashing the pillow beside Malfleur's face, sending bloodied feathers into the air. The queen gasps and rolls off her bed as the animal continues to wail—a sound like a rent in a glacier: half scream, half growl.

Dawn's cool light barely illuminates her royal chambers, but it's just enough to catch the glint of her dagger, unsheathed, on the window ledge. She crawls to it, her right arm shaking from the shock of her wound. Clinging to the ledge, she pulls herself up. The panther has noticed her movement. It lunges, a blur of white fur and fangs—the letter opener still jutting out of its face at an angle, like the tusk of the fabled unicorn.

Malfleur sucks in a breath, then strikes with the dagger, which jolts raggedly into the beast's rib cage.

A wild, gargling howl fills the air, seems to swallow up all the light in the room. Time slows. Malfleur sways with the aftershock. The panther's claws catch the skirt of her nightgown as the beast thuds to the floor, forcing the queen down onto her knees.

Still it struggles, legs scrambling, claws scraping stone.

She breathes roughly, leaning over the body as it

continues to writhe for several moments more; her night-dress is torn, covered in blood, half the panther's and half her own. She can't feel her shoulder.

Finally the panther goes still, steam still rising from its nostrils. The queen's breath begins to calm too as she stares at the majestic creature, who always seemed to her like an incarnation of winter, full of pale fury and long, cold solaces. How ugly it has become now, where once the animal was all grace, its purr deep as a subterranean tremor.

This was her favorite pet—her companion, her *creation*—but it turned on her. Betrayal rings in Malfleur's bones, so familiar by now it has come to feel like a passing season. For a moment, it is not her shoulder wound that aches and pangs but the sudden depth of her loss, echoing through her.

She collects herself, calculating the facts as she staggers slowly to her feet.

There was nothing truly sentient driving the attack, that much is obvious. Malfleur can still sense the animal's panic and hunger lingering in the air like the electricity of a storm. The large white beast—pristine, dangerous, loyal, *trained*—must have forgotten itself while it slept, forgotten the humanity the faerie queen had breathed into its mind, using the powerful magic she has accumulated over the years.

The panther had even warned Malfleur about the sleeping sickness, and the gaping purple flowers surrounding the palace of Deluce, before falling into its own slumber several weeks ago. *Hungry for hungry for*, the cat had said in their last conversation, struggling to isolate the words.

Poor animal. Most humans cannot find words for such things either.

Still, the question that tugs at Malfleur's mind—as she steadies herself to force the dagger from the panther's flesh—is not why her pet attacked her, but why it broke free from its long sleep in the first place.

And how?

The smell of guts and bile is stifling; it's as though the queen herself has been consumed. She sways, then stumbles to the wall and pushes open her shuttered window.

She heaves a breath of fresh air. The smoky undulations of LaMorte seem, at just that moment, almost peaceful, swept in a morning gauze just shy of blue, no longer silver.

There can only be one answer to her question, she realizes.

The faerie curse has been lifted.

Princess Aurora has awakened.

———

"Happiness is like starlight, my Marigold," Malfleur's father told her one summer evening when she was very little. King Verglas had always enjoyed the sound of his own voice. But Malfleur thought he was right, in a way: we do what is necessary, for our joy in this world is scarce and must be wrestled down from the black vault of all that is random and meaningless.

And so, less than a week after Aurora's awakening and the panther's attack, the queen and a small retinue of soldiers—using information she gleaned from her squeamish and simpering cousin, Violette—push their way into the royal forest of Deluce, dense with the heady coniferous scent of pine needles and sap. Even in the dead of night, the abandoned cottage isn't hard to find. The breath of memories comes to her, soft and stirring, but she does not let it touch her.

Now Malfleur stands in the doorway of the nursery she once shared with her sister, Belcoeur. There sits the spinning wheel, its gold contours flickering in the light of her torch. The instrument had been a gift to her beloved sister . . . and, later, a symbol of all that had splintered between them. She gazes at the rare, beautiful spindle. She takes her time; imagines threading her desire through the eye of the flyer, then carefully pedaling and pulling, pedaling and pulling, until the cord of revenge grows strong and taut and fine.

Until it shines.

2

Isabelle

Isbe shudders in the cold as she and several royal attendants pick their way across a field at dawn in the unpleasant business of scouring for survivors—and taking account of the lost. She is thankful, just now, for being blind. But then again, she doesn't need to be able to see the sun push up through the fog hanging over the strait in order to know the unflinching cruelty it brings, doesn't have to see the bones of the dead blanching in the grass, either—bodies forever fallen among thorny, shriveled vines, forming miniature castles for sparrows and mice.

It has been a week since the sleeping sickness officially ended, but it has left Deluce in shambles. The moment Aurora shifted, gasped, and grasped her sister's hand, everything changed: the purple flowers along the crenelated palace walls began to wither. Scattered servants and nobles throughout the palace startled into consciousness, though the vast majority remained still, their lungs frozen from the chill of winter, or their throats slit by pillagers. The list of the dead within the castle village has grown by eighty-three since yesterday. That number does not even include the eleven council members who died. The only one who lived is the chief of military, Maximilien.

"Another courtier, Miss Isabelle," says one of the servants in her party. A woman takes her arm and guides her to a body.

Isbe kneels down and feels a sunken rib cage, covered in a surcoat of ermine and velvet. She scrambles for the buttons—something light, like fine gold, and something glossy, perhaps pearl—removing each one expertly with her bare hands. "Add them to our store."

When William first told Isbe that they must scour and save, she scoffed. "Deluce has more gold than any nation in the known world," she told him. "Surely you know that."

"In war, every single jeweled ring in the land may be melted into a metal that could save a man's life. Or a woman's." His comment made her think of the nasty Lord Barnabé—*Binks*—an ostentatious noblefaerie who wears ten ruby rings at once, one for each of his fat fingers.

"My lady." A servant tugs on her sleeve, and Isbe recognizes the kitchen maid's voice, the buttery scent of her hair and clothes.

"Yes, Matilda?" At least it isn't Gertrude, who used to beat Isbe when she stole biscuits. Gertrude, like so many of the others, perished during the sickness. There'd been a rolling pin trapped in her clenched fist when her body was found.

"The prince is asking for you. May I lead you to him?" She sounds a little out of breath.

Isbe hesitates before answering. "Of course." She places her hand on the older woman's weathered wrist and allows Matilda to lead her back across the castle yards.

Early spring has a bite to it. The wind stings and cools Isbe's flushed face as she thinks of the prince. How there had been a miracle, a yes, on the tip of her tongue, a gift of a word. A yes that would have allowed her to skip right over a lifetime of no, over the impossibility of being born a bastard and not a princess. A yes that would have made her a queen, that would have made her William's.

The Aubinian prince has left an imprint on Isbe: she keeps replaying the way his words and hands tindered her, how she burned and was left shaking. But then Aurora awoke, and that alive thing—that inner self, that yes—withered on Isbe's tongue, dissolved into dust. She feels overcome now with a bashful shame, stunned by the sickening glare of the obvious: Prince William of Aubin was never hers except in that brief instant, in the wine caves, when they felt they were truly at the end of all hope. He is not hers anymore, and she is certainly not his.

But she has her sister back, and that is all that matters.

"You've been avoiding me," William announces quite accurately, as soon as she's deposited in the king's tower meeting room.

"I've been doing exactly what you've asked of me," Isbe replies, keeping her voice calm. She reaches out to steady herself, touching the back of an elaborately carved chair.

"Exactly that and only that," William responds, and she could swear she feels his gaze sweep across her skin, lighting it on fire. He is always so cutting with his words, so frustratingly precise, so pointed—like darts driven into a map to mark a location.

"You've expected more, then."

"Expected. Hoped." He clears his throat. "As you know, there have been clashes in the western villages. Bouleau and Dureté have fallen, and we were unprepared."

We.

"Queen Malfleur may be holding back the extent of her forces for now," he goes on, "but I have persuaded Maximilien that our next step is to shore up our defense along the Vallée de Merle. In the meantime, we are sending scouts into the mountains to assess the cause of Malfleur's delay. I've shown my new bombard design to the forge, and we're moving forward with—"

"William," Isbe inserts. "If I may interrupt."

"You've certainly never asked permission before." There's a familiar amusement in his voice.

It's intolerable! He finds these little ways to insinuate that he knows her intimately, when in fact, as of a month ago, she was hardly aware that a third prince of Aubin existed and, to be sure, he'd never heard of *her*.

Never mind what had happened between them just seven nights ago—the kisses that left her lips swollen; his fingertips on her shoulders, her neck, her collarbone. . . . Never mind the fact that she too feels the same connectedness—feels that even when he surprises her, he does so in a way that further clarifies and satisfies her sense of his *Williamness*.

"Sarcasm is ill fitting on you," she says now with a huff. "I don't believe, William, that our problem is one of strategy."

"What do you mean, our *problem*? Our problem is Malfleur."

"*Or* maybe Malfleur is just a symptom."

"That symptom is murdering your people."

"Only those she has not persuaded to her side."

"The sword's blade can be very persuasive," William says dismissively, but she can hear the rhythm of his pacing as he considers what she said. "So too can the bands of thugs doing her dirty work, much like the ones who captured us back in Isolé."

"Perhaps," Isbe admits, remembering how they'd been seized and tied together by the wrists, how certain she'd been that they were going to die. "But what if there's more to it than that? Everyone knows Bouleau and Dureté are the worst villages."

"Worst?"

She cringes. "Poorest, I meant. Unhappiest. I heard

a story about Dureté. That the lord who rules there is a faerie whose tithe is compassion. I heard he lived for years in constant tears, while all those who worked his fields grew angrier and more heartless by the tithe. As he took their compassion, they became hard. Is it any surprise, with such inequities, that they fell to Malfleur? Perhaps our greatest weakness is not a lack of assets or intelligence but an issue of, well, attitude. I can't help but think of the many tales we heard along the Veiled Road. . . ."

The atrocities performed by Malfleur's mercenaries are countless—barons and lords throughout the land, brutally murdered and strung up in the village greens, a mockery made of their wealth and power: bodies stripped bare and mutilated (eyes removed, bloody guts leaking out of the M-shaped wounds carved into their exposed fat bellies), their fancy furnishings torn to shreds. Most horrifying of all were the fresh recruits, Delucian peasants dressed in fabrics made from the destroyed possessions of those lords, raiding and torching their manors, or sometimes hundreds of them taking up residence and wreaking havoc, feasting and celebrating while Malfleur's soldiers offered them weapons and promises of liberation.

To anyone who knows anything about Queen Malfleur, those promises should seem thinner than the brittle layer of ice that laces the creek Isbe used to scramble across in winter, delighting in the crackle as it shattered beneath her—yet another one of her dangerously foolish (or if you asked her, fearless) pastimes. So what's making people believe the faerie queen's promises, if not a deep, preexisting anger within them? This, Isbe is convinced, is Malfleur's greatest weapon: a dangerous flame that lives inside all of us, that blooms and burns when stoked.

And there is something worse, Isbe knows, than suffering backbreaking work, a hungry belly, or the burden of enormous levees and taxes, and that is the experience of being treated as though one's life simply does not matter. Isbe knows that feeling.

William has approached her; the velvet swish of his floor-length cloak against the stone floor mirrors the warm rustle of his voice. "I remember the rumors, yes. And everything we witnessed." He pauses.

Isbe is momentarily overcome by the prince's limelike musk—part bitter, part sweet. She now associates that scent with a prickling sensation throughout her body, sort of like pins and needles, but searing as the spray of stray sparks from a forge.

"And I don't disagree with your assessment," he admits. "However, the problem you've identified is one that can only heal over time, with the careful rebuilding of Delucian society. We will lose thousands of lives in the meantime if we are not focused on aggressive tactics, fortifying the biggest and wealthiest fiefdoms first, along with those most exposed to Malfleur's path to the palace. We must stall her advance until we can detect a weakness, which we will then go after with clean, swift, vicious action."

Clean. Swift. Vicious.